He moved to the next window. Living room: hearth with fire burning, white cat sleeping on the rug in front of it, black leather  the sofa, her feet prop bowed as she went manuscript pages. A ha beside her; she reached at the window. Involuntarily Matt stepped back, even though he knew she couldn't possibly see him. She set the glass down, turned her head, and spoke to someone outside his range of vision. Appeared to be waiting for an answer.

Still pretty, Gwennie, even after fourteen years. You've taken good care of yourself. Of course, with money, that's easy.

He began to snap photographs.

PRAISE FOR *CYANIDE WELLS* AND FOR AWARD-WINNING AUTHOR MARCIA MULLER

"Stunning . . . a pure, ice blue diamond. . . . Muller turns suspense into fine art. . . . One of the world's premier mystery writers."
—*Cleveland Plain Dealer*

"Irresistible. . . . Muller's best plotting in years."
—*Kirkus Reviews*

"An intriguing . . . entertaining whodunit."
—*Booklist*

more . . .

"Four stars! . . . . A tight, crisp tale. . . . Matt and Carly are wonderfully drawn. Another triumph for Muller."
—*Romantic Times*

"One of the treasures of the genre."
—*Chicago Tribune*

"Muller vividly paints the rugged northern California coast."
—*Publishers Weekly*

"Marcia Muller quietly keeps getting better and better."
—**Charles Champlin,** *Los Angeles Times Book Review*

"Muller is building up steam, not running out of it."
—*Newsweek*

CYANIDE
WELLS

MARCIA MULLER

CYANIDE WELLS

WARNER BOOKS

NEW YORK   BOSTON

This book is a work of fiction. Names, characters, places, and incidents are the product of the author's imagination or are used fictitiously. Any resemblance to actual events, locales, or persons, living or dead, is coincidental.

If you purchase this book without a cover you should be aware that this book may have been stolen property and reported as "unsold and destroyed" to the publisher. In such case neither the author nor the publisher has received any payment for this "stripped book."

Copyright © 2003 by Pronzini-Muller Family Trust
Excerpt from *The Dangerous Hour* copyright © 2004 by Pronzini-Muller Family Trust
All rights reserved. No part of this book may be reproduced in any form or by any electronic or mechanical means, including information storage and retrieval systems, without permission in writing from the publisher, except by a reviewer who may quote brief passages in a review.

Cover design and illustration by Tony Greco.

Warner Books

Time Warner Book Group
1271 Avenue of the Americas, New York, NY 10020
Visit our Web site at www.twbookmark.com

The Mysterious Press name and logo are registered trademarks of Warner Books.

Printed in the United States of America

Originally published in hardcover by Mysterious Press
First Paperback Printing: July 2004

10 9 8 7 6 5 4 3 2 1

ATTENTION CORPORATIONS AND ORGANIZATIONS:
Most WARNER books are available at quantity discounts with bulk purchase for educational, business, or sales promotional use. For information, please call or write: Special Markets Department, Warner Books, Inc. 135 W. 50th Street, New York, NY 10020-1393.
Telephone: 1-800-222-6747 Fax: 1-800-477-5925.

For Robin and John Reese—
members in good standing of the Top-of-the-Hill Gang

Thanks to:

Barbara Bibel, for aid in researching;
Victoria Brouillette, my Minnesota connection;
Joe Chernicoff, for information on antique firearms;
Charlie Lucke and John Pearson, for their
photographic expertise;
And Bill Pronzini, who makes me work much too hard!

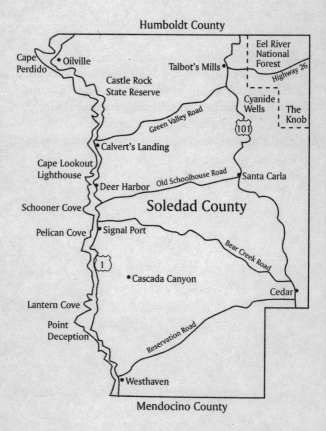

Humboldt County

Cape Perdido
• Oilville

Castle Rock State Reserve

Talbot's Mills •

Eel River National Forest

Highway 26

Cyanide Wells

The Knob

Green Valley Road

101

• Calvert's Landing

Cape Lookout Lighthouse

Deer Harbor • Old Schoolhouse Road • Santa Carla

Schooner Cove

Soledad County

Pelican Cove • Signal Port

Bear Creek Road

• Cascada Canyon

1

Cedar •

Lantern Cove

Point Deception

Reservation Road

• Westhaven

Mendocino County

Saugatuck, Minnesota
Thursday, July 28, 1988

atthew Lindstrom?"

"Yes?"

"This is Sheriff Cliff Brandt of Sweetwater County, Wyoming. Are you married to a Gwen
Lindstrom?"

". . . Yes, I am."

"And she drives a white Toyota Tercel, this year's
model, Minnesota license number four-four-three-
B-C-Y?"

"That's correct. What's this about, Sheriff?"

"Her car was found in my jurisdiction, parked by
the side of County Road Eleven, eight miles from
Reliance. That's a farming community north of Interstate Eighty. Nothing wrong with the vehicle, but

there were bloodstains on the dash and other signs consistent with a struggle. A purse containing her identification and credit cards was on the passenger's seat."

"And Gwen? What about Gwen?"

"No sign of her. Tell me, Mr. Lindstrom, does she know anyone in Reliance? Or Sweetwater County?"

"As far as I know, she's never been to Wyoming."

"When did you last see Mrs. Lindstrom?"

"Two weeks ago, on the fourteenth."

"Two *weeks* ago? And you've got no idea where she's been since then?"

"We're separated. Have filed for divorce. We met on the fourteenth to go over the property settlement."

"I see. Messy divorce?"

"Amicable. We have no children and very little in the way of assets."

"There was a student ID from Saugatuck College in your wife's purse."

"Yes, she's a senior in the journalism department."

"And what do you do, Mr. Lindstrom?"

"I teach photography there, operate a small studio on the side. Mostly wedding portraits, that sort of — Why are you asking me these questions? And what are you doing to find Gwen?"

"Just familiarizing myself with the situation. I take it you can account for your whereabouts during the past two weeks?"

"Of course I can! I was here in Saugatuck, teaching summer courses. Now, what are you doing to find —"

"Don't get all exercised, Mr. Lindstrom. My last question was strictly routine. As for finding your wife, we plan to circularize her photograph, but we're hoping you can provide a better likeness than the one on her driver's license."

"I'll overnight several to you. If you find her, will you please ask her to call me? Or if . . ."

"*If* Mr. Lindstrom?"

"Well, if something's happened to her . . ."

"Don't worry. We'll be in touch."

Thousand Springs, Nevada
Thursday, July 28, 1988

hat's a bad place to hitchhike. Somebody could pick you off coming around the curve. Where're you headed?"

"West. Where're you going?"

"All the way to Soledad County, California."

"Good a place as any, I guess. If you'd like some company . . ."

"Hop in."

"Thanks, I really appreciate it. I was starting to get spooked, all alone here."

"Why were you alone, anyway?"

"My last ride dropped me off. I kind of . . . had trouble with him."

"That'll happen. Hitching's not the safest way for a woman to travel."

"I know, but it's the only way I've got."

"How long have you been on the road?"

"A couple of days."

"Coming from where?"

"East. What's this place — Soledad County — like?"

"Pretty. Coast, forest, foothills, small towns."

"Lots of people live there?"

"No. We're one of the most sparsely populated in the upper half of the state. Isolated, too; it's a four-hour drive to San Francisco, even longer to Sacramento because of bad roads."

"Sounds nice."

"Well, you've got to like the quiet life, and I do. I live in the country, near a little town called Cyanide Wells."

"So you think Soledad County is really a good place to live?"

"If you want, I'll sing its praises all the way there. By the way, my name's Carly McGuire."

"Mine's Ardis Coleman."

Port Regis, British Columbia
Sunday, April 21, 2002

atthew Lindstrom?"
      "Yes?"
      "I'm calling about your wife."
   "I have no wife."
   "Oh, yes, you do. Gwen Lindstrom —"
   "My wife disappeared fourteen years ago. Our divorce went through shortly after that."
   "I know, Mr. Lindstrom. And I know about your legal and professional difficulties surrounding the situation. They must have been very painful. Put an end to your life as you'd known it, didn't they?"
   "Who is this?"
   "A friend. My identity's not important. What's important is that your wife is very much alive. And very

cognizant of what she put you through when she disappeared."

"Listen, whoever you are —"

"Aren't you curious? I'm sure I would be if I were you."

"All right, I'll go along with your game. Where is Gwen?"

"Soledad County, California. Has lived there for the past fourteen years near a place called Cyanide Wells, under the name of Ardis Coleman."

"Ardis Coleman? My God, that was Gwen's mother's maiden name."

"Well, there you go. Let me ask you this, Mr. Lindstrom: Will revenge taste good served up cold, after the passage of all those years?"

"Revenge?"

"Surely you must feel some impulse in that direction, considering . . ."

"What the hell are you trying to do to me? Who *are* you?"

"As I said, a friend."

"I don't believe a word of this!"

"Then I suggest you check it out, Mr. Lindstrom. Check it out."

Cyanide Wells, California
Sunday, April 21, 2002

ey, Ard, you're awfully quiet. Something wrong?"

"Nothing that I can pin down, but I feel . . . I didn't sleep well last night. Bad dreams, the kind you can't remember afterwards, but their aura lingers like a hangover."

"Maybe it's your book. It can't be easy reliving that time. And from what I've read, it's a much more personal account than what you wrote for the paper."

"It is, but that's how I want it, Carly. Besides, I don't think this is about the book — at least not completely."

"What, then?"

"Matt, maybe."

"After all these years?"

"I've been thinking of him a lot lately. Wondering . . ."

"And feeling guilty, I suppose."

"In a way. When I found out they suspected him of murdering me, I should've come forward."

"You found out way after the fact. And when you did try to contact him, he was gone, no forwarding."

"I know, but instead of trying to find out where he'd gone, I just felt relieved. I didn't want to hurt him any more than I already had."

"So he's better off."

"No, he'd've been better off if I'd been honest from the first. I could've —"

"As my aunt Nan used to say, '*Coulda*'s, *woulda*'s, and *shoulda*'s don't amount to a hill of beans.'"

"I guess. But I'm concerned for Natalie. My anxiety's obvious, and it upsets her."

"She hasn't said anything about it to me."

"You know her; she's a child who holds everything inside. Carly, d'you think I'm being irrational?"

". . . You're stressed. You'll get over it once the book is done."

"Will I? Sometimes I think that given all the terrible things I've done, I **don**'t deserve another good night's sleep in this lifetime."

Matthew Lindstrom

Port Regis, British Columbia
Wednesday, April 24, 2002

att Lindstrom watched the tourists struggle along the pier, laden with extra jackets, blankets, tote bags, and coolers. City people, up from California on holiday and unaccustomed to the chill temperatures and pervasive damp that characterized the northern tip of Vancouver Island at this time of year. Americans were also unaccustomed to going anywhere without a considerable collection of unnecessary possessions.

Smiling ruefully, he turned around, his gaze rising to the pine-covered slopes across the small harbor. When had he stopped identifying with the few U.S. citizens who ventured this far up-island? At first he hadn't been conscious of his waning allegiance; it had simply crept up on him until one day he was no longer one of them, yet not a Canadian either. Stuck somewhere in between, perhaps permanently, and in an odd way his otherness pleased him. No, not pleased so much as contented him, and he'd remained contented until the past Sunday evening. Since then he'd felt only discontent, and a sense of unfinished business.

"Matt?" His deckhand, Johnny Crowe, stood by the transom of the *Queen Charlotte,* Matt's thirty-six-foot excursion trawler. A full-blooded Kootenay, Johnny was a recent transplant from the Columbia River Valley. He asked, "You want me to button her up?"

"Yeah, thanks." Matt gave him a half-salute and started along the dock, past fishing boats in their slips. The tourists he'd taken out for the morning's charter were bunched around their giant Ford Expedition, trying to fit their gear among the suitcases piled in its rear compartment. They'd spent the night at Port Regis Hotel at the foot of the pier—an establishment whose accommodations one guidebook had described as "spartan but clean," and from the grumblings he'd overheard, he gathered that spartan was not their first, or even second, preference.

When he reached the end of the pier, he gave the tourists a wide berth and a curt nod and headed for the hotel. It was of weathered clapboard, once white but now gone to gray, and not at all imposing, with three entrances off its covered front porch: restaurant, lobby, and bar. Matt pushed through the latter into an amber-lighted room with beer signs and animal heads on the walls and rickety, unmatched tables and chairs arranged haphazardly across the warped wooden floor. The room was empty now, but a few hours before, it would have been filled with fishermen returning at what was the end of their working day.

"Hey, Millie," Matt called to the woman behind the bar.

"Hey, yourself." Millie Bertram was a frizzy-haired blonde on the far side of fifty, dressed in denim coveralls over a tie-dyed shirt. The shirt and her long beaded earrings revealed her as one who had never quite made a clean break with the sixties. When Matt moved to Port Regis ten years ago, Millie and her husband, Jed, had co-owned and operated the hotel. Two years later Jed, who fancied himself a bass player of immense if unrecognized talent, ran off with a singer from Vancouver, never to be seen again. Millie became sole proprietor of the hotel, and if the prices had gone up, so had the quality of food and service.

Now she placed a mug of coffee in front of Matt. "Early charter?"

"Only charter. Those guests of yours from San Jose."

"Ah, yes, they mentioned something about a 'boat ride.' " The set of Millie's mouth indicated she was glad to have seen the last of them. "Fishing?"

"Not their thing. Bloody Marys, except for one woman who drank mimosas. Point-and-shoot cameras and a desire to see whales."

"On a day when there's not a whale in sight."

"I pointed out two." Matt sipped coffee, burned his tongue, and grimaced.

"Let me guess," Millie said. "Bull and Bear Rocks."

"You got it."

"You're a con man, Lindstrom."

"So they're leaving happy and will tell all their friends to look me up."

Millie went to the coffee urn, poured herself some, and leaned against the backbar, looking pensive. Probably contemplating the summer months that would bring more tourists with a desire for whales, who would become drunk in her bar, look askance at her chef's plain cooking, and leave her spartan guestrooms in a shambles.

Matt toyed with the ceramic container that held packets of sugar and artificial sweetener. "Mil, you're from California, right?"

"Yeah."

"You know where Soledad County is?"

She closed her eyes, apparently conjuring a map. "Between Mendocino and Humboldt Counties, on the coast. Extends east beyond the edge of the Eel River National Forest."

"You ever hear of a place called Cyanide Wells?"

"Sure. Back when Jed-the-asshole and I were into our environmental phase, we protested at Talbot's Mills. Lumber town. Company town. Identical little houses, except for the mansions the thieving barons built on the labor of the loggers and millworkers they exploited."

Matt made motions as if he were playing a violin.

"Okay," Millie said, "so I'm still talking the talk even though I'm not walking the walk. Anyway, Cyanide Wells is maybe thirty miles southeast of there. Former gold-mining camp. Wide spot in the road back in the seventies, but I guess it's grown some by now. I do know it's got one hell of a newspaper, the *Soledad Spectrum*. Owned and edited by a woman, Carly McGuire. About three years ago they won the Pulitzer Prize for a series on the murders of a gay couple near there. How come you asked?"

"I just found out that somebody I used to know is living near Cyanide Wells."

"Somebody?" Now Millie's tone turned sly. She was, Matt knew, frustrated and puzzled by his lack of interest in a long-term relationship with any of the women she repeatedly shoved into his path.

"Somebody," he said in a tone that precluded further discussion.

Somebody who, fourteen years ago, had put an end to his life as he'd known it.

Matt sat on the deck of his cabin, looking out at the humped mass of Bear Rock, which was backlit by the setting sun. It *did* look like a whale, and he was glad he'd given the tourists their photo op this morning. Clouds were now gathering on the horizon, bleaching the sun's brilliant colors, and a cold breeze swayed the three tall pines that over the past ten years he'd watched grow from saplings. Feeling the chill, he got up and took his bottle of beer inside.

The cabin was snug: one room with a sleeping alcove on the far wall, and a stone fireplace and galley kitchen facing each other on the side walls. A picture window and glass door overlooked the sea. The small shingled building had been in bad shape when he'd first seen it, so he'd gotten it cheap, leaving enough of the money from the sale of the Saugatuck house for the down payment on the *Queen Charlotte*. During two years of drifting about, his life in ruins, he'd taken what odd jobs he found and scarcely touched the money.

He lighted the fire he'd earlier laid on the hearth, sat down, and watched the flames build. Dusk fell, then darkness, and he nursed his warmish beer without turning on a lamp.

Fourteen years. A way of life lost. A home gone. A career destroyed.

Then, finally, he'd found Port Regis and this cabin and the *Queen Charlotte,* and he'd created a new way of life, built another home and career. True, he was not the man he'd intended to be at thirty-nine, and this was not the life he'd expected to lead. But it was a life he'd handcrafted out of ruin and chaos. If it was as spartan as one of Millie's guestrooms, at least it was also clean. If his friends were little more than good acquaintances, so much the better; he'd learned the small worth of friendship those last two years in Minnesota. He was content here—or had been, until a late-night anonymous phone call destroyed all possibility of contentment. . . .

He wasn't aware of making a conscious decision, much less a plan. He simply turned on the table lamp and went to the closet off the sleeping alcove, where he began going through the cartons stacked in its recesses. When he located the one marked P EQUIP., he carried it to the braided rug in front of the hearth, sat down cross-legged, and opened it.

Memories rose with the dust from the carton's lid. He pushed them aside, burrowed into the bubble-wrapped contents. On top were the lenses: F2.8 wide angle, F1.8

and F2.8 telephotos, the F2.8 with 1.4x teleconverter, and even a fish-eye, which he'd bought in a fit of longing but had seldom needed. Next the camera bag, tan canvas and well used. And inside it, the camera.

It was an old Nikon F, the first camera he'd ever bought and the only one he'd kept when he sold his once-profitable photography business. Heavy and old-fashioned next to the new single-lens reflexes or digital models, the markings were worn on the f-stop band, and the surfaces where he'd so often held it were polished smooth. He stared at it, afraid to take it into his hands because if he did, it would work its old magic, and then what he now realized he'd been subconsciously considering would become a reality. . . .

Don't be ridiculous. Picking it up isn't a commitment.

And just like that, he did.

His fingers curled around the Nikon, moving to long-accustomed positions. They caressed it as he removed the lens cap, adjusted speed, f-stop, and focus. He sighted on the flames in the fireplace, saw them clearly through the F3.5 micro lens with a skylight filter. Even though the camera contained no film, he thumbed the advance lever, depressed the shutter.

The mind may forget, but not the body.

She'd said that to him the last time they made love, in a sentimental moment after being separated for two months, but he sensed that her body had already forgotten, was ready for new memories, a new man. She'd told him she needed to be free—not to wound him, but with deep regret that proved the words hurt her as well. But now, after allowing him to think her dead for fourteen years, it seemed she was alive in California, near a place called Cyanide Wells. He had no reason to doubt his anonymous caller, who had taken the trouble to track him down for some unexplained reason.

"... *your wife is very much alive. And very cognizant of what she put you through when she disappeared....*"

Matt's fingers tightened on the Nikon.

Picking it up had been a commitment after all.

Soledad County, California
Tuesday, May 7, 2002

ain clouds hovered over the heavily forested ridgeline that separated central Soledad County from the coastal region, reminding Matt of home. As the exit sign for Talbot's Mills appeared, he took his right hand off the wheel of the rented Jeep Cherokee and rubbed his neck. It had been a long drive north from the San Francisco Airport, and he was stiff and tired but keyed up in an unpleasant manner that twice had made him oversteer on Highway 101's sharp curves.

It had taken him two weeks to put the charter business in order so that it would run properly under Johnny Crowe's supervision, as well as to prepare his cabin should his absence be a long one. All the time he was going about his tasks, he felt as if he were saying good-bye: to Millie, to Johnny, to the woman at the bank where he arranged for payment of what few bills would come in, to the clerks at the marine supply he patronized, to the mechanic at the gas station where he had his truck serviced for the drive to Vancouver. Once there, he left the truck in the garage of a woman with whom he'd had an on-and-off affair for years, and she drove him to the airport. As his plane took off and his adopted country receded below him, he wondered what kind of man he'd be when he returned there.

Now he rounded a bend in the highway and sighted the lumber company town nestled at the base of the ridge. Clustered around the interchange were the ubiquitous motels and gas stations and fast-food outlets, and beyond them a bridge spanned a wide, slow-moving river. Two huge beige-and-green mills sprawled for acres along its banks, and small houses rose on the terraced slope above them. Higher on the hill were larger homes, including one whose gables cleared the tallest of the trees.

Matt exited on a ramp whose potholed surface threatened to jar the Jeep's wheel from his hands. Logging rigs lined the frontage road's shoulder on both sides, in front of a truck stop advertising HOT SHOWERS AND GOOD EATS. He'd pulled off for a burger hours ago in a place north of the Golden Gate Bridge called Los Alegres, but the keyed-up feeling had prevented him from eating most of it. He knew he should have a solid meal, but his stomach was still nervous, so he drove past the truck stop, looking for a motel.

There was a Quality Inn sandwiched between a

Denny's and a Chevron station about fifty yards ahead. Grease and exhaust fumes were a potential hazard, but its sign advertised vacancies, and if he didn't like it, he could move. He pulled in, rented a surprisingly spacious room, and then set to work with the county phone book.

No listing for an Ardis Coleman. Listing for the *Soledad Spectrum* on Main Street in Cyanide Wells. No public library there, but Talbot's Mills had one, located in the Talbot Mansion on Alta Street. Best to make that his first stop, gather information, and map out strategy before visiting the smaller town.

He wasn't concerned that he'd run into Gwen and she'd recognize him. Immediately after making his decision to come to Soledad County, he had begun growing a mustache and beard, neither of which he'd ever worn before. The heavy growth rate of his facial hair, which he'd cursed his whole life, produced both quickly and respectably. The dark-brown dye he had applied to his naturally blond hair the night before he left Port Regis had further changed him, and as proof of the tepid quality of his relationship with the woman friend in Vancouver, her only comment on his new look was, "I don't like beards."

Even without these changes it was possible Gwen wouldn't know him should they come face-to-face. For one thing, she wouldn't expect to find him here. And he was older, his weathered skin a deep saltwater tan. His once-stocky body had been honed lean by his active life on the sea. He walked differently, with the catlike precision necessary to maintain balance on an often heaving deck. He spoke differently, with the slowness and economy of one who spends a great deal of time alone.

No, he was not the man Gwen used to know.

While he was crossing the bridge, the pretty picture of the old-fashioned company town that he'd formed from a distance deteriorated. One of the long mills was still in operation, a thick, steady stream of smoke rising from its tall stacks, but the other was in poor repair, surrounded by broken, weed-choked asphalt and twisted heaps of rubble. As he climbed higher on the slope, he found that the small, identical frame cottages on the terraced streets had peeling paint, sagging rooflines, and many boarded windows; their patches of yard were full of disabled vehicles, trash, cast-off furnishings. Still higher, a small business district contained mostly dead storefronts and empty sidewalks. Even the equipment in a playground had been vandalized.

Matt drove slowly through the business district, looking for Alta Street, found it at the very end, and turned uphill again. The homes there were of Victorian vintage—mostly modest, but larger and in better repair than the cottages below. At its end tall, black iron gates shielded a parklike area, and beyond rose the mansion he'd glimpsed from the freeway: three stories of forbidding gray, with iron railings, verdigrised copper gables, huge stained-glass windows, and balconies with trim as delicate as the icing on a wedding cake. Although it must have been built in the Victorian decades, it bore little resemblance to the recognizable styles of that era; if anything, it was a hodgepodge of architectural features that only a serious eccentric would incorporate into the same edifice. A sign on the gate identified it as the Talbot Mansion, now the Central Soledad County Public Library and Museum.

Matt studied it for a moment, wondering what kind of lunatics the Talbots had been to create such a place, then drove through the gate, parked in the small paved lot, and went inside. After an hour and a half he'd amassed a surprising amount of information about Gwen and her new life as Ardis Coleman.

He went to bed early that night but found he couldn't sleep, not even after the double shot of Wild Turkey he'd poured from the bottle he'd bought at a nearby liquor store. Finally he got up and dressed and drove back to Talbot's Mills. There he prowled the deserted streets, looking for . . .

What?

He didn't know, so he kept walking until he found an open tavern in the half-dead business district—a small place with a single pool table and a jukebox playing country songs. Only three old men hunched over their drinks at the bar, and the bartender stood at its end, staring up at a small, blurry television screen. Matt ordered a beer and took it to a corner table, where dim light shone down from a Canadian Club sign.

Canada . . .

Most people led one life. They might move from place to place, marry and divorce and remarry, change careers, but the progression was linear, and they basically remained the same persons from birth to death.

Until fourteen years ago Matt, also, had been one person: He'd enjoyed an overprivileged childhood in Minnetonka, a suburb of Minneapolis; learned boating from his father, an accomplished sailor, at the family's cabin near Grand Marais, on Lake Superior; attended Northwestern University, majoring in prelaw while studying photography under a master of the art in nearby Chicago. When photography won out over the law, his teacher recommended him for a position at small but prestigious Saugatuck College in his home state. The pay was also small, so his parents offered to loan him the money to establish his own commercial studio. Two years later he married a journalism student who had taken a course from him, pretty Gwendolyn Standish. Life should have been good.

Yet it wasn't. After their marriage, Gwen's personality changed, so much that she seemed like two persons encased in one skin. Caring and passionate, withdrawn and cold. Cheerful and optimistic, depressed and pessimistic. Open and filled with confidence, closed and filled with self-doubt. Eventually the negative side overwhelmed the positive, and despite Matt's assurances that he would do anything to save the marriage—counseling, therapy, walking barefoot over hot coals—she insisted on a divorce.

Even the divorce hadn't ended what he now thought of as his first life, though. That was brought on by her disappearance and its aftermath.

Suspicious minds . . .

The words echoing from the jukebox meshed with his thoughts. The first hint of suspicion had come during the call from the Wyoming sheriff, Cliff Brandt: "I take it you can account for your whereabouts during the past two weeks." And he'd too quickly replied, "Of course I can! I was here in Saugatuck, teaching summer classes." Too quickly and also dishonestly, because of an ingrained fear of the authorities that stemmed from his older brother Jeremy's arrest and eventual conviction for dealing cocaine in the mid-seventies; Matt was thirteen at the time and had watched the officers brutally subdue Jeremy when he attempted to resist them.

In truth, Matt had been nowhere near Saugatuck during those two weeks. The summer of 1988, a drought year, was the hottest and driest Minnesota had experienced since the 1930s. Matt's temper grew shorter with every July day, and he found it difficult to maintain focus on his work. So he closed down the studio, turned his summer classes over to a colleague, and went on a solo driving and camping trip designed both to escape the heat and help him put the failure of his marriage in perspective. It was his bad luck that the trip, which ended in Arches National Park, on Utah's Green River, took him home through Wyoming along Interstate 80 at approximately the same time Gwen's car was abandoned by the side of a county road north of there.

Sheriff Brandt found that out, of course, when he called the college to verify Matt's alibi and then checked the paper trail of credit card and gas station charges. His department lifted Matt's fingerprints from the abandoned Toyota (which he had occasionally driven) and inside Gwen's purse (where he had occasionally placed items of his own too large for his pockets). The Lindstroms' property settlement showed that Matt had consented to pay Gwen half the value of his photography business. And, most damning, Matt had lied to the sheriff during their first conversation. Brandt, unable to produce any trace of Gwen, seemed determined to prove Matt a murderer.

Eventually, of course, Brandt had given up. Even in Sweetwater County, Wyoming, he had more pressing matters to attend to, and the district attorney convinced him that no-body cases were difficult to prove in any jurisdiction. But by then, the damage had been done.

The police in Saugatuck watched Matt's every move; he was repeatedly stopped for nonexistent traffic violations, and it became common for him to see squad cars cruising past his house and place of business. Gwen's disappearance and his possible involvement were worked and reworked by the media. Initially friends and neighbors were supportive, but after a while they stopped calling him. Halfway through the fall semester, a television show, which both described in sensational terms his romantic involvement and marriage to a sophomore and raised questions bordering on the libelous about her disappearance, prompted several students to withdraw from his classes. In the spring the college's governing board unanimously decided it would be advisable that he take a year's sabbatical without pay; if the "regrettable situation" was resolved before the year was up, his pay would become retroactive.

And yet there remained no trace of Gwen.

By the anniversary of her disappearance in July, Matt's former friends were crossing the street to avoid him. Requests for his services at weddings, anniversary parties, and bar mitzvahs dropped off sharply. New mothers no longer brought their babies to his studio for their first portraits. Engaged couples took their business to his competitor across town. At Christmastime he shot a photograph for only one customized card: an elderly woman and her "family" of three toy poodles. The dogs yipped and snarled and peed on the carpet, and when the woman was leaving, she told him she'd only come there because she couldn't get an appointment with the other photographer.

At least, Matt thought, his competitor had a clean rug.

He stubbornly hung on in Saugatuck, however, living off his savings. It was his home; he'd done nothing wrong except stupidly lie to a Wyoming sheriff. Sooner or later he would be vindicated.

When his savings were about to run out, he phoned home to ask for a loan; his mother agreed but then called back the next day.

"Your father and I have discussed the loan," she told him, "and we have come to the conclusion that it's time we stopped spoiling you. Look what happened to your brother because of our indulgence: He's down in New Mexico, taking drugs again." When Matt started to protest that Jeremy was in Albuquerque working as a counselor in a program for troubled youth, she cut him off. "No, hear me out. Your father and I know you couldn't have killed Gwendolyn. We didn't raise you that way. But the negative publicity has made it very difficult for us—"

Matt hung up on her.

Still, he remained in town, selling off cherished possessions and then the photography business. With some of the proceeds he hired a private investigator to look for

Gwen; the man delivered sketchy reports for a month and then ceased communication; when Matt called his office, he found the phone service had been discontinued.

Then, three weeks after the second anniversary of Gwen's disappearance, a chance encounter in the supermarket ended his first life.

He was in the produce section, filling his cart with the vegetables that had become staples of his diet now that he could no longer afford meat, when he looked up into the eyes of Gwen's best friend, Bonnie Vaughan, principal of the local high school, a heavy but attractive woman with long, silky hair and gray eyes. Eyes that now cut into him like surgical instruments.

"So you *are* still here, you bastard," she said in a low voice that was more unsettling than if she'd shouted.

"Bonnie, I—"

"Shut up, you murderer!"

The words and her tone rendered him speechless.

"We know what you did," she went on. "And we know why. You'd better get out of Saugatuck before somebody murders *you!*" Then she whirled and walked away.

Matt stared after her. Bonnie had always been a gentle, caring woman: She tended to her friends' homes and pets while they were out of town; she could always be counted on in an emergency; she brought thoughtful, handcrafted gifts when invited to dinner. The last time he'd seen her, eleven months after Gwen disappeared, she'd hugged him and said he had her full support. If the hatred that had infected the rest of the community could also infect a woman like Bonnie Vaughan, he wanted nothing more to do with Saugatuck—

"Hey, mister."

Matt started and focused on the woman who had spoken. He'd been so deeply mired in his memories that he hadn't noticed her come into the bar. She was in her early twenties, too thin, with long brown hair that could stand a washing, and an unhealthy grayish pallor to her skin.

"Buy me a drink?" she asked with a tentative smile.

He didn't want company, particularly her brand of company, and his expression must have said so, because her smile faded.

"Listen," she said in a different tone, "I'm not selling anything, if that's what you're thinking. I just need somebody to talk to."

Something in her voice convinced him she was telling the truth. Besides, her earnest, pleading expression made him feel sorry for her. Maybe listening to her troubles would help him keep his own pain at bay.

"Okay." He motioned at the chair opposite him. "What'll you have?"

"Whatever you're having."

He took his empty mug to the bar and ordered a round. As he was paying, the bartender said in a low voice, "Be nice to the kid. She's going through a bad time."

He nodded and went back to the table.

"Thanks, mister." She raised the mug in both hands and drank.

"You're welcome. I'm John." As in Johnny Crowe,

the name that he'd borrowed for the journey, with his deckhand's blessing. "What's yours?"

"Sam. Short for Samantha. Thanks for not making me drink alone."

"Drinking alone's no good."

"But you were."

"Yes, I was. So tell me about yourself, Sam."

"What d'you want to know?"

"Anything you care to reveal. You said you needed somebody to talk to, and you seem upset."

"Yeah, I'm upset. Got every right to be. My father . . . died last week."

"I'm sorry, Sam."

"Not as sorry as I was for Dad. He had it rough there toward the end. Twenty-one years with the mill, and they laid him off. No severance pay, and then they told him we had to be out of the house in thirty days. Dad sweated all his life for the company, and that's how they repaid him. He worked his fingers to the bone for them—and us."

"Who's 'us'?"

"Me, my brother, and my mom. My brother got out, joined the army. I don't even know where he is now. Mom died two years ago, cancer. I was all Dad had left."

Matt took the empty mug from her hands and went to the bar for a refill. Sam was hurting, that was for sure, and a few beers seemed poor comfort. But he wasn't used to comforting others, especially strangers; that particular activity had never been a part of his life, except for the brief time he'd been married to Gwen.

When he went back to the table, Sam was sitting very still, eyes focused on a beer sign depicting a mountain meadow. The tilt of her nose was delicate, her cheek-bones and forehead high. She'd've been pretty if she weren't in a disheveled, grief-stricken state. Matt set the beer in front of her, and she nodded thanks, keeping her gaze on the sign.

She said, "I'm thinking maybe I'll get out, too."

"And go where?"

"Anyplace there's a future. Everything's dying here—the mill, the town. Pretty soon it'll just be a wide spot on the freeway for people who want a cheap motel and the kind of crap I serve up at the Chicken Shack."

"I noticed one of the mills is closed."

"Yeah, and the other one'll close later this year."

"Environmental regulations causing that?"

"Not really. Talbot's never relied on old-growth forests, like Pacific Lumber up in Scotia did. No, what happened is, it got sold. Ronnie Talbot, the last of the family that owned it, he didn't give a rat's ass about the business. He was a faggot, and all he wanted was a lot of money so he could live high on the hog with his lover. This Portland company bought it, and they're letting it fail so they can get the tax write-off." Her lips curved up in a malicious smile. "At least Ronnie didn't get to enjoy the money. Three months after the sale was final, some-body shot him and his lover at their house over by the Knob. Killed them both, right there in their bed."

That afternoon at the library, Matt had read the *Soledad Spectrum*'s Pulitzer Prize–winning series on the murders in a secluded home east of Cyanide Wells with more than usual interest. Many of the accounts had borne Gwen's assumed name. In a way, it hadn't surprised him; she was a talented reporter, and it was the logical thing for her to be doing here.

Sam's use of the word "somebody" didn't jibe with the published accounts, though. "I thought they caught the guy who shot them."

"Well, Mack Travis confessed to it and hanged himself in his jail cell, but nobody here believes he did it. There was evidence that he'd been in Ronnie and Deke's house that night, but Mack was always a couple of cards short of a full deck, and he was the type who'd confess to anything if anybody gave him half a chance. He had a peculiar relationship with his momma, if you know what I mean. Confessed because he thought the cops had him dead to rights, then offed himself because he didn't want to shame her."

"That paper over in Cyanide Wells won a Pulitzer for their coverage of the murders, didn't they?"

"Uh-huh. Biggest thing that ever happened around here—of the good kind, I mean. I liked those articles. I'm no fan of faggots, but that Ardis Coleman, who wrote most of the stories, actually made me understand how lousy their situation is in a place like this."

"You ever meet her?"

"Me? Do I look like somebody who hangs with Pulitzer Prize–winners? I've seen her in the supermarket, is all. And, of course, I used to read her."

"Used to?"

"She quit the paper right after they won the prize, is writing a book about the murders."

Evidently had been writing it for close to three years now. She'd probably never finish it, let alone get it published. Gwen had lacked the ability to handle large projects; she agonized over term papers but was able to knock off a good newspaper article under extreme time pressure. But if she wasn't working for the paper, how was she paying her bills?

"Mister . . . John, what d'you think I should do?"

The question startled him. "About what?"

"Should I stay here or just chuck everything and go? What would you do in my place?"

He thought for a moment, then imparted the sum total of his wisdom.

"I'd go, but I'd also keep it in mind that no matter where you are, you'll still be you. You'll still be carrying the same old baggage."

Wednesday, May 8, 2002

y the time Matt delivered Sam to the small company home that would soon cease to be hers—gently refusing her offer of a nightcap—it was after one. He drove back to his motel, stripped off his clothing, and got into the shower. After drying off, he wiped the steam from the mirror over the vanity and once again appraised his somewhat altered appearance.

Yes, he was definitely a different man. A man created out of pain.

After finally leaving Saugatuck, he thought he'd experienced enough pain for any one lifetime, but he hadn't counted on his brother, Jeremy, compounding it.

When in distress, Matt's first impulse had always been to turn to family, and even after being rebuffed by his mother and father, he had thought he could count on his big brother. So he set out on the long drive to Albuquerque, what few possessions he hadn't sold packed in his old Chevy Suburban. He didn't bother to write or call; the brothers had extended standing invitations to visit each other without advance notice.

Jeremy's house was on Vassar Drive, a stucco ranch-style with a yard filled with gravel instead of grass, cacti instead of flowers. Four years before, Matt and Gwen had visited there, and the spare key Jeremy had given him was still on his keychain. When Jeremy didn't answer his ring, Matt checked the garage, saw no car, and let himself inside. In the kitchen he helped himself to a beer and sat down at the table to leaf through the help-wanted ads in a copy of the *Journal* that had been left there. Although the Southwest had never particularly charmed him, it was a long way from Minnesota, and distance was what he now craved.

Some fifteen minutes later he heard the front door open. Footsteps came along the hallway, and Matt looked up in anticipation of seeing his brother's face. Instead a woman came into the room, carrying a sack of groceries. She was short, blond, and slightly over-weight, with a bland, pleasant expression that changed radically when she saw him.

She gave a little cry, dropped the grocery bag, and shrank back against the doorjamb. Oranges rolled across the floor. Matt stood up, so quickly that he knocked over his chair.

"Hey," he said, holding his hands out. "Don't be frightened. I'm Jer's brother, Matt. I guess I should've phoned—"

The woman whirled and fled down the hallway, sobbing.

That was the end of Matt's hopes of making a new start in Albuquerque.

"She's damaged," Jeremy said later of his new wife, Marty. "I met her when I was doing volunteer work at a center for victims of violent crimes. Two years ago a man invaded her home, shot her husband, and held her captive for twenty-two hours. Repeatedly raped her. Can you imagine what she thought when she found a total stranger in our kitchen?"

"I'm not a 'total stranger.' And how come you didn't let me know you'd gotten married?"

Jeremy's expression became remote, as it always did when he was preparing to lie. "We've only been married six weeks. I planned to tell you the next time we talked."

But when would that have been? During the past year and a half their phone conversations had tapered off to once every three months or so. "Do the folks know?"

"Why would I tell them? The last time I spoke with Mom was when I bought this house. I thought she'd be proud of me for getting my act together. Instead she all but accused me of making the down payment with profits from drug deals."

"I've tried to explain to them—"

"I know you have. But they're not going to listen to what they don't want to hear. They've always been good at labeling people, and my label was pasted on the day I was convicted of dealing."

"Well, you're not alone in that. They've labeled me, too. About Marty—is she gonna be okay?"

"She'll be fine. She's cooking her special spaghetti for dinner, in honor of your visit."

But Marty wasn't fine. That night at dinner she fidgeted and refused to make eye contact with Matt and finally excused herself before they were finished eating. As he and Jeremy loaded dishes in the washer, Matt said, "Something's still bothering her, and it's not because I scared her this afternoon."

"I don't know what you mean."

"I think you do. She's afraid of me, your wife-killer brother."

"Oh, Matt, don't go there."

"In spite of what you've told her, she believes I did it."

Jeremy began scrubbing a pot, steam clouding his glasses.

Matt said, "You *did* tell her I'm innocent?"

No reply.

"You *do* believe I'm innocent?"

Jeremy looked up, shut off the water. Steam coated his lenses, but through it Matt could see the fear in his eyes.

Give him an out. Don't let this turn ugly.

"Well, don't feel disloyal, brother," he said. "Maybe I did do it."

The next morning he left his brother's house for good.

After that, what he thought of as his wandering years began. From New Mexico he drove across Arizona and into Southern California. In San Diego he worked two months for a contractor, mainly doing demolition work, then moved on north. All the way up the coast to Oregon he camped out or stayed in cheap motels or hostels, spending frugally, then cut inland to Portland.

In the window of a Portland secondhand bookshop he

saw a Help Wanted sign. He worked there as a clerk for six months while living at the YMCA. The city was nice enough, but he became restless and once again headed north, stopping in Seattle. He'd always been drawn to cities on the water, and he liked the hills and sweeping vistas, so he rented a room in a residential hotel and got on with another contractor; within two months he began scanning the want ads for more permanent quarters. But then a chance encounter near Pioneer Square changed his plans.

"Matt! Matt Lindstrom!" a man's voice had called out.

He turned and found himself face-to-face with Dave Kappel, one of his former students. Dave, ever the motormouth, grasped his hand and pumped it, chattering.

"So this is where you're living now. Guess you wanted to get away from that rotten town, and I sure don't blame you. Shitty, the way people treated you after your wife disappeared."

Matt opened his mouth to say that he wasn't living in Seattle, was merely a tourist, but Dave went on, oblivious. "I came out here last fall. I'm a staff photographer on the *Post-Intelligencer*. Married, too. Kid on the way. Fast work, huh? Why don't you give me your phone number? We'd love to have you to dinner."

Automatically Matt gave him the number of the phone that only rang for work-related calls.

"Great, man," Dave said as he scribbled it down. "You know what I'm thinking? I'll talk to a reporter I work with about doing a feature on the shit deal you got back in Saugatuck. Use photos I've got of the place, take others to show you in your new life. Unfounded rumor, innuendo, wrecking a life, but in the end you triumph. Way cool. People eat up that kind of thing."

Just his luck, Matt thought. The only person from Saugatuck who was on his side—and only for purposes of personal gain—had to be on the staff of the major newspaper in a city where he'd flirted with the idea of settling.

He was on the ferry to Vancouver, B.C., the next morning.

For the next year he traveled about British Columbia: east to the Rockies, up to the edge of the Northwest Territories, down to Prince Rupert, then back to Vancouver. He stayed mainly in small towns, picked up work when and where he could, and was charmed by the friendliness and courtesy of the people. By the time he boarded the B.C. Ferry for Vancouver island, he was seriously considering taking up permanent residence in the province.

Another chance encounter, this one more fortunate than the incident in Seattle, turned possibility into reality. While strolling along the pier in Port Regis the morning after he'd checked into the hotel, he met Ned Webster, owner and operator of the *Queen Charlotte*. A garrulous man in his mid-sixties, Ned responded with pride and pleasure to Matt's questions about his handsome craft and allowed him to pilot her during a free harbor tour. Later, over drinks in the hotel bar, his interest in Matt became apparent: He was looking for a partner who would buy the business when he decided to retire—but not just any partner. The *Queen Charlotte*'s new captain would have to be a man who would appreciate her and maintain her in the style to which she was accustomed. Matt, Ned told him, had passed the test.

By the next afternoon Matt had requested that his

Minnesota bank wire the funds necessary to buy into Webster Marine Charters. The following morning the local real estate agent took him to look at the run-down cabin with the view of the sea and Bear Rock. By that afternoon he'd put in a second request to his bank for the funds to buy it.

His second life, the wandering years, was over, and his third life had begun.

As he stood staring into the mirror in his motel room in Talbot's Mills, he reflected that by leaving British Columbia he'd ended that life and embarked upon yet another. His fourth life would not be nearly as pleasant as the last, but it would surely make up for the pain that had ended his first.

Cyanide Wells lay in a wide meadow some twenty-five miles southeast of Talbot's Mills, near the Eel River National Forest. High grass, as yet unbrowned, rippled on either side of the well-paved two-lane highway, and clusters of ranch buildings appeared in the distance. Ahead, under a clear blue sky, lay the rolling, pine- and aspen-covered foothills of the forest, and above them towered a bald, rounded outcropping that Matt assumed was the formation called the Knob.

The previous afternoon in the library he'd read about the town and learned it was a former gold-mining camp, once called Seven Wells because of its abundant underground springs. In its heyday in the 1860s its population had numbered nearly ten thousand, and it had boasted of five hotels, three general stores, various shops, twenty boarding houses, twenty-seven saloons, seventeen brothels, and two churches. The rocky Knob contained one of the richest veins of ore in the northwestern part of California, but the mines were eventually played out and abandoned. Seven Wells was on the verge of becoming a ghost town when, in 1900, cyaniders, as they were known, from a Denver mining company arrived, equipped with knowledge of how to use the deadly poison to extract gold from the waste dumps, tailings, and what low-grade ore remained in the earth. A bitter rivalry between one of their engineering team and an old Cornish miner with a small, poor claim had resulted in the poisoning of the seven public wells for which the town was named—an incident so notorious that the popular appellation of Cyanide Wells took hold and was years later made official, even though the water supply had long since been cleansed. By now most of the wells had run dry.

The town and its contrast to Talbot's Mills took Matt by surprise. The business district consisted of two blocks of restored false-fronted buildings, and on the side streets tidy, Victorian-era cottages mingled with larger, more contemporary dwellings. Bed-and-breakfasts abounded. Although Starbuck's hadn't yet invaded, Aram's Coffee Shop was doing a turn-away business; Dead People's Stuff offered "fine antiques"; the Good Earth Bakery advertised fresh focaccia; Mamma Mia's featured lobster ravioli; the Main Street Diner looked to be a takeoff on the Hard Rock Cafe. Everything was freshly painted and too tidy and seemed a counterfeit of the real world. As he drove along, Matt began to feel nostalgia for Port Regis's rough edges.

He soon located the *Soledad Spectrum* in a white frame building with Wedgwood blue trim, sandwiched between

M'Lady's Boutique and the Thai Issan restaurant. Cars and trucks and campers lined the curbs, and there wasn't a parking space to be had, so he pulled off onto a side street and walked back, his camera slung around his neck. As he merged with the people on the sidewalk, he took in details with his photographer's eyes. For twelve years he'd shunned his true calling, but he'd never stopped looking at his surroundings as if through the lens.

Couples in shorts and T-shirts, holding hands the way they did when on their own in a strange place, took in the sights. Locals in casual or business attire entered and exited Bank of Soledad, First American Title, State Farm Insurance, Redwood Cleaners, and Tuttle Drugs. Children, on some sort of field trip from grade school, walked in line behind their teacher, clutching at a colorful braided rope like a litter of puppies on a lead. Old men lounged on a bench in a park by a stone-walled well—presumably one of the seven that had been poisoned over a century before. Several women in flowered dresses sipped cappuccino at a wrought-iron table in front of the Wells Mercantile. At the post office, newspaper racks were lined up on the sidewalk: everything from the *New York Times* to the *Soledad Spectrum*.

He bought a copy of the local paper and, at the Mercantile, an area map. Then he walked over to the park and sat down on a bench by the well to study both. The front section of the *Spectrum* was devoted to county news; national and world items off the wire services and syndicated material filled the second; the third covered the arts. Nowhere was Ardis Coleman's byline. He turned to the op-ed page, and immediately his eye was drawn to a boxed ad at its bottom.

Wanted: General assignment photographer for
Soledad Spectrum. *Small paper experience, refer-*
ences required. See C. McGuire, 1101 Main Street.

Sheer coincidence? Fate? He didn't believe in either,
yet a chill was on his spine.

Photographer? Yes.

Small-paper experience, references? No.

But those he could acquire.

After half an hour on the phone to Port Regis, making
explanations to Millie Bertram that were at best half-
truths and giving instructions that she carefully wrote
down and repeated, Matt stepped through the door of the
Soledad Spectrum. An unmanned reception desk confronted him, flanked on its left by a gated railing barring
access to the area behind. Four computer workstations,
three of them unoccupied, filled the rest of the room, and
a trio of closed doors led to the rear of the building.
When Matt came in, a slender, dark-haired man who was
pounding on a keyboard at the station farthest from the
reception desk glanced up and snapped, "Help you?"

"I'm looking for C. McGuire."

"You're the only one, buddy. Carly's on a tear, and
everybody but me has taken off early for a long lunch.
I'd've gone to earth, too, if I didn't have to finish this
goddamn story on the new logging regs." He lifted his
hands from the keyboard, flopped them beside it in an
exaggerated gesture of helplessness. "But my man-
ners—where are they?"

"You tell me."

The man smiled and got up, came over to the rail, and extended a hand. "Severin Quill, police/political reporter. Don't laugh at the name. It's ridiculous, but few people forget it."

"John Crowe, wanna-be general assignment photographer."

"All right!" Severin Quill's mouth quirked up. He was no more than twenty-five, with a puckish face and, apparently, a sense of humor to match. "You just may be our salvation, Mr. Crowe. One—though by no means all—of the reasons for Carly's bearish mood is the defection of our former photographer. He took off last week without a word of notice. Not that I blame him."

"Why don't you?"

"Because on her best of days Carly McGuire is a pain in the ass to work for. I feel duty-bound to warn you of that before you go back there"—he jerked his thumb at one of the closed doors—"into the harpy's nest."

"So why are you here?"

"Because to any newspaper person worth his or her salt, Carly's standards and expectations are challenges others only dream of."

"Then maybe I'll take my chances."

The first word Matt heard out of Carly McGuire's mouth was *"What!"*

Loud, even through the closed door, and very irritated. But also low-timbred and sultry—the kind they used to call a "whiskey voice." One that, whatever potential abuse lay behind that door, made him determined to see its owner.

"I'm here about the photographer's job," he called.

"So don't just stand there. Come in!"

He pushed through into a small, cluttered room. A huge weekly calendar scrawled with notations covered the far wall. Tearsheets and lists and photographs were tacked haphazardly to the others. The floor was mounded with books and papers; in its center sat a large, equally mounded metal desk. And in *its* center a woman in black jeans and a T-shirt sat cross-legged, glaring at him.

Carly McGuire was around forty, slender and long-limbed, with honey-colored hair that fell straight to her shoulders. Her skin glowed with what looked to be a year-round tan, and her oval face framed rather severe features. Or maybe they only appeared to be severe because of the horn-rimmed half-glasses that perched on the tip of her nose, and the frown lines etched between her eyebrows.

"Well?" she said.

"I saw your ad—"

"Of course you did. Get to the point."

"I want the job."

"And why do you think I should hire you?"

"Small-paper experience—eighteen years. A reference—from my editor and publisher. And I'm a damned good photographer."

She seemed to like his response. At least her scowl didn't deepen, and she took off the glasses, twirling them around as she studied him.

"Name?" she asked.

"John Crowe."

"From?"

"Port Regis, British Columbia."

"Here for?"

"A change of scene."

"Reason? Fired? Divorced?"

"Neither. Leave of absence for now, but it could become permanent."

She nodded. "Okay, none of my business and rightly so."

"I'm glad you realize that."

She compressed her lips and studied him some more. Then she unfolded her long legs and scooted over to the edge of the desk, knocking several files to the floor but sliding off gracefully. "Let's have you fill out an application, and then I'll put you to the test."

"What test?"

"You'll see."

Carly McGuire seated Matt with an application form at the still unmanned reception desk and disappeared into her office. Before he could get started, Severin Quill expelled a dramatic sigh and swiveled away from his workstation. "The piece is finished, and so am I," he announced. "Lunchtime—a long, liquid one. Sorry to leave you here to fend on your own, Mr. Crowe."

"If you hear screams, come running."

Matt waited till Quill had left the building, then scanned the desk where he sat. A Rolodex, fat with cards, stood on one corner. Quickly he turned it to the *C*'s, located Ardis Coleman's name, and copied the address and phone number onto a piece of scratch paper.

Easy, but things are if you think them through.

He then turned his attention to the job application.

Former employer: the—fictional—*Port Regis Register*. Contact: Millie Bertram, editor and publisher.

Position: chief photographer.

Employed: 1984–2002.

Education: BA, English and prelaw, Northwestern University. McGuire wouldn't check with the college, given the passage of time.

Address and phone number—

Damn! He'd registered at the motel under his own name. But . . .

He reached for his wallet, took out the slip of paper that Sam—last name D'Angelo—had written her phone number and address on when he'd delivered her there the night before. He'd phone, ask her to field his calls. If necessary, he'd take her to dinner as payment for the favor. No, he'd do it anyway; the kid could use a good meal.

He was signing the application with Johnny Crowe's name when Carly McGuire emerged from her office, smiling fiendishly.

"What's this?" Matt asked, staring at the red Ford pickup with the white camper shell on its bed and a Save the Redwoods sticker on its bumper. It was pulled up against the wall in the alley behind the building.

"The test," she said.

"You want me to take pictures of a *truck*?"

"I don't want you to take pictures of anything." She seized the strap of his camera bag and relieved him of it, then slapped a key into his hand. "I want you to make it start."

"Huh?"

She tapped the toe of her cowboy boot on the gravel. "You said small-paper experience. I don't know about the *Port Royal Register*—"

"Port Regis."

"Whatever. But here at the *Spectrum* we all pitch in to do whatever it takes to get the paper out. And if I can't get this truck started, I can't get the week's issue to the printer down in Santa Carla by six o'clock tonight. In all the years I've owned the *Spectrum* we've never missed press time."

"So if everybody pitches in to get the paper out, why haven't any of them already gotten the truck started? Or offered you the use of their vehicles?"

McGuire's mouth drooped and she suddenly looked tired. "A couple of them tried and gave up. And I don't like to drive other people's vehicles."

Meaning other people didn't like to lend theirs to her. "How about calling a garage or Triple A?"

"I have a . . . problem with the local garage. And I accidentally let my Triple A membership lapse. Can you fix it or not?"

Fortunately, he'd spent most of his life poking his nose into various engine compartments. "I can fix it."

It wasn't an old truck—1999 Ford Ranger, and appeared to be well maintained. But when he eased himself into the driver's seat and tried to turn it over, the idiot lights flashed and bells rang, but there wasn't even a click, just the faintest of hums.

"It's not the battery," he said.

"I know that! It was the first thing the others checked."

He jiggled the gearshift lever, depressed the clutch,

turned the key again. Nothing. "This an alarm system?" he asked, pointing to a unit with a blinking red light mounted beneath the dash.

McGuire came over and peered through the open door. "Yeah. The dealership put it on because there had been a lot of thefts off their used-car lot. I didn't want to pay for it, and they were supposed to make an appointment to have it taken off, but they never got back to me. I don't even know how it works."

"Raise the hood, will you?" While she did, he set the ignition to Start. When he went around to the front of the truck, he found McGuire staring at its innards with a bewildered frown.

"I hate mechanical things," she said.

"Maybe if you knew more about them, you'd like them better. D'you have some pliers?"

"There's a toolbox in the bed. I'll see." She went away, came back with a pair. "These okay?"

"Yep." He took them from her and went to work connecting the ignition wire directly to the solenoid. The engine roared, then began to purr.

McGuire smiled as if the sounds were the opening notes of a favorite symphony. "What was wrong with it?"

"Well, it could be a problem with your starter, but my guess is that the truck's paranoid."

"It's *what?*"

"The kind of alarm you have prevents theft by keeping the vehicle from starting. Apparently your truck decided somebody was trying to steal it and activated its own alarm."

She scowled. "Is this a joke?"

"Truck's running, isn't it?"

She transferred her scowl to the Ford. "Is it fixed for good?"

"No. I bypassed the alarm for now, but it should be disconnected."

"Can you do that?"

"It depends."

"On what?"

"On whether I have the photographer's job."

McGuire sighed. "You have the job, Mr. Crowe."

A difficult woman, Carly McGuire. Puzzling and contradictory, too. But Matt couldn't afford to dwell on her. After he spent half an hour disconnecting the Ford's alarm, he had more immediate matters to attend to.

First the call to Sam, who was so eager to help him that she hadn't asked why he needed to use her address and phone number, and so happy to be invited to dinner that she offered to cook for him. He didn't think it was a good idea, but when she insisted, he agreed.

Next he went to the Jeep, removed the standard lens from the Nikon, and attached the F2.8 telephoto with 1.4x teleconverter—a combination that afforded the equivalent of a 400 F4.0 lens without the bulk and length. On the area map he'd bought earlier, he located Drinkwater Road, northwest of the Knob, along the creek of the same name. Before he left town, he bought a sandwich and a Coke at a deli and ate while he drove.

Aspen Road led him across the eastern side of the meadow toward the Knob. To either side of the pavement, houses spread behind rustic split-rail fences: new, with much glass, yet weathered to blend in with their surroundings. An exclusive development to match the tricked-up little town, here in what he'd learned was a poor county where the economic bases of logging, mining, and commercial fishing were eroding. Perhaps luxury dwellings and services for retirees and second-homers would provide the answer to Soledad County's dilemma, but to Matt it seemed they would only create a dangerous gap between the haves and the have-nots.

Ahead, the Knob rose against the clear sky: tall, rounded on top, slightly atilt, eroded and polished by the elements. He couldn't help but smile. Perhaps it had resembled an upended doorknob to the settlers who named it, but to him it looked like a huge erect penis. God knew what the retirees in their expensive homes thought about spending their declining years in the shadow of an enormous dick!

Drinkwater Road appeared some two miles from town. He followed its curves as it meandered north along the creek bed. The stream was swollen with runoff from the mountain snowmelt, and its water rushed over rocks and foamed between them. To the road's left, wooden bridges led to dwellings on the creek's other side; eucalyptus and pine and newly leafed aspen blurred the buildings' outlines. To the right of the pavement rose a rocky slope, broken occasionally by dirt driveways with mailboxes. He didn't need to consult the slip of paper on which he'd written Gwen's—no, Ardis Coleman's—address; he'd already committed it and the phone number to memory.

He drove slowly for several miles, taking careful note of his surroundings: blind curves, sheltered places to turn off, areas where there were no houses or driveways.

When he saw a wood-burned sign at the end of a bridge on the creek side, bearing the number 11708, he didn't stop. Instead he drove for another mile, still observing, then turned back.

The house where his ex-wife lived—possibly had lived for all of the fourteen years he'd presumed her dead—was set back from the creek and screened by trees and other vegetation; the plank bridge was not wide enough to accommodate a car or truck, but there was a paved parking area to its right, currently empty. Matt stopped there, took up the Nikon, and scanned the property.

One-story redwood-and-stone house with chimneys at either end and a number of large bubble-type skylights. Flagstone patio in front, equipped with a hot tub, table and chairs, chaise longues, and barbecue. Rope hammock in an iron stand under an oak tree to the other side of the walk.

Nothing at all like the modest home he and Gwen had shared in Saugatuck.

After a moment, he moved the Jeep to a different vantage point. There was a rose garden beyond the hammock, fenced off, probably against the incursions of deer. Gwen had always loved roses. And beyond that sat a child's swing set. Gwen, unlike him, had never wanted children. . . .

A car, coming along the road from the south, taking the curves swiftly and surely.

Matt started the Jeep, pulled away as the other vehicle crested a rise and sped past. Not Gwen, but it wasn't a good idea for anyone to see him here. There was a place about fifty yards to the south that he'd spotted earlier, where he and the Jeep would be concealed from all traffic—a place that commanded a view of Gwen's parking area.

That was where he'd wait for her.

By four-thirty he was cramped and tired and suffering from a severe tension headache. Best to pack it in and head back to the motel. After all, he'd waited fourteen years; another day or two wouldn't kill him. He was now gainfully employed—general assignment photographer and truck mechanic for the local paper. That gave him a bona fide reason for prowling the countryside.

But still he waited. Five minutes, ten, fifteen . . . Cars and trucks and SUVs passed—residents returning to their homes. He counted them, one through twenty, and then a white SUV appeared, slowed, and turned off into Gwen's parking area. One of those new Mercedeses he'd seen written up in the automotive section of the Vancouver paper; suggested retail price was in the neighborhood of seventy-three thousand U.S. dollars.

Doing well, Gwennie.

He took up the Nikon again as the driver's-side door opened. Leaned forward with the lens aimed through the Jeep's windshield. A woman came around the vehicle—tall and slim, with a model's erect posture and a dancer's graceful step. Gwen's posture. Gwen's step.

She went to the passenger-side door and opened it. Said something to someone inside and turned. Now he had a clear view of her face. Her once-smooth skin bore fine lines at the corners of her eyes and mouth, and her long dark-brown hair had been cut so that it curved in smooth wings to her jawbone, but he recognized her instantly. He gripped the Nikon hard, and his nervous finger depressed the shutter.

As Gwen moved to the rear of the SUV and opened the door, the passenger stepped down. A girl of nine or ten, dragging an enormous backpack of the sort all the kids seemed to favor these days. Her skin was honeytan, and her features and curly black hair indicated African-American heritage. Had Gwen married a black man? Adopted a mixed-race child?

Gwen was taking a folded metal cart from the rear of the vehicle. As the child approached, smiling up at her, Matt took another photograph. Gwen set up the cart and began filling it with grocery bags. After she finished and shut the door, she tried to take the backpack from the little girl, who resisted, laughing. Gwen laughed, too, ruffling the child's hair; the love in her eyes was reflected in her daughter's. The two started across the footbridge, Gwen pulling the cart with one hand, the other resting on the girl's shoulder.

Matt snapped a picture of them before they passed out of sight behind an overhanging fringe of pine branches.

Well, now you know, Lindstrom. She's got herself a nice home, nice little girl, probably a nice husband. The good life that she somehow couldn't find with you.

Now you know. And you know what you have to do.

Back at his motel, he had one drink of Wild Turkey and then another. They did nothing to take the edge off. Even though he'd expected to see Gwen's image through the camera's lens, its actual appearance had shocked him. Altered him, too, in ways that he couldn't yet begin to guess at. His hands were shaking as he poured another drink and the memories crowded in, their former bittersweet flavor now charred by rage.

"Let me help you. Gwennie. Whatever's wrong, I can help you through this if you'll let me."

"Nobody can help. Least of all you."

"Is it my fault? What's wrong with me?"

"It's not you. Just leave it."

"Gwen—"

"Just leave it. And leave me alone!"

"Why don't you want kids? Give me one good reason why."

"For God's sake, Matt, look at the world we're living in. Do you really want to bring children into it?"

"Ah, the standard line."

"What does that mean?"

"It's everybody's excuse when they're—"

"When they're what? Too selfish? Is that what you think of me?"

"No, but maybe you're afraid of the responsibility."

"Well, what if I am?"

"I'd share the responsibility. You wouldn't be alone."

"I don't know. I just don't know. Kids, they make everything so . . . permanent."

*   *   *

"The way you're looking at me, Gwen, it's as if you hate me."

"Matt, no . . ."

"Well, that sure isn't the way a woman looks at the man she loves."

"I do love you; that's not the problem."

"Then what is the problem?"

"Matt, I want a divorce."

"You say you love me, but you want a divorce?"

"I want a divorce because if I don't leave you, I will hate you."

"The mind may forget, but not the body."

"Then stay. Refresh your memory."

"It's not that simple, Matt."

"Why not?"

"Because it just isn't."

When he reached for the Wild Turkey again, he saw the bottle of wine that he'd bought along with his lunch at the deli in Cyanide Wells.

Sam! Jesus Christ . . .

He'd been due at her house at seven, but now his watch showed eight-forty. *Better phone. No—go. Think of some plausible excuse on the way.* Poor kid, she'd been so excited; he couldn't brush her off with a call.

Sam's little frame house was dark when he stopped at the curb, and for a moment he felt relieved. He could just drive away, call her in the morning. But then he spotted a flicker of light on the porch, and a figure moved in the shadows. After he cut the Jeep's engine, Sam's voice called, "Well, John Crowe. The roast I spent my hard-earned money on this afternoon is as tough as beef jerky by now, and the fresh asparagus have turned gray. So what's your excuse?"

He got out of the Jeep and mounted the steps. The light he'd seen came from a candle in a glass globe on a small table between two broken-down wicker chairs. Extending the wine bottle to her, he said, "I'm sorry."

She took the bottle and turned toward the door. "It's my fault, for making a big deal out of having a guy I met in a bar over for dinner."

"No, it's my fault. I lost track of the time." The elaborate excuse he'd concocted about his new job and a time-consuming first assignment seemed a shabby lie now.

Sam said, "I'll open the wine and get us glasses. Maybe after we drink some, the beef jerky won't seem so tough, and I can probably get the asparagus up on their feet with some salad dressing."

In a couple of minutes she came back. Wordlessly she handed the open bottle to him, set down two glasses, and indicated he should pour. When she sat, the candle's light touched her face, and he saw her eyes were puffy and red.

"You've been crying."

"Crying's kind of my thing these days."

"Sam, I should've called. I was thoughtless, and I'm sorry."

"One 'sorry' is enough, thank you. How much bourbon have you drunk, anyway?"

"Too much."

"You shouldn't've driven in your condition. I don't like drunks behind the wheel. My girlfriend's little boy died because of somebody like you."

"I'm—"

"Yeah, I know—you're sorry. Give me your car keys."

"What?"

"Your car keys." She held out her hand, snapped her fingers. "You can stay here tonight, because I plan to drink this wine and then some more, so I won't be able to take you back to your motel."

"But—"

"It's not a proposition. My dad's bed is made up fresh."

He reached into his pocket, surrendered the keys.

She nodded in approval. "So why the communion with the bottle?"

He had an easy answer prepared. "Celebrating too much."

"Celebrating what?"

"My new job as general assignment photographer for the *Spectrum*."

"Hey, that's great!"

"I'm pretty happy about it."

"That what you did up in Canada?"

"For a much smaller paper."

"Then you know about all the world-shattering events you'll be taking pictures of: the hog judging at the county fair, old folks celebrating their fiftieth wedding anniversaries, the groundbreaking for the new Denny's."

"Listen, in order to get the job I had to fix Carly

McGuire's truck. After that, everything else'll seem exciting."

Sam laughed. "She bullied you into it, huh?"

"Sort of."

"I hear she's not easy to work for, but if you've got a good idea she'll turn you loose on it. That's what she did with Ardis Coleman on the series that won the Pulitzer. And she ran an arty shot by the last photographer every week. You give her something she likes, she'll print it."

"You sound as if you know her."

"I don't really know anybody in Cyanide Wells."

"What about Ardis Coleman?"

"I told you last night, the closest I've gotten to her is being in the next line at the supermarket."

"You must've heard something about her. She's a local celebrity."

"How come you're so interested?"

"I guess it's kind of like hero worship. This is the closest I've gotten to a Pulitzer winner—being in the same county with her."

"Well . . . They say she's reclusive. Lives out on Drinkwater Creek on a big piece of property. Doesn't give interviews or make public appearances. I think somebody told me she has a kid, but I don't remember whether it's a girl or a boy. She must have money, though; that's one expensive, snooty town. I don't know why that paper's there. They crusade for all the things rich people are against: financing decent health care and welfare programs through higher taxes, making big corporations pay their fair share. They're for preserving the environment, too, but they don't go overboard; they recognize that people like loggers and fishermen have to make a living. What they want is a reasonable balance, and I like that. I also like it that the paper's owned by a woman. It's the kind of thing I'd've wanted to do if I'd gotten a decent education and had the kind of money Carly McGuire must."

In the light from the candle Sam suddenly looked melancholy. She added, "Lots of *if*s, huh? But *if*s don't count. I'll be working at the Chicken Shack till I keel over serving a Supreme Combo with cole slaw and fries."

"You told me last night that you were thinking of getting out of here."

"I *think* about a lot of things. It's the doing that's hard." She sipped wine, more pensive. "So you'll be staying around. Got a place to live?"

"Not yet. On my salary I couldn't even afford a closet in Cyanide Wells, so I'm thinking of looking here. I like Talbot's Mills better, anyway."

"Why?"

"It's real."

Sam smiled grimly. "Oh, it's real, all right. My dad could've told you how real it is. But listen, I know of a room for rent, with kitchen privileges."

"Oh?"

"Yeah. Very cheap, if you volunteer for some chores, like fixing the drippy bathroom faucet and cleaning out the gutters."

"When can I look at it?"

"Right now, if you want." She stood and moved toward the door.

"I thought you had to be out of here next month."

Sam looked uncomfortable. "I didn't tell you the

whole truth about my dad. He . . . shot himself. Just couldn't take being laid off at his age. After the funeral, one of the *Spectrum*'s reporters, that Donna Vail, interviewed me. I didn't exactly hold back about the way the mill treated him. The manager there found out they were printing the story, so he called this morning and said I can live here rent-free till the end of the year, and if I want to stay longer, they'll negotiate a fair price."

"And of course their P.R. department called the paper as soon as you agreed."

"Of course, but what the hell do I care? It's a roof over my head, and if you move in I might actually be able to save some money."

He considered. Sam struck him as both levelheaded and easy to get along with. She wasn't especially curious about either his prior or his present life and seemed disinclined to initiate a sexual relationship with him. Plus, she was an excellent source of information about the community. But best of all, he could get out of the motel, where he'd registered under his own name.

"I don't need to inspect the room," he said. "I'm sure it'll be fine. I'm good with plumbing, so the leak should be fixed by this time tomorrow. Give me a little longer on the gutters."

Thursday, May 9, 2002

tour of the *Spectrum*'s offices, under the guidance of Severin Quill, was the first activity of the new day. Matt, nursing a hangover, suffered most of it in silence, saving his strength for Quill's introductions of their fellow staff members. He'd already been greeted at the reception desk by the office and subscription manager, Brandi Webster, a young woman with the good looks of a high school cheerleader and the mannerisms to match; normally he would have found them delightful, but today they just seemed wearisome.

As Quill got up from his desk and came to meet him, a heavyset woman in a purple straw hat and voluminous flowered clothing rushed past Matt, calling out, "Vera

Craig, arts editor. Welcome aboard!" The scent of violet perfume trailed after her.

Quill smiled. "Appearances to the contrary, Vera's a damned good reporter and an astute critic. This morning she's off to chronicle the opening of the new Thomas Kinkade gallery."

"Kinkade?"

"California's 'painter of light.' Mass-produced 'originals.'"

"Like Keane paintings?"

"No, more palatable. Idyllic scenes instead of glassy-eyed children. Very popular in the nineties; less so now, and his enterprises are overextended—hence a gallery in our provincial little community."

A woman came through one of the doors at the rear of the room, and Quill called, "Donna, meet John Crowe, our new photographer. John, Donna Vail, general assignment reporter. You'll be working closely with her."

Donna Vail was small, blonde, and attractive. She wore shorts and a tee, and her frizzy shoulder-length hair was topped by a baseball cap. Her blue eyes surveyed him with frank interest, and she said in a husky voice, "Good to meet you, John. I'm sure I'll enjoy working *closely* with you." Then, like Vera Craig, she was out the door.

Quill chuckled, and Matt realized his mouth had fallen open. "Don't mind Donna," Severin said. "She likes to project a bad-girl image. In reality, she's a dedicated soccer mom and wife of the golf pro at the Meadows."

"The Meadows?"

"A big planned community on the road east of town.

The way to handle Donna is to serve back to her what she dishes up. She won't know if you're serious or not, so she'll back off and treat you like a buddy."

"Well, that's a relief."

The tour went on to a large back room full of cubicles, where Matt met the display ad manager, advertising sales representatives, and mail-room personnel. As they were passing through the front room again, Quill introduced him to the religious/education and sports reporters. The door to Carly McGuire's office was closed, and a Do Not Disturb sign—courtesy of Ramada Inn—hung on its knob.

"She's hiding?" he asked.

Quill rolled his eyes. "Yes, thank God. She came in loaded for bear."

"Why?"

"Who knows, with Carly?"

"The truck got her to Santa Carla and back okay, didn't it?"

"If it hadn't, my friend, you wouldn't be alive."

Quill led him through another door, to a room where the production manager and chief of page makeup and their assistants congratulated him on joining the staff. Beyond their areas were a couple of desks, a bank of file cabinets, and a light table. A door labeled DARKROOM was set into the wall opposite them.

"Your bailiwick," Quill said, with a flourish of his hand. "Your assistant, Joe Maynard, is currently in the inner sanctum, printing what he claims are perfectly egregious photographs he took at the Calvert's Landing mayoral press conference this week."

"Calvert's Landing?"

"It's the largest town on the coast. An Alaskan company wants to float gigantic, ugly plastic bags at the outlet of the Deer River to collect water to sell to southern California. Mayor's all for the deal; he claims the water belongs to the state, not the municipality, so they can't stop it. Which means he's been paid off by the Alaskans. His constituency is concerned about environmental issues and visual pollution. The mayor's effort to convert them to his point of view ended up in an unfortunate egg-throwing incident, which Joe captured on film."

"Egregiously."

"He tends to underestimate his talents. Anyway, I'll leave you to await his emergence."

Matt had hoped, now that the tour of the facilities was at its final destination, to ask Quill about Ardis Coleman. But when he invited him to sit down and chat till Maynard was done, the reporter said he had an appointment in fifteen minutes. Maybe they could have a beer after work? Matt suggested. Sure, Quill said, if they finished at the same time. Hours at the *Spectrum* were irregular at best.

Joe Maynard was built like a linebacker, with a shock of unruly brown hair, a nose that looked as if it had been broken more than once, and almost no neck. His hands were so large and clumsy-looking that Matt wondered how he could manipulate the settings on his camera. As they began trading histories in the cautious manner of men who know they must get along in order to work together, he found that Joe had indeed been a linebacker, at UCLA, where he'd earned a degree in fine arts.

"So what brought you to Cyanide Wells?" Matt asked.

"A chance to work at a paper in a place where I could also hunt and fish. After college I played a couple of seasons on special teams for the Pittsburgh Steelers, but I hated the weather back there. And I wasn't really pro caliber, anyway. So I saved my money, came back to California, and worked for the *Long Beach Sentinel*. Then I heard about an opening here and applied. They'd just won the Pulitzer, and McGuire had an interesting reputation. Plus, I could live cheap."

"How come McGuire didn't promote you when the last guy left?"

"She tried to, but I turned her down. I don't want to work full-time. I invested well before the dot-com bubble popped, took my profits, and put them into conservative holdings. And a year ago my wife presented me with twin boys. I want to be as much a part of their lives as I can."

"Good for you." Matt proceeded to give him the same abbreviated details of his made-up life that he'd told Carly McGuire, then said, "Now, let's see how those shots of the egg-faced mayor have turned out."

Maynard's photographs were so good that Matt wondered what he might have accomplished had he had the desire to apply his talent. But talent alone, he knew, wasn't enough to ensure success; success took drive and dedication, which his new assistant plainly lacked.

"So," he said as they emerged from the darkroom, "you came to the paper before it won the Pulitzer?"

"Afterwards. That was one of the things that attracted me. I mean, how often do you get to work for a small country weekly that's achieved the granddaddy of journalistic honors? The only other one that comes to mind is the *Point Reyes Light,* for their exposé of Synanon, and that was decades ago."

"I understand the bulk of the *Spectrum*'s prize-winning articles were written by a reporter called Ardis Coleman. You know her?"

"I've met her."

"What's she like?"

"Quiet. Unassuming. Self-deprecating, actually. She once told me she didn't do anything special, she was just handed a great story. But under the circumstances, I'd say her coverage was extraordinary."

"What circumstances?"

"Ronnie Talbot and Deke Rutherford, the murder victims, were good friends of Coleman's, and she was the one who found their bodies. Yet she was able to separate herself from her emotions and write extremely balanced, well reasoned stories. I admire that kind of control."

And how had Gwen achieved such control? The picture that Maynard painted was not of the woman Matt had married.

"What's Coleman like personally? She married? Have kids?"

Maynard smiled. "What, you thinking of asking her for a date?"

"I'm just curious about how a woman like that balances work and family, if she has any."

Maynard seemed unconvinced of his reply. "Look," he said, "she's a good friend of McGuire's. Why don't you ask her?"

He'd have more success prying information out of the

Great Sphinx. "I guess I'd better wait till she's having a better day."

"Good luck, buddy."

Within fifteen minutes, a memo from McGuire was delivered to his desk by a young man with magenta-and-green hair and multiple body piercings, who identified himself as the office gofer. "Name's Nile, like the river."

"No last name?"

"Don't need one. How many people're called Nile? Besides, Nile Schultz sounds just plain stupid." He gave him a little salute and walked away.

Matt picked up the memo and studied it. It was computer-generated, printed on the back of what looked to be copy for a story, which had a big black X through it. McGuire clearly didn't waste paper—or type very well, either.

John, I called your former editor this a.m. and she gave you a glowing recommendation. I hope you can live up to it. Here's the schedule of your assignments for today. I want to meet with you at 4:30 after you've completed them. 11:30a--meet Vera Craig at the new Kinkade gallery, Main St. next to the Book nook. Vera will tell you what shots she needs. 1:30p--Gundersons silver wedding anniversary shoot, their home, 111 Estes St. I assume you have a map, if not purchase one. 2:15p--Pooh's Corner, next to Aram's, need shots of new line of anatomically correct dolls that are causing the current flap. Avoid private parts, the parents are up in

arms and we don't want to further incite them.
Thanks, Carly.

It was now a little after ten; since his first assignment wasn't until eleven-thirty, he had time to slip away and check out Gwen's home more closely. Grabbing his camera bag, he left the office and drove off toward Drinkwater Road.

The expensive SUV sat in the paved area by the footbridge but in a different place than on the previous afternoon; probably Gwen had driven her little girl to school. Matt drove past, turned, and zoomed in on it, snapping a photo showing its license plate number. Then he drove to where he'd parked before and moved along the road, taking random shots to either side. A casual observer would probably have assumed he was documenting the regional plants and trees, but the true objects of his shots were Gwen's mailbox, the footbridge, and the extent of her property. When he finished the roll, he drove back toward town and his first appointment, wondering whether he could persuade Vera Craig to have lunch with him. The arts editor seemed open and friendly, exactly the sort of person who might be willing to answer his questions about the paper's prize-winning former reporter.

"Hell, honey," Vera Craig said, "none of us see much of Ard these days." She speared a lobster ravioli from the plate she and Matt were sharing at Mamma Mia's, bit into it with her eyes closed, and made a sound of pure sensual delight.

Matt tasted one. It was good, but not enough to nearly induce an orgasm. "Why not?"

"I guess she's just holed up at home, working on her book. It's giving her trouble. At least that's what Carly says."

"You know her well?"

"Nobody knows Ard well, except for Carly, and sometimes I wonder about that. I've been acquainted with her since she came to town, and after fourteen or fifteen years, I still don't know what makes her tick."

"She worked for the paper right from the first?"

"Yeah, as a gofer, then general assignment reporter. Good one, willing to take on anything. She just got better and better, till Carly finally promoted her to roving-reporter status, meaning she basically covered any story in the county that she found controversial or interesting. Then came the murders."

"I understand she was the one who found the bodies."

Vera Craig's face grew somber, and she set her fork tines on the edge of the plate. "Yeah. Bad for her in a couple of ways. Finding two men slaughtered in their bed was pretty horrific. And they weren't strangers; they were her friends. But besides her grief she had to deal with community reaction."

"I don't understand."

"Cyanide Wells and the county as a whole are pretty conservative. You've got your rich people, mostly retirees; you've got your religious people, your young families, your working-class people, and your assholes who like to drink and shoot their guns and would consider a good evening's fun burning a cross on somebody's front lawn—or blowing away a couple of 'faggots' in their own bed. And, like anyplace else, you've got your gays who mainly keep a low profile. Ronnie Talbot and Deke Rutherford didn't, and Ronnie compounded the general dislike by selling off the mill. When it came out that Ard was their friend, the dislike was transferred to her."

"That must've changed when the paper won the Pulitzer."

"It changed when people started reading her stories. They were so powerful, they made the readers under-stand—or at least think about—the problems of gays who live in this type of environment."

"So now she's writing a book."

"Has been for over two years. It's contracted for and is due to be turned in pretty soon, but like I said, she's having problems with it."

"It can't be easy, dealing with that kind of material."

"I guess not." Craig picked up her fork and attacked the ravioli with renewed vigor. "But enough about Ard. Tell me about yourself, honey. What brought you to our little village, anyway?"

Lying, Matt reflected as he packed up his gear and said good-bye to the proprietor of Pooh's Corner, could be an exhausting business. Today he'd given various versions of the life and times of John Crowe to at least five peo-ple. He was glad that his final encounter would be with Carly McGuire, Severin Quill having canceled their ten-tative plans for drinks—he had to go someplace called Signal Port on a story. McGuire, Matt assumed, knew everything about him that she wanted to know, and would be more interested in his work than his personal history.

He had roughly an hour and a half before their meeting, so he headed back to the darkroom to develop his films. The contact sheets showed he hadn't lost his eye, although there were certain technical skills that weren't as sharp as they'd once been. He particularly liked the last batch of photos: the inanely smiling girl and boy dolls that were causing such controversy among local parents. Innocence, if not downright stupidity, radiated from their faces, and the private parts—which he'd shot for his own amusement—were no more threatening and much less realistic than those that the children of Cyanide Wells surely witnessed while playing the time-honored game of "doctor."

Four-thirty on the dot. Armed with his contact sheets, Matt went to McGuire's office. The door was slightly ajar, and before he could knock, he heard Carly's raised voice.

"Don't you threaten me, Gar!"

"That was a mere statement of fact, not a threat." The man's voice was deep and full-bodied—and vaguely familiar.

"Facts, I'm afraid, are open to personal interpretation."

"Perhaps, but you should realize that there are complex issues at work here, which you can't possibly begin to understand."

"Complex issues. Which I can't understand. I don't think so."

"You're not infallible, Carly. If you don't believe me, look to your own life."

There was a silence, and then McGuire spoke, her voice low and dangerous. "Get the fuck out of my office, Gar."

"You're being unreasonable—"

With a shock, Matt remembered where he'd heard that voice.

"Out. Now!"

The door opened, grazing Matt's shoulder. The man who pushed through was tall and lean, with a thick mane of gray hair. The cut of his suit, and his even hothouse tan, spoke of money; an old, jagged scar on his right cheek and the iciness of his eyes were at odds with his gentlemanly appearance. His gaze barely registered Matt's presence as he strode from the building.

McGuire came to the door, her face pale, mouth rigid. She started when she saw Matt. "I suppose you heard that," she said.

"I heard you telling him"—he jerked his thumb at the door—"to get the fuck out of your office. Good for you. I don't like the look of him."

"What's to like?"

"Who is he?"

"Our mayor, the esteemed Garson Payne. An asshole who, in four years, hopes to be our district's representative to the state legislature."

At least now Matt had a name for the man who had made the anonymous call to him in Port Regis. But why would an elected official do such a thing? And how had he found him?

He tried to ask more questions about Payne; McGuire

declined to discuss him further. Instead she invited Matt into her office and went over the contact sheets intently, staring at them through her half-glasses, circling the shots she wanted him to print. When she came to the doll series, she said, "Oh, my God! *This* is what all the commotion's about?"

"Maybe you'd like to run one of them as your arty shot of the week?"

She grinned. "I've half a mind to. No, instead I think I'll run one with Sev's article. He said the same things you've captured here. This one." She circled it. "And also this, where their faces look like they're flirting with each other. The smug mommies and daddies of this county can use a shaking up."

"You like messing with people's heads."

"If it serves a purpose. That's what a good newspaper should do: Challenge the readership's opinions; make them think. I'll need these by tomorrow at one. Nice first day on the job, John."

"Thanks, I enjoyed it. The people I talked with really like and respect the paper. Of course, not every town of this size can boast of a Pulitzer-winning publication."

"True." She handed the sheets back to him and stood.

"I've read the series, and I liked it a lot, particularly the stories written by Ardis Coleman."

"Ard's a terrific writer. We'll never see the likes of her again."

"She quit to write a book on the murders?"

"Uh-huh."

"You still see her?"

McGuire had been gathering papers and putting them in her briefcase, but now her hands stilled. "Look, John, we'd better get one thing straight right off the bat. This is a small paper, and a small community. When you live at close quarters with your coworkers and fellow citizens, you've got to draw boundaries. The one I insist on is the separation of one's professional and personal life."

"I couldn't agree with you more. The only reason I asked about Ms. Coleman is that I'd like to meet her, talk with her about the articles."

"That's not possible. Ard's at a difficult place in her work right now, and she doesn't wish to be disturbed."

"Maybe later, when the book's finished?"

"Maybe, if you haven't moved on by then."

"Why would I move on?"

She busied herself with the papers again, avoiding his eyes. "You moved on after eighteen years with your former paper."

"Eighteen years is a long time."

"You're what—thirty-eight?"

"Thirty-nine."

"Well, in my experience, that's an age when men tend to get antsy. Move from woman to woman, job to job, place to place. Right now you could be at the beginning of a long journey."

As he worked on the leaky faucet in Sam's small bathroom early that evening—didn't the woman know that washers eventually wore out?—Matt thought about McGuire's comments. She'd sensed his restlessness but interpreted it in conventional terms—and wrongly. His was a condition born of a desire to wrap up old business rather than to seek out the new. And the long journey he'd undertaken was not geographical, but one that would take him deep inside himself to confront things that now were only shadowy and unsettling. The prospect of that confrontation made him turn such a vigorous hand to tightening the pipes under the sink that one joint began to spit water.

Just what he needed. Sam had no plumbing supplies on hand, and although he'd noticed an Ace Hardware in one of the strip malls near the freeway interchange, he hadn't planned to spend all his evening performing handyman's duties. He went to the kitchen, rummaged in the drawer where Sam kept her tools, and found a roll of duct tape. In his opinion, duct tape was one of the greatest inventions of the past century, a quick fix for everything; he'd used it for such diverse purposes as temporarily repairing a camera and hemming a pair of jeans. After he taped the pipe joint, he left a warning note for Sam, who was working till ten, and set out for Drinkwater Creek.

Gwen's house was wrapped in shadow when he arrived, its lighted windows a pale glow through the surrounding trees. He freed the Nikon from its bag, reattached the telephoto, adjusted the settings. It wasn't till he looked up that he noticed there were two vehicles in the paved area by the footbridge: Gwen's luxury SUV and a red Ford Ranger with a Save the Redwoods sticker on its rear bumper. Carly McGuire's truck.

Paranoia seized him. His explanation for his interest in Ardis Coleman hadn't rung true to McGuire, and she'd come here to discuss him with her friend. Somehow Gwen would figure out who he was, and . . .

Don't get ahead of yourself. McGuire's probably here for a perfectly normal visit.

He turned off the switch on the truck's dome light, slipped out, and ran lightly across the pavement. The footbridge was easily visible from the house, so he walked downstream until he found a narrow place where he could cross on stepping-stones. After scrambling up the opposite bank, he stopped to get his bearings. The house was on a forty-five-degree angle to his right, screened by a windbreak of eucalyptus. He moved toward them and stood in their shelter, sighting on one of the lighted windows with the telephoto.

Kitchen: granite tiles, wood cabinets, lots of stainless steel. Table with remains of a meal for three set in a cozy nook.

He moved to the next window. Living room: hearth with fire burning, white cat sleeping on the area rug in front of it, black leather furniture. Gwen sat at the end of the sofa, her feet propped on a coffee table, her head bowed as she went over some papers, probably manuscript pages. A half-full wineglass sat on the table beside her; she reached for it and sipped, looking up at the window. Involuntarily Matt stepped back, even though he knew she couldn't possibly see him. She set the glass down, turned her head, and spoke to someone outside his range of vision. Appeared to be waiting for an answer.

Still pretty, Gwennie, even after fourteen years. You've taken good care of yourself. Of course, with money, that's easy.

He began to snap photographs.

Gwen said something else, set down the papers, and curled her legs beneath her. She was wearing a long blue robe, and she pulled its hem over her bare feet—a gesture he remembered.

Now Carly McGuire came into view, moving around the sofa and setting a glass of wine on the coffee table before she sat. Gwen spoke again, and Carly shrugged, her mouth set. Gwen frowned, said something else to Carly. Even though he couldn't hear her words, Matt remembered that look and the tone that accompanied it. McGuire closed her eyes, shook her head.

God, it was like witnessing a scene from his marriage: Gwen angry, himself on the defensive.

Gwen's lips tightened, and she looked away from Carly. Matt could now see her face-on, and this, too, was familiar. For a moment her mouth remained in a firm line, but then it began to crumble at the corners; her teeth nipped at her lower lip as her eyes filled. She squeezed them shut, and the tears overflowed, coursing down her cheeks as she remained perfectly still. She was, he knew, making no sound. Her silent weeping had always unnerved him, made him want to flee.

Apparently it had the same effect on McGuire. As Matt moved the lens to her face, he saw panic. But just as his own panic had quickly dissolved, so did Carly's. She closed the space between them and took Gwen into her arms.

How many times had he done just that? He watched, fascinated, as a part of his first life was reenacted before the powerful lens of his camera.

Carly stroked Gwen's hair. Her lips murmured words

that had belonged to him in years past: *"It's going to be all right. You'll see. It will be all right."*

Gwen's face was pressed into Carly's shoulder. Soon she would raise her head and ask in a little girl's voice, *"Do you mean that? Do you really mean it?"*

And Carly, like Matt, would be forced to lie: *"Yes, of course I do."*

As he watched the scene through his lens, a chill touched Matt's shoulders, took hold of his spine. He was years in the past, comforting his wife. He was here in the present, a voyeur. He was about to step into a future he wasn't sure he cared to visit. . . .

Gwen raised her head, asked her question. Carly gave her response. Gwen's face became suffused with hope.

Then, forcefully, the women's lips met and held.

And with a jolt, Matt realized the nature of the relationship between them.

Friday, May 10, 2002

e was halfway to Santa Carla, the county seat, driving blindly while trying to absorb what he'd learned about Gwen and Carly McGuire, when the Jeep ran out of gas. He coasted onto the shoulder, set the brake, and leaned forward, his arms resting on top of the steering wheel. The dashboard clock showed it was twelve-seventeen in the morning, and he hadn't seen another car for at least ten minutes.

Briefly he debated leaving the Jeep and walking south to find a service station, but decided against it. Some miles back the highway had narrowed to two sharply curving lanes, dangerous to walk along in the darkness. Besides, stations were practically nonexistent between towns, and the last sign he'd noticed said he was thirty-five miles from the county seat. Instead he set out an emergency flare, shut off the Jeep's headlights, and settled in to wait for a Good Samaritan.

His thoughts kept turning to Gwen, picturing the look of hope on her face before she and Carly kissed. So his former wife had formed an intimate relationship with another woman after leaving him. A long-term, stable one from the looks of it. There was a child. Gwen's? Carly's? Natural? Adopted? Who had fathered her?

Had Gwen been involved with women before and during his marriage to her? He knew about the men she'd been with earlier, and up to now had felt reasonably certain she'd remained faithful to him until she disappeared. Surely he'd have known had it been otherwise. Or would he? The possibility of his wife having a lesbian affair is not the first to occur to a man, even when his marriage begins to deteriorate.

Did the trouble that had arisen so quickly in the marriage stem from Gwen's confusion about her sexual orientation? From her inability to discuss it with him? From her guilt over an affair?

How long after she left Saugatuck had she met Carly? Where and how? Did Carly know that Gwen's former husband had been suspected of murdering her? Gwen had known, according to his anonymous caller, now identified as Mayor Garson Payne.

And now to the big question: Would the current situation alter his feelings toward Gwen? His plans? Should it? He'd waited such a long time for . . .

Headlights flashed around the curve in front of him. The vehicle slowed, its driver spotting the flare. It U-turned and pulled onto the shoulder, beams blinding in the rearview and side mirrors. Matt stepped out of the Jeep.

A woman walked toward him, moving in a deliberate but cautious manner, as a cop does when approaching a stopped vehicle. When she came closer, he saw she had closely cropped black hair and a pretty, fine-boned face; she wore a dark suit and had her right hand thrust inside her shoulder bag, as if it might contain a gun.

"Need some help?" she asked in a guarded but friendly tone.

"I'm out of gas. Can you give me a lift to the nearest service station?"

"Sure can, but I'll have to ask to see your license and registration first. Detective Rhoda Swift, Soledad County Sheriff's Department." She flashed her identification at him.

He got the rental papers from the Jeep, removed his license from his wallet.

The detective examined them in the headlights' glare. "British Columbia, huh? Nice country up there. What brings you to Soledad County, Mr. Lindstrom?"

"I've taken a job here, as a photographer for the *Spectrum*." As soon as he spoke the words, he realized he'd made a bad mistake. John Crowe, not Matt Lindstrom, had taken the job.

"Good publication. How's Carly these days?"

"Prickly as ever, but fine."

Rhoda Swift smiled faintly and said, "Well, Mr. Lindstrom, let's get going before the sun comes up. I was headed north for Green Valley Road, but I can just as easily take Old Schoolhouse out of Santa Carla."

"I don't want to make you go out of your way—"

"Insuring the public's safety is what we're here for. Green Valley's a better road, but Old Schoolhouse is more direct to where I'm going. I'll deliver you to the service station there, and they'll give you a lift back."

Matt barely had time to get his seat belt fastened before Rhoda Swift accelerated onto the highway, clearing the Jeep's bumper by scant inches. He glanced at her, and she grinned wickedly—a good, fast driver who took pleasure in showing off for her passenger.

There was a police radio mounted beneath the dash, its mutterings indistinguishable to him. Swift turned down its volume, and he was about to ask her about her job when she reached for the mike, keyed it, and said, "Yeah, Valerie, what've you got for me?"

A pause, then a sigh. "I've told him my cell doesn't work on this side of the ridge. . . . Okay, patch him through to me." She rolled her eyes at Matt. "Men! Yes, Guy. . . . I told you— Oh, never mind. . . . The meeting ran longer than I thought it would, but I'm on my way. Just have to deliver a motorist in distress to a service station first. . . . Don't worry, I'll be careful. . . . Yes, *dear.*"

As she hung up the mike, Rhoda Swift laughed softly.

"Overprotective husband?" Matt asked.

"Overprotective gentleman friend. He's a New Yorker, spends part of the year at his vacation home near Deer Harbor. When he's in Manhattan, he thinks nothing of wandering the streets at two in the morning, but should I be driving one of our rural byways at night, his mind conjures up all sorts of peril."

"Men like to think we're fierce protectors even when we're not, I guess. Where's Deer Harbor?"

"On the coast, north of Signal Port."

"One of our reporters was covering a story in Signal Port today."

"That would be the Dawson case. Hugh Dawson, owner of the Sea Stacks Motel. Miserable cuss, and last night his wife finally decided she'd had enough of his abuse and shot him. I've just come from a meeting with the D.A. in Santa Carla; we're in agreement that it was justifiable homicide."

For the remainder of the trip into town Matt chatted with Rhoda Swift about the county, learning more about the coastal area, which, by virtue of being cut off by the ridgeline, seemed a world unto itself. When she dropped him at the Chevron station at Old Schoolhouse Road, she said, "Welcome to Soledad County, Mr. Lindstrom. Take my advice, and fill up often from now on."

"I will. And thanks for the lift."

Her big eyes clouded. "No problem. A couple of years ago I didn't give a stranded motorist a lift, and I very much regret it. I try to make up for it every time I can."

The encounter with the sheriff's detective had calmed Matt. After the Chevron station attendant returned him, with a supply of gas, to the Jeep, he drove to a small motel near the county courthouse in Santa Carla and took a room. As soon as the government offices opened the next morning, he was there and, with the help of a kindly clerk, began researching the public records.

The house on Drinkwater Creek, it turned out, belonged to Carly McGuire. She'd bought it in 1983, the same year she bought the *Soledad Spectrum*. By his estimate, Carly couldn't be more than forty-five, which would put her in her twenties at the time of the purchases—large purchases for one that young. Money there. Perhaps she was a trust fund baby.

He had no name for the child he'd seen with Gwen, so he asked the clerk to show him how to access birth records by the parent's name. No child had been born to Ardis Coleman or Carly McGuire in Soledad County during the four-year period when he assumed the birth would have taken place. Adopted, perhaps?

One question answered. More raised.

He headed back to Cyanide Wells.

"So you think you can just show up at your leisure, do you, Crowe?" McGuire stood outside her office door, arms folded, expression severe.

"Car trouble," Matt said. "Sorry."

Boss trouble, he thought. Big time.

"You can fix my piece-of-shit truck in half an hour, but something goes wrong with that fancy Grand Cherokee that keeps you away all morning?"

"I said I'm sorry."

"Your assignment sheet's on your desk. Get cracking."

God, what did Gwen see in the woman?

*   *   *

"Got time for that drink this evening?" Matt asked Severin Quill.

The reporter looked up from his keyboard. "You could probably use one right now, after the contretemps with Attila the Hun." He looked at his watch. "I have to attend a press conference in Santa Carla at two. Why don't we meet at Rob's Recovery Room at five-thirty. You know where that is?"

"Uh-uh."

"Just south of the Talbot's Mills exit on the east side of the freeway."

"Kind of far from here."

"Yes, but it's on my way back. Plus, it's seedy enough that Attila wouldn't deign to set foot there."

"Are we hiding from her?"

"Not exactly, but her policy of separation of work and private life makes for uneasy encounters here in town."

"I'll see you at five-thirty, then."

Rob's Recovery Room was a country tavern, and fully as seedy as Quill claimed. The bar was gouged with initials and other penknife graffiti; the upholstery of the black leatherette booths had been eviscerated in places. The customers were mainly men with work-hardened hands and weathered faces, wearing faded clothing and baseball caps with logos. Whiskey and something called Knob Ale seemed to be the drinks of choice. After Matt shouldered through the knots of patrons by the bar, he asked for a Knob, no glass, and took a booth from which he could survey the crowd.

On the surface, the atmosphere was convivial. The

men laughed and joked and made suggestive remarks to the lone busy waitress; a trio of women occupied the booth next to him, and their conversation was punctuated by shrill giggles. But soon he began to detect a curious hollowness to the sounds and noticed that the smiles stretched people's lips but didn't reach their eyes. When voices rose in anger near the door, the thin, sallow-faced woman to Matt's left winced and said to her companions, "Doug's gonna be a handful tonight; I just know it."

"Got his notice, did he?"

"Yeah."

"What're you guys gonna do?"

"My brother thinks he might be able to get him on at the mill where he works up in Washington. But things're bad there, too."

"Fuckin' tree-huggers."

"Yeah, but they're not the only ones to blame for what's happenin' here. Maybe if the mill had a better manager it wouldn't be failing."

"Wrong, honey. The manager follows orders from the top, and what they're orderin' him to do is shut the place down. They'll make more money that way than if they ran it proper. Ain't that always how it is? The people who've got money get more, and the rest of us . . . Well, that's how it is."

By six-thirty Severin Quill had not appeared, and Matt was growing weary of the bar scene. He had decided to give him another fifteen minutes, then pack it in, when he heard the bartender call, "Is there a Matt Lindstrom here?" Automatically he rose and went to take the receiver the man held out to him.

"Well, Mr. *Lindstrom*, what do you have to say for yourself?" Carly McGuire's voice, low and furious.

"How did you . . . ?"

"Find out your real name? Funny story. Sev Quill went down to the county seat for a press conference at the sheriff's department about a murder case he's covering in Signal Port. He got to talking with the investigating officer, and she told him she gave a lift last night to a Matt Lindstrom, who claimed he'd taken a job as a photographer for this paper. Sev knew something was wrong, so he came to me and told me where I could find you. I know who you are and who you've come here to hurt."

Damn! He hadn't had any choice but to reveal his true name to a law enforcement officer, given his lack of identification as John Crowe.

McGuire went on, "I don't know how you found Ardis or what your plans are, but I'm putting you on notice: You are to stay away from her, our child, this newspaper, and me. If necessary, we'll get a restraining order against you, and if that doesn't work, I own a handgun and I'm not afraid to use it."

Anger of the sort he hadn't felt since Saugatuck flared. "What does Gwen have to say about that?"

"*Ardis* doesn't know you're here yet. I plan to tell her, but she's fragile, and I'll have to handle it carefully. My first order of business is to protect her and our little girl. And that means keeping you away from them."

"This is none of your business. It's between Gwen and me."

"What is it I said that you don't understand? Perhaps you've never heard of a restraining order?"

"I wonder if a judge would look favorably upon a woman who deliberately disappeared and left her husband under suspicion of murdering her. A woman who sat back and allowed his life to be ruined."

"You're not listening to me, Mr. Lindstrom. I will do anything to protect Ardis and our daughter. Is that clear?"

"Is that clear? You bet. Am I going to roll over for you? No way."

McGuire hung up on him.

He slammed down the receiver and went outside. Leaned against the Jeep, shaking with rage. Gwen had a fierce protector in Carly McGuire, but not fierce enough. No one had been there to protect *him* fourteen years ago. No reason it should be any different for Gwen.

The house on Drinkwater Creek looked much as it had the night before—windows lighted, but only Gwen's SUV in the parking area. He entered the property by the same route, clutching his Nikon. Again he sighted on the windows, but this time he saw no sign of Gwen or the child.

Around him the shadows were deepening. Springtime scents drifted on the warmish air—freshly growing things, pungent eucalyptus, and something sweet that he had always associated with his first love. Behind him he heard the rush of the creek, the hum of tires on the pavement. Before him the house's windows glowed, but without motion. As he waited, staring through the telephoto, unease stole over him. The house seemed too quiet. . . .

He slipped out from the trees' shelter and sprinted across the open ground between them and the kitchen window. A half-full glass of red wine sat next to a cutting board; a knife and a heap of green beans lay on the board, some of them trimmed. The table was set with three placemats and napkins, but the cutlery was scattered across it.

His unease was full-blown now. He moved to the living room window. No one there.

After a moment he went around the corner to the front door. It was ajar. He stepped inside, waited until he could make out lines among the shadows. A small table lay on its side, a broken lamp beside it. A rug was bunched against one wall.

A chill took hold of him. He stood very still, listening. No sound except the rush of the creek in the distance. No one moved here. No one breathed.

After a moment he felt beside the door for a light switch, flipped it on. He was in a hallway, rooms opening to either side. Terra-cotta tiled floor, puddled with red. Red on the bunched-up rug. Red smears on the beige wall . . .

Sound of a vehicle on the road. Engine cutting out by the footbridge. Quick steps on the path.

He reached for the light switch, but his arm felt leaden, and his hand fell to his side. He was about to step into the doorway behind him when a voice exclaimed, "Oh, my God!"

He whirled and stared into Carly McGuire's eyes.

Their pupils were huge black holes, and the blood was draining from her face. Her gaze jumped from him to the puddles on the floor, to the stains on the rug, to the smear on the wall, and back again.

"You bastard!" she screamed. "What have you done to her?"

Carly McGuire

Friday, May 10, 2002

rdis's former husband stood in a circle of light in her front hallway, staring at her as if he couldn't comprehend the meaning of her words. Her eyes again moved to the bloody smears on the wall, and she felt a growl rising from deep in her throat. She launched herself at him, pushing off on the balls of her feet, intent on doing him serious damage, but at the last second he feinted to the left, caught her from behind, and pinned her arms between them. His rough, strong hand covered her mouth.

He's killed Ard, and now he's going to kill me!

"Be quiet," he whispered. "Whoever did this may still be in the house."

She struggled against him, but he tightened his grip and dragged her into the living room. In the mirror above the mantelpiece she saw his face: pale under its tan, its planes honed sharp by tension. And his eyes . . .

He was afraid, too.

Without taking his hand from her mouth, he said, "I did not do this, Carly. You've got to believe me. I did not do . . . whatever was done here tonight."

Of course you'd deny it, you bastard.

"Think," he added. "You called me at Rod's at— what? Six thirty-five? There wasn't enough time for me to drive here and cause this kind of damage before you arrived."

She calculated. Thirty minutes max. Thirty minutes to drive here and kill a woman. Her woman. And what about Natalie? Where was she?

Slowly Lindstrom took his hand from her mouth, turned her so she faced him. "Look at me," he said. "Do you see any blood? Whoever did this would be covered in blood."

She shook her head, stepped away from him, sank, weak-kneed, on the edge of the sofa. Lindstrom moved toward her, and she snapped, "Get away from me."

He backed off, his expression watchful.

She perched on the cushion's edge, poised to spring should he make another move toward her. "If you didn't cause that"—she motioned at the hall—"what're you doing here?"

"I wanted to talk with Gwen."

"Talk?"

He looked down at his feet. "All right, confront her."

"And?"

"The house seemed unnaturally still when I got here.

The door was partway open. So I came inside. A minute or so before you arrived."

"And you think whoever's responsible might still be in the house. So why didn't you stay outside and call nine-one-one? And why are you talking in a normal voice?"

"I just said that to make you stop fighting me. There's nobody here but us. I can feel it. So can you."

Nobody alive, anyway . . .

"Carly," he added, "we ought to search the house."

For a body. Or bodies.

She took several deep breaths and pushed up from the sofa. "You go first, so I can keep an eye on you."

Ard's office, across from the living room: compulsively neat, as always.

Kitchen: no sign of a struggle except for the flatware strewn across the table. Setting the table was Natalie's responsibility. . . .

Don't go there.

Formal dining room, seldom used, but Ard loved the cherry-wood table and silver candlesticks. . . .

All in order.

"Bedrooms?" Lindstrom asked.

"That way." She pointed him toward the hall that led to the house's other wing, motioned for him to precede her.

Guest room: tidy, waiting for visitors who seldom came.

Her at-home office: as chaotic as the one at work.

Back in the hall he asked, "Where does this door lead to?"

"Natalie's room. Our little girl." She steeled herself, pushed it open, stepped inside.

No girlish pink or yellow for Nat. Instead, bright-green walls with stencils of jungle animals, and a dark-blue ceiling with her favorite constellations painted in silver Day-Glo.

"She could be hiding," Lindstrom said.

Carly nodded, crossed to the closet while he checked under the bed. Together they searched the few nooks and crannies but found no trace of Nat.

Finally they moved along to the last door. Beyond it was the master suite with two baths and a fireplace. It had seemed too large when she'd bought the house, a lone and lonely young woman, but now it often seemed too crowded. . . .

"Carly?"

Even though she knew she must, she did not want to go into that room. What if Ard was lying dead there and Lindstrom had lured her on this search with the intention . . . ?

She looked up at him, met his gaze.

No, there was no danger in him. One of her assets as a journalist was the ability to see into people through their eyes. And what she saw within Matt Lindstrom was what she felt within herself: fear of what he might find there.

She said, "Let's go."

The spacious blue-and-white room was much as she'd last seen it that morning: bed linens rumpled, comforter askew, yesterday's cast-off clothing tossed over the armchairs by the fireplace. Ard, a late riser, usually tidied up, but today she hadn't. The *Sacramento Bee,* which she liked to read in front of the fireplace with her morning coffee, sat unopened in plastic wrap on the big table between the chairs, her Mr. Peanut mug—a birthday gift from Nat—resting beside it. She'd apparently relighted last night's fire; the smell of wood smoke was strong. On the padded window seat overlooking the meadow lay Gracie, the little white cat that had wandered in during a rainstorm eleven years ago—a flighty but endearing creature they'd named after the comedienne Gracie Allen.

Surely nothing horrible could have happened in this room.

Carly crossed to Ard's bathroom. All was in order there. The same was true of the room containing the shower and oversize tub that connected Ard's bath with hers. Her bath was in its usual state—one that frequently made the cleaning woman roll her eyes in despair.

Lindstrom was holding Gracie when she returned to the bedroom. He set her down, said apologetically, "She crawled up my leg, yowling."

"It's her only trick."

"So what happened here, McGuire?"

". . . I don't know."

But an unpleasant suspicion was forming in her mind, and much as she tried to push it away, it took hold and grew.

Lindstrom said, "We ought to call the sheriff's department."

"Not just yet."

"Why not? It looks as if they've been attacked and abducted. Every minute you hesitate in calling the sheriff puts them at greater risk. I read someplace that the first two hours are critical to recovering kidnap victims alive."

"There's something I need to check first." Something she'd earlier glimpsed, but not fully registered, in the kitchen. She turned and hurried down there.

In the brushed-chrome sink sat a freezer bag containing a steak. Its top was open, but there was none of the blood that usually drained out of defrosted meat. A mixing bowl, stained red, sat beside it.

A horrible certainty took hold of her as she crossed to the refrigerator, looked into the freezer. A few bags of vegetables and fruit, some fish, but no meat. She went back to the sink and opened the cabinet beside it, where two trash receptacles were mounted on a pullout rack. Empty. With Lindstrom's voice at her back she went outside to the garbage and recycle bins in their enclosure next to the kitchen door. They were full of freezer bags containing spoiling steaks and roasts and ground beef and chicken parts—but no blood.

Ard had planned this in advance, then. Carly pictured her coming downstairs this morning, in such a hurry that she hadn't put the bedroom to rights. She'd removed all the meat from the freezer, left it to defrost, and later, maybe after she'd picked Nat up from the school where Carly had dropped her in the morning, she'd poured the blood into the bowl and created the scene in the hallway. Created the scene in the kitchen, too.

Where had Natalie been while Ard was doing that? In

her room or outside, Carly hoped. Still, she must've known something was wrong. . . .

And then Ard hadn't even hidden the evidence of what she'd done. The bowl and bag in the sink, the meat in the garbage—they were a tip-off to one who knew her well.

Or did she want me to know what she'd done? Did she want to hurt me yet another time?

"Carly?" Lindstrom had come up behind her. "Do you want to check around out here before we call the sheriff?"

"There's no need to make a call. The blood is animal, not human." She swept her hand at the garbage bins.

"I don't understand."

"Ard did this. She set up a violent disappearance. She staged the whole thing."

Of course Lindstrom couldn't understand, not without knowing the history of their relationship. He didn't press for an explanation, though, just followed along silently as she checked Natalie's room and the master suite for items Ard might have taken with them. There were telling gaps in the clothing in both closets, and Nat's prescription medication for asthma was gone. The largest travel bag in Ard's matched set was also missing, as were Natalie's duffel and backpack.

Carly picked up the bedside phone and called the town's taxi service: Had Ardis Coleman been picked up on time that afternoon? No, the dispatcher said, she hadn't called them. A similar inquiry of the local car rental agency produced the same result: Ms. Coleman had not reserved a vehicle with them.

Of course not; her partner was clever—and devious. Most likely she'd rented a vehicle in another town, or even bought one. Long-range planning, then.

As she hung up the receiver, she saw that Lindstrom had grown impatient. He said, "Will you please tell me what's going on here?"

Could she trust him with this? Could she trust him at all? But who else could she turn to?

"We need to talk," she said.

They returned to the living room. As Lindstrom sat on the sofa, she studied him. He didn't look like the man whom Ard had described as "handsome in a pretty-boy way. A typical Minnesota Swede." This man's face was weathered, with lines etched by hard experience; his hands were work-roughened, his body lean and muscular; he'd dyed his blond hair an unbecoming shade of brown. No more pretty boy, but character and presence made him attractive in a rough-hewn way.

"Tell me," she said, "what is it you actually do up there in British Columbia? You're not a newspaper photographer, are you?"

"No, I run a small charter business—one boat, one deckhand. Tourists, mostly wanting excursion cruises. Some fishermen. Now, what do we need to talk about?"

She sat on the opposite end of the sofa, tucking one foot under her. "Ardis. I don't know if she was this way while she was married to you, but as long as I've known her she's exhibited a pattern of behavior that I call cut-and-run. Whenever things get unpleasant or she's overwhelmed by a situation, she just takes off."

"Has she done this often?"

"Often enough. The first time was when we'd been together less than a year."

"And you've been together how long?"

"Nearly fourteen years."

"Since right after she disappeared, then. D'you mind if I ask how you met?"

"She was hitchhiking in a dangerous place outside of Thousand Springs, Nevada. I picked her up."

She remembered Ard, standing bedraggled by the side of a two-lane highway in northeastern Nevada. She was wearing dirty jeans and a tee with a ripped-out shoulder seam and was sitting on a big blue duffel bag. Her face was sunburned and peeling, her long dark hair straggling down from a ponytail.

Normally Carly wouldn't have stopped for any hitchhiker without the sense to wear a hat in the glaring sun, or one too lazy to stand up when a vehicle approached. In fact, she seldom picked up hitchhikers at all. But the way Ard's face had suddenly filled with hope made her put her foot to the brake pedal. . . .

"Did she tell you her true name?" Lindstrom asked. "Or why she left home?"

"Not at first. She just said she was going west and asked if Soledad County was a good place to live. I brought her here, gave her a job as a gofer, found her a cheap place to live. It wasn't till months later, after we became lovers, that she told me her story."

Lindstrom flinched at the word "lovers" but quickly

recovered. Was he homophobic? Disgusted at the images that came to mind? Or was he simply wounded, even at fourteen years' remove, that his wife could so easily make a new life for herself?

"Why did she up and disappear from Saugatuck?" he asked.

"Her business," she said. Then, more gently, "It had nothing to do with you—at least, not directly. She loved you."

"I wish I could believe that." He was silent for a moment. "Okay, the first time she took off . . . ?"

"I'd promoted her to general assignment reporter. She'd covered the trial of a woman who had killed her abusive boyfriend, and I criticized her stories for lack of objectivity. She insisted that we owed it to our readers to take a firm stance against abuse of any sort, and I said that was what the editorial page was for, and if anybody took a stance it would be me. We fought, and the next morning she was gone. Two weeks later she showed up, contrite, saying she'd gone away to get her head together."

"And you took her back."

"Yes. She disappeared a few other times for varying periods over the next couple of years. Then, in the fall of ninety-one, she left and stayed away for fifteen months."

"What precipitated that?"

I'm not going there—not with you.

"That's private. Anyway, she returned with Natalie, who was under a year old. Seems Ard had gone to San Francisco, taken up with a black musician who played at a jazz club where she was waitressing. Nat is the result of their union." A familiar bitterness welled up, clogging her throat.

"But you still took her back."

"You criticizing me, Lindstrom?"

He shook his head. "I'd've probably done the same. There's a quality to Gwen—Ardis—that makes you want to help her no matter what she's done."

Yes, she knew that quality well—had for years tried to analyze it. Often she'd thought that if she could pin it down, she would become immune to it, gain control over her situation, but its exact essence remained elusive.

"Well, then you know," she said. "I not only took her back but welcomed her. I'd never wanted children and was concerned about what kind of mother Ard would make, but I thought Natalie might settle her down, bring stability to our relationship. And by and large she's done that. Ard's a good mother, and I've found I enjoy having a kid around."

Lindstrom eyed her keenly. "But?"

"Did I say 'but'?"

"You didn't have to."

"All right!" Her irritation gave way to relief. It felt good to unburden herself, even though the recipient of her confidences couldn't have been more unlikely. "I love Natalie, but sometimes she's a reminder of how much Ard has hurt me."

"I understand. This running off—has it stopped since she had Natalie?"

"No. But it's not as frequent, and of shorter duration—usually only a day or two."

"It's enough of a pattern, though, that you think

this"—he nodded toward the hallway—"might be more of the same."

"I'm sure it is. Ard's been under a lot of pressure lately. I think I told you the book she's writing is due at the publisher soon, but it's not going well." She hesitated. "And we haven't been getting along."

"Why not?"

"My business, Lindstrom."

He held up his hands, palms toward her. "Sorry, I didn't mean to pry. Has she ever done anything like this in the past? Staged a violent scene?"

"No, and she's never taken Natalie along, either. Frankly, I'm worried about her mental health. She claims somebody's been watching her, that somebody's been in the house while we were gone."

"You don't believe it?"

"No. There's no evidence of forced entry, and I haven't noticed any prowlers. Besides, she's always been a little paranoid."

"When did she first mention this?"

"Yesterday."

"Well, that explains it. I was out here then, and today, taking pictures with a telephoto lens. Maybe she sensed my presence. But I never got any closer than that grove of trees to the south. Tonight's the first time I've been in the house."

She studied him thoughtfully. He was either an honest man or an adept con artist.

He added, "If you're worried about her mental health, you really ought to call the sheriff's department."

"No." She shook her head. "I can't do that to Ard. The department didn't like her coverage of the 'faggot murders,' as they privately called them. God knows how they'd handle this, what they'd say to the media. And I'll admit to more than a little self-interest—my newspaper is the one voice of reason in this county, and I don't want it discredited because its editor couldn't control her personal life."

He nodded in understanding. "That detective who gave me a lift last night—Rhoda Swift—she seems nice, a sympathetic person. Nonjudgmental, too. Maybe you could ask for her."

"No, I couldn't. Rho only works cases in the coastal area."

"But as a favor?"

"Rho's all the things you say she is, but she's also a by-the-book cop. She'd have to bring the local deputies in on it. I know how she operates because I did a special interview with her a couple of years back about an old murder case that she cracked. Besides, she's romantically involved with a best-selling journalist; if he got wind of this, Ard and I might end up as the subjects of his next book."

"Which neither of you needs." Lindstrom frowned. "Me, either."

For the first time she considered how the situation might affect him. "Let me ask you this," she said. "What did you plan to do about Ard? Obviously you came here with an agenda."

He looked away from her. "I guess you could say so."

"And that was . . . ?"

"To take pictures."

"Pictures of her?"

"Right. I wanted to make an identification. Document her new life. Then I was going to take the photographs to the Sweetwater County, Wyoming, Sheriff's Department—where there's still an open file on her disappearance naming me as the prime suspect—and vindicate myself. Vindicate myself in the eyes of my family and former friends. Vindicate myself in the national media as well."

He paused, gaze turned inward. "And," he added, "I wanted a confrontation with her. Wanted to wring out of her the reason she disappeared and left me to face a possible murder charge. Wanted to make sure she knew what a despicable human being I think she is."

Despicable? Carly turned the word over in her mind. From his point of view, she supposed it was appropriate. But from hers, *damaged* was the better choice.

"If it's any consolation," she said, "she abandoned her car and purse hoping you'd think she'd been killed and not look for her. She had no idea you'd be suspected—or that you had been, until long after you'd left Saugatuck. When she found out, she tried to call you, but you'd vanished as completely as she had."

"She could've set the record straight with the authorities."

"Maybe, but by then the case had received major publicity. She was afraid of more."

"Why?"

". . . She had her reasons."

"And again, they're none of my business."

Carly was silent, thinking bitterly of those reasons. Had she cut Ard entirely too much slack all these years? Probably. But wasn't that what you did when you loved someone?

Lindstrom said, "Well, never mind. That's long past, and what's happened today changes the situation. I've got my photographs, and if I can get a statement from you—"

"You're not thinking of leaving?"

"Of course I am. There's nothing to hold me here."

"Oh, yeah? You can't just walk away from this mess. After all, you admitted she probably took off because of your sneaking around here."

"So what am I supposed to do about that?"

"Help me find her. You and I are in this thing together, Lindstrom, and together we are going to see it through."

Once Lindstrom's astonishment at her pronouncement had faded, he smiled mockingly. "Ready to take her back again, are you?"

She glared at him.

"My advice is to embrace her philosophy: Cut your losses and run."

"You forget, there's another factor in the equation: Natalie. She's a delicate child, has asthma. If Ard's become unbalanced, she may neglect Nat's health. I need to find them, bring them home, or at least to someplace safe. Afterwards I'll decide about the relationship."

"And you think I can help you find her?"

"Maybe. You could have some knowledge about her that I don't. Something that will suggest what she might've done."

But do I really believe that, or do I just want him here so I won't feel alone?

He smiled, gently this time, as if he intuited her thoughts. "Okay, I'll stay and try to help you—for a while. Where do we start?"

"Well, the major problem in Ard's life recently—except for you showing up—is the trouble she's having with the book. I think we should both go over the manuscript and her notes."

He looked at his watch. "How long will that take?"

"Hours, probably."

"Then I'd better make a phone call."

Carly showed him to the cordless unit in the kitchen, listened as she ground beans and brewed a pot of coffee.

"Hi it's— Yeah, I should've called. Don't be upset. Something— No, not some*one*. I spent last night in Santa Carla— What d'you mean, the duct tape's not holding? It's a miracle fix. . . . Well, just slap some more on, then. I'll buy the joint I need on the way home tomorrow. . . . No, I'm working on a major assignment and likely to be out all night. . . . Assignment, not *as*signment! I'll see you in the morning, and don't forget about that tape."

As he replaced the receiver, Carly folded her arms and regarded him with mock severity. "You don't waste any time when you hit a new town, Lindstrom."

"That was my landlady. I fix things in exchange for cheap rent."

"Uh-huh."

"Well, it *was*."

"And just what did you put the duct tape on?"

"The pipe under the bathroom sink. It leaks, and I didn't have the right— What's so funny?"

"You. And believe me, Lindstrom, right about now I

could use a laugh, however feeble." She paused. "By the way, I think I should continue to call you John Crowe in public. People here know you as that. A change could complicate things."

"Sev Quill knows I'm Matt Lindstrom."

"I asked him not to tell anyone, and he won't. Where'd you come up with your alias, anyhow?"

"Johnny Crowe's the deckhand I mentioned. I figured if anybody here wanted to check on whether such a person used to live in Port Regis, he's in the directory. And he said he'd cover, claim to be subletting his place from me."

"This Millie Bertram, your alleged publisher—who's she?"

"Owner of the Port Regis Hotel."

"She was well coached."

He was as clever and devious in his own way as Ard was in hers. And Carly herself had her moments. Perhaps together she and Lindstrom could outwit her missing partner.

"Okay, Matt," she said, "grab a cup of coffee and let's get started on Ard's papers."

Saturday, May 11, 2002

 he stood naked on the threshold of the gold-and-cream ballroom, and one by one the beautiful, formally attired people turned to stare. Silence fell, punctuated only by the tinkling of the crystal chandeliers. She turned to flee, but the doors had become a solid wall, barring exit. As she searched frantically for a way out, a woman behind her said, "She is not one of us," and a man agreed, "Definitely not one of us." Then the others began chanting, "Not one of us, not one of us—"

Carly jerked up from where she was slumped on the wide armrest of the chair. Her shoulder throbbed, and her neck was stiff. She blinked, looked around, saw sunlight streaming through the windows of Ard's office. Looked down and saw she was swaddled in one of the afghans from the living room. Her reading glasses hung over one ear.

The dream . . .

She hadn't had it in more than two decades, since she willfully banished it during her senior year in college. But now it was back in vivid detail, reminding her of her humiliation. . . .

Don't go there. Not today. You have to stay focused.

Focused on what?

Oh . . .

The events of the previous night returned to her in a painful rush of memory. She groaned, put her hands to her face, winced at the tenderness in her neck. After a moment she looked around, saw a note propped on the keyboard of Ard's computer, extricated herself from the afghan, and went to read it.

Carly:
I've finished the manuscript and gone to fix my landlady's leaky pipe. (I really do fix stuff in ex-change for cheap rent!) Didn't want to wake you. I'll call or come by as soon as I can.
"Johnny"

She crumpled the note and tossed it in the wastebasket, anchored her glasses atop her head, and went to the kitchen for coffee. The maker was still on, and the dregs of the carafe she'd brewed last night had distilled to sludge. She ran water into it and, while it soaked, got out the cleaning supplies that she'd need to remove the evidence of Ard's latest betrayal.

An hour later—after purging the hallway, taking a quick shower, and dressing—she was back in Ard's office looking for the manuscript Crowe had been reading while she'd examined the legal pads and index cards full of notes. It was neatly stacked in a tray on the workstation. When she picked it up, its slenderness surprised her, and she flipped to the last page, numbered 130. Less than half the amount of pages Ard had led her to believe she'd written, and even at twice that number she'd've had trouble meeting her July first deadline.

At what page had Ard told her she'd rather she didn't read any more until the book was done? One hundred, and that had been over six months ago. Yet nearly every night she proofed her day's work after dinner. Where had those pages gone?

Carly moved to the file cabinet and scanned the disks in their holder: financial records, copies of stories going back to when she worked for the paper, correspondence, idea files—but nothing beyond page 130 on the manuscript, working title *Cyanide Wells*. Strange. Ard was paranoid about losing her work in case of a crash; she put it on disk every day.

My God, has she been sitting here for six months, staring at a blank screen? Proofing the same pages night after night? Are those one hundred thirty pages all she has to show for two years' efforts? Granted, she had to do a lot of research, but . . .

Ard must've been hopelessly blocked and afraid to admit it. But why? Because she was afraid of botching her first book—one that she considered a memorial to their murdered friends? Because it meant so much to her? What was it she'd said a few weeks ago?

"Reality's starting to interfere with the writing. I have nightmares about that morning."

And Carly had replied, somewhat unsympathetically, "You're bound to come face-to-face with reality. The book's a fact-based account."

Ard had given her a look whose meaning she couldn't decipher and had gone back to proofing what she claimed was the current batch of pages.

Now Carly returned to the armchair and located the stack of legal pads containing Ard's handwritten notes. Some had slipped to the floor; another was mashed down the side between the cushion and the arm. She smoothed out its rumpled pages and—

"Carly?"

She started, looked around. Lindstrom, back from the plumbing wars.

"Sorry for just walking in on you," he said. "I left the door unlocked in case you were still asleep when I got back. Hope that was okay."

"That's fine. We always left our doors unlocked before Ronnie Talbot and Deke Rutherford were killed. Our friends felt free to just walk in."

"But that changed."

"Yeah, it did. Everything changed."

"In what way?"

"You really want to know?"

"I do."

"Why? Ard's your ex-wife; I'd assume it would be painful to hear about her new life, particularly because . . ."

"Because she made that new life with a woman?"

She nodded.

He went over to the computer, examined the screen saver. "Roses," he said, "she's always loved them."

Biding his time, because whatever he wants to say has to be said just right, or we'll lose the connection that's growing between us. And he wants that connection because he's still unsatisfied with what he's found out about Ard's disappearance.

He turned the desk chair around, sat facing her. "You know, I was thinking about her new life the whole time I worked on the plumbing. And I concluded that Ardis Coleman is no longer Gwen Lindstrom. She's someone else entirely, the evolution of a woman I once loved but probably didn't know. In a sense we reinvent the people we love to our own specifications, and that's what I did with Gwen."

"Then why're you here now? Having realized that, you could've walked away."

"To tell you the truth, I'm not sure. Maybe it's because I like you. Or I feel for your little girl. And even though I didn't know Gwen, I loved her very much. I suppose I care about the woman she became."

"Or maybe you still want that confrontation. To tell her what a despicable woman she is."

He shook his head. "Doesn't seem important now. The woman you describe is troubled, needs help. It occurred to me while reading her manuscript that what she did yesterday may be less related to me than to a disturbance brought on by having to relive your friends' murders. Maybe if you tell me more about the circumstances surrounding them, we can figure out what's happening with her."

A good man. A kind, thoughtful man. Possibly better than his Gwen, my Ardis, deserved.

"Thank you," she said. "Where would you like me to begin?"

"Wherever you care to."

"Well, Ronnie and Deke were closer to Ard than me, although we were friends, too. Deke was a painter, very innovative and talented. Ard met him when she interviewed him about a big show he was having at a San Francisco gallery. Ronnie inherited the mill before he met Deke, and put its management into Gar Payne's hands, claiming he didn't have a good head for business, but I think that was just an excuse to get out, because a few years later he took over as Deke's manager and did a great job. He dealt with the galleries, arranged for the shipping of the canvases, handled their finances and investments."

"Gar Payne—that's the mayor?"

"Right. The mayor's job is only part-time. Of course, when Ronnie sold the mill, Gar had to go back to trying to peddle the unsold lots in the Meadows. As you witnessed on Thursday, he's been cranky ever since."

"Is he just a salesman there or the developer?"

"The developer, along with a partner, Milt Rawson. Only about half the lots have been sold in the ten years since they bought and subdivided the land, and there've been problems with the homeowners' association over how the place should be run." Lindstrom gave her a questioning look, and she added, "Don't ask. The Meadows is a hotbed of petty intrigue. Too many affluent people with too much time on their hands. But why're you so interested in Payne?"

"When the two of you were arguing at the paper, I recognized his voice. He's the man who made an anonymous phone call to me and told me where to find Gwen."

"Gar? Why would he do that? And how did he know about you in the first place?"

"That's what I've wondered. Is it common knowledge that Ardis was married before she came here?"

"Only her close friends are aware of that, and most of them don't know your name."

"And Payne's not one of those friends?"

"Hardly."

"Then how . . . ? Well, no use speculating on it now. You were telling me about Ronnie and Deke."

"Right. Ard hit it off with both of them, and pretty soon they were in and out of here all the time, as we were at their house near the Knob."

"I thought the Knob was in the Eel River National Forest."

"It is. Ronnie and Deke's house backs up on the forest—very secluded, on nearly a hundred acres that Ronnie inherited from his father."

"Ardis's newspaper accounts made the two of them sound like special people."

"They were." She pictured Ronnie delicately removing a painful foxtail from the nose of Gracie the cat. Deke, doing his campy Toulouse-Lautrec impersonation. Ronnie, picking up and comforting Natalie after she took a tumble from the pony he kept for the enjoyment of friends' children. Deke, producing with a flourish his "world infamous" chorizo enchiladas. Ronnie, in a ridiculous pink bunny suit at their annual Easter egg hunt. Deke, clumping the seven miles from his house to theirs on snowshoes to bring them a sackful of candles and emergency rations during an unusually severe winter storm.

She said, "They were caring. Loyal. They'd go out of their way to help a friend—or a stranger. In all the time I knew them, I never heard them exchange a harsh word." She paused. "Of course, we all know appearances can be deceiving. Ard and I have never exchanged a harsh word in public, but at home they fly."

Lindstrom seemed to prefer to let the comment slip by. He said, "Okay, the murders. I've read both the newspaper accounts and the account in Ardis's manuscript. They're quite different."

"Well, the facts are the same, but the newspaper accounts are controlled; she let her professionalism take over. But she deliberately made the book's version emotional. Too much so, in my opinion. I suspect she was working something out through the writing."

The morning she discovered their friends' bodies, Ard had called her, gasping for breath, her words practically unintelligible. Carly wouldn't have been able to figure out where she was, except she'd mentioned at breakfast that she planned to stop by to deliver a load of the zucchini she'd overplanted. "Even if Deke and Ronnie aren't crazy about the stuff, I'd rather share the bounty with friends than be forced to sneak around leaving it in strangers' parked cars and mailboxes," she'd joked.

When Carly arrived at the spacious redwood-and-glass home in the shadow of the Knob, she found Ard lying on the front lawn beside a pool of vomit. Ard was more coherent than before, but her words were punctuated by sobs and dry heaves. "The house was . . . too quiet. It felt . . . weird. I called out to them, then . . . went looking. They're in the bedroom, both shot in the head, and the blood . . ."

Carly went inside, verified what Ard had told her, and—when her hands stopped trembling enough to dial—called the sheriff's department.

By the time the first deputies arrived, however, Ard was on her feet and had pulled herself together. When they emerged from the house, grim-faced and shaken, she had her notebook and tape recorder in hand and set about covering the biggest story in the history of the *Soledad Spectrum.* Carly watched in awe; she'd always been aware of a core of strength in her partner, but Ard's erratic behavior and emotionalism usually eclipsed it. That day Ard proved the often-cited principle that extreme circumstances often force a person to call upon the better side of his or her nature.

"Carly?" Lindstrom said.

"Oh. Just remembering. Anyway, after that day everything changed. The gay and lesbian communities here had always kept a low profile, but suddenly we felt targeted. Those of us who never locked our doors installed deadbolts and alarms. We were even more circumspect than usual in public places. Our hetero friends felt the need to shield us. I even found I was self-censoring my editorials about the crime. The only bright light was Ard, who'd been the most traumatized by the killings. She wanted our readers to understand Ronnie and Deke's situation, the situation of every gay person in this county. And she illuminated it beautifully in her stories, by making the reader see the two of them as human beings rather than just gay victims."

"My landlady says she's 'no fan of faggots,' but that the series gave her some understanding of their problems."

"Well, that's progress of a small sort, isn't it?"

"I guess. How did the paper winning the Pulitzer affect things?"

"Well, the prize brought a lot of attention to the county and made some people proud. But it pissed off the small-minded folk who thought it branded the place as a hotbed of homosexuality. And the gay community still locks its deadbolts and sets its alarms."

"Is it common knowledge you and Ardis are partners?"

"You can't hide something like that in a place like this."

"People sure hid it from me. The staff members at the paper brushed off my inquiries about her, and Sev Quill cited your dictum that employees' professional and personal lives are to be kept separate."

She smiled. "Well, sure. That's because of the memo from me that they all found on their desks the morning you started work. From the first I felt something wasn't quite right with you, so I warned them to be on their guard. Even after I spoke with your Millie Bertram I had my reservations."

"And here I thought I was such a good actor."

"Well, you aren't all that bad. And you're good-looking, even if you do seem to be having a permanent bad-hair day."

Carly customarily worked in her office at the paper on Saturday afternoons, and she decided, in the interest of keeping Ard's flight a secret, that today should be no different. She and Lindstrom could continue their conversation there behind a closed door, so she told him to follow her into town.

When she was passing the Mercantile, however, her plan abruptly derailed. A crowd clustered around the old well in the park across the street, and two men were leaning over its high stone wall. Her newswoman's instincts kicked in, and she pulled her truck to the curb. Lindstrom pulled in behind her. Without waiting for him, she hurried across the street and into the park, asked a man on the fringes of the group what was going on.

"Looks like some kid's fallen into the well and drowned."

Natalie!

The response was irrational because by now Natalie was probably far away from here, and there wasn't enough water in the well to drown a mouse. Still, adrenaline coursed through her as she pushed forward. One of the men at the well straightened and turned. Timothy Mortimer, an old drunk who frequented the park's benches. She recognized the other man by the green-and-blue wool stocking cap whose tassled tip hung over his face as he stared downward: a shabbily dressed newcomer who had moved into the town eyesore, the

Golden State Hotel, a few weeks ago. He'd taken to hanging out with Timothy, who also lived there.

Now Timothy's red, bleary eyes focused on her. "You all right, Ms. McGuire?"

"What's happened here?"

"Looks like there's a dead kid in the well. Me and Cappy're tryin' to—"

"Let me look," Lindstrom said. He shouldered Timothy aside and leaned over the wall. The man called Cappy straightened and glared at him.

"That's not a child down there," Lindstrom said, his voice echoing. "It's a backpack. Green, I think."

Like Nat's backpack. Why . . . ?

Lindstrom turned, and his eyes met hers. She nodded slightly. He frowned, unsure of her meaning, but said, "If somebody's got a heavy rope, I can get the pack out."

"There's one in my van," Will Begley, owner of the Mercantile, said.

Matt peered up at the peaked roof that sheltered the well. There was, Carly knew, an iron bar anchored between its supports, which was once used to lower and raise a bucket. He reached up, tested it, then came over to her.

In a low voice he asked, "What is it?"

"Natalie's backpack is green with purple trim."

"I see. Well, if this one is hers, you've got to tell the sheriff's deputies."

"But then I'll have to tell them what Ard did. And that I destroyed the evidence of it. I don't know why she would've put the pack in the well, but I sense it's part of a plan."

He considered, eyes moving from side to side. "Okay, I'll deal with it."

Will Begley returned with the rope, helped Lindstrom secure it to the bar, held it fast as he climbed down the thirty-some feet to the well's bottom. He was there some time before he climbed back up and heaved the pack over the wall. Carly knelt to examine it.

Definitely Natalie's. It had purple trim, and she recognized a tear in one of the outside pockets. Her hands trembled as she opened it and looked inside.

Pencils. Colored Magic Markers. Drawing pad. Packet of decorative stickers. Gym socks. Apple. Kit-Kat bar. Half an egg-salad sandwich.

Carly had placed the sandwich Ard made on Thursday night, plus the apple and a small bag of potato chips, in the pack on Friday morning. She couldn't positively identify the other items as Nat's, but the little girl liked to draw and had a great fondness for Kit-Kat bars, which could be purchased in the school cafeteria. The backpack had also typically contained textbooks, various spare items of clothing, and a Palm Pilot that Ard had insisted on buying for Nat the previous Christmas, all of which would show—by bookplate, name label, or user—who their owner was.

Carly looked up at Lindstrom. He winked, indicating that he'd been responsible for the disappearance of those things.

And then, just as she was feeling relief, a male voice behind her said, "I'll take that, Carly."

Deputy Shawn Stengel was, in Carly's opinion, the biggest asshole in the sheriff's department. Someone must have phoned the substation at Talbot's Mills, and he'd rushed over here, intent on being first on the scene of what he thought could turn into a major case. Unfortunately, while Stengel was short on interpersonal skills, he wasn't stupid; and he had three young children, so he knew how much stuff kids carried in their heavy backpacks. How long before he realized this one was suspiciously light and checked the well, where Lindstrom must've dumped the items that would identify it as Natalie's?

She glanced at Matt, but he seemed unconcerned.

Stengel ran his hand over his neatly cropped blond hair. "I hope nobody moved the kid's body."

Carly said, "There's no one in the well."

"The call that came in said there was a dead kid down there."

"The men who spotted the backpack only thought it was a child."

"Where are they?"

She looked around. With the arrival of the law, Timothy and Cappy had vanished. She told Stengel who they were, and that they lived at the Golden State.

The deputy grimaced. "Somebody oughta torch that place, get rid of it and the vermin that stay there."

"Shawn, are you advocating that one of our citizens commit arson?"

His jaw knotted. "You know damn well I'm not! And if you dare print anything of the kind, I'll haul your ass in for obstructing an investigation."

The threat was too absurd to warrant a response.

Stengel scowled down at the backpack. "Doesn't surprise me that those two thought that was a kid. They're both probably boiled." He hefted the pack, shook his head. "Not much stuff in here, is there? My kids're always toting at least half a ton of crap. I worry it'll ruin their spines."

She said, "Maybe somebody got a new pack, thought it would be fun to toss the old one down the well."

Stengel squatted, went through the contents. "That doesn't seem right. I can see them getting rid of a dried-up sandwich and socks with holes in them, but Kit-Kat bars and this other stuff? I don't think so."

"So what *do* you think?"

He straightened, looked self-importantly at the bystanders. "At the moment I'm not at liberty to say. Especially to a member of the press."

Carly closed her office door and leaned against it, expelling a long sigh. Matt went over to her desk and began unloading objects from the pockets of his jeans, shirt, and jacket.

He said, "The books are wedged under a pile of debris at the bottom of the well, and I ripped out the bookplates. Everything else that could identify Natalie as the pack's owner is here."

"Thank you, Matt." She examined what lay there. Gym shorts and blouse, with labels. Bead necklace spelling out "Natalie." Graded papers, art club membership card, soccer team uniform shirt with her name and number embroidered across the back. No Palm Pilot.

Ard let her keep her favorite thing.

Lindstrom leaned against the desk, arms folded, frowning. "I tell you, McGuire, I don't feel comfortable hiding things from the authorities—even though Stengel's an idiot."

"He's not an idiot; he's an asshole. There's a difference."

"He didn't seem too bright to me."

"You'd be surprised. Even though he was the deputy who coined the term 'the faggot murders,' he worked damned hard on the case. In fact, he brought in the lead on Mack Travis."

"I've heard that some people don't think Travis killed your friends."

She sat down on her desk chair. "Isn't that always the way when there's no trial or resolution? But to be fair, Ard didn't think so, either. When she started working on her book, she told me she hoped her research would shed light on what really happened."

"And you—what do you think?"

"I think Ard and the others who believe in the killer-who-got-away theory have been taking the Mystery Channel much too seriously."

"Well, to get back to what I was saying, I don't like withholding information from the cops."

"Even after what the cops did to you when Ard—Gwen—disappeared?"

"Even after that. Lying to a Wyoming deputy was what got me into trouble in the first place."

"No, Gwen's actions were what got you into trouble."

"I don't care to debate the point. And since when have you taken to calling her Gwen?"

"Since when have you taken to calling her Ardis?"

". . . I guess we're each trying to reconcile who she was with us with who she was with the other. Calling her by the name she used at the time we're talking about helps. But frankly, it's not an easy job, and it's giving me a headache."

His words made her aware of a dull throb above her eyebrows. "Me, too. Let's get out of here."

"And go where?"

"Someplace that will cure our headaches and allow us to speak in total privacy."

"This is beautiful," Matt said in a slightly winded voice.

"Isn't it?" Carly sat down on the outcropping on the western side of the Knob, feet dangling over the precipitous drop. "More than a hundred and eighty degrees visibility from here. The first time I climbed up, I thought I could see all of California."

"How'd you ever find the trail?"

"Ronnie Talbot showed it to Ard and me. Not too many people know about it. Ronnie did a lot of hiking and exploring here in the forest."

"You must do a lot, too. You're less winded than I am, and I lead a very active life. Don't tell me Ardis hiked with you."

"Only the one time." She realized she sounded curt, as she tended to when anyone strayed too close, however innocently, to the aspects of her life she chose to keep private. Such as the discord at home that drove her to solitary hiking.

In a gentler voice she added, "Ard's thing is gardening. It doesn't seem like much exercise, but when you're hauling around huge bags of fertilizer and peat moss . . .

Anyway, she keeps in shape that way, and I hike. News-papering's a pretty sedentary occupation."

"Gardening. She always loved it." He came over and sat beside her. "Point out some landmarks to me. Except for being able to see the Pacific out there, I'm disoriented."

Glad he'd settled on a neutral topic, she swept her hand to the south. "The coastal ridge, the valley between it, and these foothills run down through Mendocino County. We're not talking very high elevations on the ridge—maybe eleven hundred to fifteen hundred feet. But look around to the east, and you'll see peaks in the national forest of up to seven thousand feet. And to the northwest"—she moved her hand again—"that's the King Range, below Eureka and Humboldt Bay. People who don't know the state always think of California as Los Angeles or San Francisco or urban sprawl. They have no idea of the vast wilderness and agricultural and ranch lands. There's endless territory to explore."

"You love it here, don't you?"

"Absolutely."

"Are you a native?"

"No. I grew up in a suburb of Cleveland, Ohio—Ellenburg. Studied journalism at Columbia, worked for a time as a reporter on the *Denver Post,* then on the *Los Angeles Times.* At the point when L.A. started to wear on me, my aunt died and left me a lot of money; I'd heard about this small-town weekly that was up for sale, and thought, Why not? So here I am."

"Quite a history. Never had any desire to return to Ellenburg, Ohio?"

"About as much as you have to return to Saugatuck, Minnesota. You and I, Lindstrom, are brother and sister under the skin."

"Meaning?"

"You left Saugatuck because everybody thought you were a murderer. I left Ellenburg because everybody knew I was a lesbian."

The corner of Matt's mouth twitched, and for a moment he didn't speak. Then he asked, "You want to tell me about it?"

"No. Not now."

"Why?"

Because for all our common suffering, I don't know you that well. May never know you that well.

"This isn't the right time. I brought you here so we could both clear our heads and have the privacy to talk about some things I found in Ard's notes."

She pulled from her daypack the legal pad on which she'd highlighted certain entries. "When Natalie was small, she had an odd conversational style. We'd be driving along in the car, for instance, and she'd be talking about something that had happened to her in school. Then all of a sudden she'd interrupt herself and exclaim, 'Oh, look—horses!' And next thing, without breaking stride, she'd go right back to whatever she'd been saying before. Some of Ard's notes remind me of that."

"Read them to me."

She flipped to the first of the pages she'd marked.

" 'Ronnie Talbot had made the decision to sell the mill a year before the deal was Meryl Travis finalized. . . .' "

"Huh?"

"Exactly my reaction. The name Meryl Travis is circled."

"Who is that?"

"The mother of Mack Travis, the man who confessed to the killings and hanged himself in his jail cell."

"Odd. What else?"

" 'Members of both the gay and straight communities came to the support of the friends of the victims as Ronnie Talbot and Deke Rutherford were laid to rest, but then the Andy D'Angelo process of fragmentation began.' "

"D'Angelo? That's my landlady's last name. Her father . . ."

"Killed himself recently. That's Andy. How'd you meet the daughter?"

"In a bar in Talbot's Mills. But it wasn't the way you think. She's a nice woman."

"Did I say anything, Lindstrom?"

"No."

"I flat-out hate people telling me what I do or don't think."

"Sorry."

"I mean, how can anybody assume—"

"Sorry."

"Oh, hell, I'm—"

"Sorry."

"We sound like a bad comedy routine."

"Maybe we should work on it, take it on the road. So is Andy D'Angelo's name circled?"

"Yes. And there's another reference of the same kind. 'Guns are common in this county, but the sheriff's department ballistics expert maintains the markings on the fatal bullets are distinctive and Rawson or Payne the missing weapon has never been found.'"

"Rawson or Payne—the developers of the Meadows."

"Right."

Lindstrom's blue eyes grew intense; they locked on hers and held. "Is she naming them as the killers?"

"I don't know."

"Are these references some kind of code?"

"I doubt it. Ard's mind doesn't work that way. She runs out of patience with crossword puzzles or rebuses. She hates mystery novels because she can never figure out their solutions. Natalie loves to do jigsaws, spreads them out on the dining room table, but Ard doesn't have the vision to fit the pieces together."

"Then what *do* these things represent?"

"Possibly reminders to herself to check something out."

"She'd break in the middle of a sentence to note them?"

"Given how distracted she's been lately, it wouldn't surprise me. Here's something else I found on the last page of this pad." Carly flipped to her marker. "It's a list: Wells Mining. They owned the Knob mine in its heyday—the eighteen sixties. Denver Precious Metals. That's the firm that bought it around the turn of the twentieth century and used a cyanide-based process to extract the remaining gold from the waste dumps and low-grade ore. They donated the land to the national parks system in the nineteen fifties. Neither company had anything to do with Ronnie or Deke. The next item is CR ninety-two. I have no idea what that is. And then there's Moratorium ten-slash-zero-zero. Again, I haven't a clue."

"Anything else?"

"Just a name—Noah Estes. And a date—nineteen seventy-four. Estes is a fairly common name in this county; the manager of the mine under Denver Precious Metals was John Estes, and he and his wife had a number of descendants. I don't recall a Noah, however."

Lindstrom nodded but remained silent. A breeze started up out of the northwest, blowing about the branches of the newly leafed aspen trees in a declivity below. Carly studied the play of light and shadow on them. She loved this time of year, when spring crept up into the foothills; its arrival always invigorated her, gave hope. But this year she felt sluggish and despondent— had felt that way even before Ard pulled her latest disappearing act.

Matt said, "Andy D'Angelo—did he have any connection to you, Ardis, or your friends?"

"I wasn't aware the man existed till he committed suicide."

"As owner of the mill, could Ronnie Talbot have known him?"

"I doubt it. He never took an active role in its management."

"Well, why don't I talk with Sam D'Angelo? See if she knows of a connection?"

"Good idea. In the meantime, I'll check on the items on Ard's list."

He stood. "You coming?"

"Not yet." They'd driven there separately. "I want to stay for a while."

"I'll call you later, then, after my talk with Sam."

After Matt's footfalls faded on the other side of the Knob, she moved to a more sheltered spot and propped her back against the smooth rock wall. Tried to empty herself of thoughts and emotions—a bastardized Zen technique that she'd developed after attending a couple of weekend retreats. It worked about forty percent of the time, but not today. Finally she abandoned it and fell back on the mantra often quoted by her brother, Alan, during their troubled teenage years: "Everything ends. Everything ends."

The mantra had helped both of them survive their parents' deteriorating marriage and their increasingly disturbed mother's unreasonable restrictions and unfounded accusations. ("I saw you with that Watkins kid. You've been smoking, haven't you?" "I caught you smiling at that boy on the street. You've been messing around, haven't you? You tramp!") It got them through long periods of punishment for the most minor of transgressions. ("You didn't make your bed right. No TV for thirty days." "You fed the cat five minutes late. No desserts this month.") And it helped them endure the long, chilly silences that were somehow more disturbing than the spates of verbal abuse.

Today the mantra didn't work at all. Instead it reminded her that, for Alan, everything had indeed ended: twenty years ago on an icy country road in upstate New York, when he'd been trying to outrun a storm to get home to his wife and baby son. A year later his wife had died of breast cancer, and the son had been spirited away by his maternal grandparents, who didn't want him exposed to the "evil influences" of the family their daughter had married into.

The foremost of the evil influences they cited being his lesbian aunt.

My brother, my best friend, the only family member besides Aunt Nan who accepted me for who I am—lost to me forever. My sister-in-law, also my friend, who understood the pain I'd been through—also lost. My nephew—I didn't know him, will never know him.

And now what if Ard and Nat are lost, too?

Old grief welled up, choking her; fresh grief made her eyes sting. She stood, hefted her pack, began climbing down the steep trail. She'd go home, get on the computer, tackle the problem.

But then, when she was in her truck, another old grief made her turn in the opposite direction.

The redwood-and-glass house stood in the shadow of pines and live oaks; the rose garden that Ard had helped Deke plant showed robust new foliage. Carly got out of her truck and breathed in the mentholated scent of the eucalyptus that lined the long driveway. Everything here was well tended, courtesy of the Talbot estate, of which Ardis was executor; in the years since the residents had been murdered, no one, not even the most pragmatic of potential buyers, had made an offer on the property.

She still had a spare key to the house on her ring; she and Ard and Ronnie and Deke had traded plant-watering and pet-caring duties during the times they traveled. She fingered the key, studying the windows whose closed blinds had blocked out the stares of the curious in the days after the killings. She hadn't been back here since Ard's frantic summons, and she found she couldn't get past the memories of her partner lying on the lawn next to a pool of vomit, her friends lying dead in their bloodstained bedroom, the impersonal bustle of the officials' activity. She would have given anything to envision Ronnie coming through the front door to envelop her in a welcoming hug, Deke following close behind to offer a glass of excellent cabernet. But while she knew such moments had occurred many times, it was as if they had happened in a film she'd seen and half forgotten. Here, in this peaceful place, she could only feel pain and the remnants of horror.

Still, she felt drawn to the house.

Don't do it, McGuire. It's not healthy.

She went up the walk, slid the key into the lock, opened the door.

The tiled hallway whose big window overlooked the swimming pool at the opposite side of the house was cool and shadowy. The living plants that Deke had cultivated under the skylights had been replaced by silk imitations, but otherwise nothing was significantly altered. She moved along, glancing into the living room, the library, the den, the exercise room, the dining room, the kitchen . . .

Something unexpected there. An odor. She sniffed, recognized it as bacon. An aroma she encountered frequently in her own kitchen on Saturdays and Sundays. One of the household bonds was a love of bacon, the crisper the better.

She moved slowly into the room, taking in small details. Stove: clean, but some streaks showing where it had recently been wiped. Scattering of crumbs on the edge of the pullout breadboard. Purple smudge on the handle of the double sink's faucet. She touched it, smelled her fingers. Blueberry jam.

Ard was a neat freak in her office, but seldom in the kitchen.

Carly went to the refrigerator and looked inside. Only a box of baking soda. But in the adjoining laundry room she found a damp and stained dishtowel inside the hamper.

She started upstairs to the bedrooms. Stopped, remembering what she'd found there the last time, then steeled herself and went on.

Guest rooms, three of them. Those who came to dinner parties here at the end of the long, winding road preferred to stay over, and Ronnie and Deke had provided accommodations. The first room showed no signs of occupancy; in the second the blinds on the two windows were closed in different directions—a mistake the realty people wouldn't have made. And in the third the comforter on the bed hung lopsided—exactly as the one on Nat's bed at home always did.

Carly didn't have the heart to search further. It was clear that Ard and Natalie had stayed here last night. Slept in a place where Ard knew no one would ever look for them, while Carly agonized and spent the night trying to find clues to their whereabouts.

They'd gotten up this morning, and Ard had prepared their traditional Saturday breakfast: orange juice, bacon, eggs over easy, toast with blueberry jam from a mail-order house in Montana. Had Nat asked why they were staying at Uncle Ronnie and Uncle Deke's house? Asked why Carly wasn't with them? How had Ard explained that?

And how had she summoned the courage to spend the night in this place where their friends were brutally murdered? Or had she visited here many times without Carly's knowledge?

Her breath came ragged and fast; then black spots danced across her field of vision. As dizziness overcame her, she sank to the floor, pressed her face into the comforter.

After a few moments her physical reactions subsided, but her emotions swung wildly—from rage to despair to rage and back to despair. She pounded the mattress with her fists, twisted the comforter with vicious fingers, and finally wept.

Why, Ard? Why?

It was after seven when she left the house. Pink and gold streaks lingered in the sky over the coastal ridgeline, but shadows enveloped the valley, and to the east the foothills were dark. The temperature had dropped sharply, and a chill was on the air, along with the scent of damp earth and growing things. . . .

Movement in the underbrush—slow, stealthy.

She stopped, listening.

"Who's there?"

No reply.

"Who's there?"

Nothing.

She must've imagined it. Probably had caught Ard's paranoia. Feeling foolish, she ran for the truck.

Once inside she turned on the dome light and twisted the rearview mirror so she could see her face. It was blotchy, her eyes red and swollen. She looked, in short, like shit. But her emotional fit—something she hadn't permitted herself in years—had proved cathartic: She was in control once more and hungry as a wolf.

At home she fixed a huge sandwich from a leftover roasted chicken, took it and a glass of Fume blanc to the table by the windows, shutting the blinds before sitting down. She ate the sandwich, drank the wine, went back to the fridge for potato salad and more wine. She was back again, in hot pursuit of ice cream, when the blinking light on the answering machine caught her attention.

Lindstrom: "Carly, I talked with Sam, and now you and I need to talk." He gave a number.

Mayor Garson Payne: "Have you given any more thought to what we were discussing the other day? Call me. You have my numbers."

Arts reporter Vera Craig: "Hey, honey. You looked kinda peaked when you and Johnny Crowe rushed in and out this afternoon. Need some of Aunt Vera's TLC?"

Sev Quill: "Hi, boss woman. What's happening with Crowe, a.k.a., well, you know? I'll be home till six, not back till morning, if I get lucky. Redheaded tourist, and she's just fascinated with newspaper reporters."

She listened to Matt's message again, then dialed the number he'd left. The phone rang ten times—no answer, no machine. The mayor's message she deleted; she was not open to further discussion with him—now or ever. Vera's message she'd ignore; if the big-hearted woman caught the slightest hint of something gone amiss, she'd be over in a flash to smother her with affection and eventually glean all the details. Sev, of course, was now busy charming the redheaded tourist.

She went to her home office and—after stepping over a stack of environmental-impact reports, a paint-stained sweatshirt, three pair of athletic shoes, and an unabridged dictionary that Nat had been perusing last week—logged on to lii.org, a site created by librarians, which listed other sites to go to for a wide variety of reliable information. An hour later she had amassed a considerable amount of printout on Wells Mining and Denver Precious Metals, none of which appeared to be relevant to anything but the dim past.

CR-92 continued to baffle her. A county road she'd never heard of, perhaps? She hurried through the still night to her truck, consulted her local map. No numbered roads; Soledad County preferred more colorful appellations. A road in another county? Another state? A search would take hours, maybe days.

She returned to the house, consulted the list. Moratorium 10/00 puzzled her as much as CR-92.

Noah Estes? A glance through the phone book

showed plenty of Esteses in the county, but no Noahs. This was something on which she could turn loose her best researcher of local matters, Donna Vail, but it was now close to eleven, so that call would have to wait till morning.

Again she went to lii.org and scrolled through the categories listed there. A few that she hadn't yet tried seemed relevant to her search, so she clicked on them and visited a couple of sites, then followed links to other sites. And as she did, a feeling stole over her. . . .

She sat up straighter, listening. Nothing but a tree branch tapping against the house's wall. She glanced at the window, saw only her own reflection. Her face bore the expression of a deer caught in the glare of oncoming headlights.

Imagining a watcher again, McGuire? You're getting as bad as Ard.

She turned back to the computer, clicked on yet another link, but the feeling persisted. Finally she left the office, went to the darkened bedroom, and peered out at the fringe of oak trees at the meadow's edge. Motion there, but it could merely have been caused by the wind or an animal. Raccoons, deer, opossum, even kit foxes coexisted with humans here in the country.

She went back to her office and drew the curtains, then sat, propping her feet on a broken-down desk chair she'd been meaning to get rid of for more than a year now, and contemplated the framed movie poster on the opposite wall. *The Last Picture Show,* a film based on a novel that had had a profound effect on her as a teenager. Larry McMurtry's vivid portrait of life in a poor, windswept West Texas town mirrored the emotional poverty of her youth and had elevated that condition to the universal. She'd taken comfort in the story's bleakness, because after reading it she no longer felt so alone.

Loneliness had been the hallmark of her childhood. When her brother, Alan, was nine and she five, their father, a successful insurance agent, had accepted an executive position with his company's home office in Cleveland and moved the family north from a small town in Georgia. While their new home in suburban Ellenburg was lovely and the neighbors hospitable, their mother refused to adapt and instead turned to the tenets of the fundamentalist church in which she was raised— a faith so out of the mainstream that even the most conservative of Christian sects viewed it with skepticism. While Stanley McGuire's job took him farther and farther afield, his wife, Mona, attempted to keep the outside world at bay; her restrictions on Alan and Carly quickly isolated them from the community, made them freaks in the eyes of their schoolmates. Even the well-meaning teachers who asked Mona to come in to discuss the children's poor socialization eventually gave up in the face of her refusals.

Alan was four years older and soon figured out how to circumvent his mother's strictures, but Carly was at her mercy. She couldn't understand why she had to return home for lunch rather than eat in the school cafeteria. She was repeatedly disappointed when her mother refused to sign permission slips for field trips. There were no after-school sports for her, no extracurricular activities; no sleepovers, birthday parties, ballet lessons, or trips to the mall. In sixth grade, when her mother tore up the permission slip for a class trip she desperately wanted to make, she complained to her father. The bitter quarrel that ensued between her parents made her vow never to do so again, but even without complaints on her part, the dissension between Stanley and Mona escalated.

A few days before she was to start junior high school, Alan sat her down and taught her his mantra: "Everything ends. Everything ends. When things get really bad, like when they're screaming and throwing stuff at each other, you say it over and over. But when he's gone and Mom's not looking, you slip and slide."

"What do you mean?"

"Say you want to go to the mall with some of the kids—"

"Nobody wants me along."

"That'll change, once you're in junior high—if you stop being Mama's baby girl. The other kids'll like you if they think you're getting away with something."

"So how do I do that?"

"Okay, Mom has her rule about being home fifteen minutes after school lets out. But you tell her, 'Mrs. Smith asked me to stay to help her set up a display. Nobody else got picked, just me. Can I?'"

"She'll say no."

"Uh-uh. She'll think it's an honor, so she'll say yes."

"What if she calls the teacher to check up?"

"She won't. Here's the key to Mom: She's afraid of people, especially people like teachers, who she thinks are better than her. Why d'you think she's never gone to PTA or Parents' Night?"

"Mom, afraid?"

"She's one of the most afraid people I know."

Carly thought about that for a moment. "Your science project, the one you have to work on after school in the chemistry lab, it isn't for real?"

"Nope. Same with the math study group on Saturday mornings."

A new world was opening up before Carly's eyes.

Alan added, "When you start high school and want to slip out at night, I'll show you my escape route."

"You go out at night, and Mom hasn't caught you?"

"Not once."

"But what if she checks your room?"

"I'm good at bunching up pillows under the covers to make them look like me. I can show you how to do that, too."

"But she might come in, to straighten the covers or kiss you good night."

"When was the last time she did that to you?"

". . . When I was really little."

"Here's another thing you should know about Mom, Carly: She liked us when we were little kids, but she doesn't like us now that we're growing up and turning into real people. That makes us just another thing in her life that she can't control. Trust me, she won't ever come into your room."

All of a sudden Alan sounded angry. Carly asked, "D'you hate her?"

He shook his head. "No. She's my mom, and I love her, and I suppose in her weird way she loves me. If I hate anybody, it's Dad, for not standing up to her. I don't feel good about the stuff I'm doing, but I've got to have a halfway normal life, and so do you."

Alan had placed a gently worded farewell note on the kitchen table and left home the day he turned eighteen. He attended college at Cornell University, took a job with an accounting firm, married, and had a child. He had created a completely normal life for himself, until it was abruptly cut off on that icy road.

Carly, on the other hand, had left home under far more dramatic circumstances and had never striven toward normalcy—at least not of the sort Alan achieved. Her definition of normalcy was self-acceptance, satisfying work, and love—and for a while she believed she'd found all three.

That belief had been an illusion, of course, but sometimes our illusions sustain us.

What, she wondered, was going to sustain her now?

Sunday, May 12, 2002

 ot one of us . . . not one of us . . . not one of us . . .

Carly jerked upright in bed, hands gripping the edge of the comforter. She was sweating, her heart pounding. Someone moved close by in the darkness—

And thumped on the bed. A voice said, "Ur? Ur?"

"Oh my God, Gracie!" She fumbled for the switch on the lamp. She and the little white cat squinted at each other in the sudden glare. Carly gathered the animal in her arms, lay back against the pillows. Gracie resisted at first but quickly settled down.

Cats were such habitual creatures, sensitive to every change in their daily routine, and Gracie's had been altered big-time. She usually slept with Natalie, but Nat had been gone two nights, and by now the cat had also noticed Ard's absence. Her questioning sounds amounted to "Where are my people, and will you go away and leave me, too?"

Carly stroked Gracie absently, still in the grip of the dream. Dammit, why was she having it again, after all these years? She'd thought last night's appearance an anomaly, but apparently it was not.

Unlike many of her dreams, this one required little interpretation; it was a symbolic reenactment of the most humiliating experience of her life—one that had caused her to sever her ties to Ellenburg, Ohio, forever.

As her brother, Alan, had predicted, once Carly devised ways to circumvent her mother's restrictions, she attracted a circle of friends, and in high school hung with a wild crowd who gathered late at night to drink beer and smoke grass at a secluded spot by the Chagrin River. She had a reputation as clever and crazy, a girl who'd try anything. Wily C. McGuire, her crowd called her. Other, more elite cliques were not so kind; they called her a slut.

By now Carly was used to being different, so she ignored their taunts and did her best to live up to the reputation; if they were going to call her a slut, she'd be the best the town had ever known. But a series of less-than-successful heterosexual experiences undermined her confidence and finally forced her to face what it was that really set her apart from the others.

It was 1976. The sexual revolution had transformed American society; gays and lesbians were openly holding hands on the streets of the cities—but not in Ellenburg, Ohio. There, homosexuality was usually the subject of smutty jokes, and teachers of the high school's euphemistically titled Practical Living Course branded it an aberration that could and should be cured by counseling. Carly kept her secret, withdrew from her friends, and developed a case of depression so severe that her homeroom teacher insisted she talk with the school district's staff psychologist.

Victoria Sherwood was a wise woman who quickly intuited Carly's problem; through their sessions she enabled her to accept her sexual orientation, while cautioning her against coming out while she was still living in Ellenburg. Given Carly's family situation and the conservative views of the community, Ms. Sherwood felt such a move would prove disastrous. Instead she put Carly in touch with a support group, and before Mona McGuire put a stop to that and all other forms of counseling, Carly had met her first female lover, a woman from a nearby town, Dierdre Paul. Soon she was slipping out at night to meet Dierdre, and though they tried to be discreet, eventually a classmate of Carly's spotted them together and figured out the nature of the relationship.

As the rumors began to circulate, the situation turned ugly.

The veiled glances and sudden silences as she passed groups in the hallways were nothing new; they'd started long ago and increased along with her bad reputation. But graffiti in the women's lounge—*McGuire is a lesbo*—was harder to take, and a note stuffed inside her locker—*We know what you're doing and who you're doing it with*—brought on a panic attack. The boys who considered themselves studs set up a betting pool to see who could score first with "the dyke," and reacted angrily when she rebuffed them; the girls who had been catty before were now downright cruel. Some of her friends stood by her, but passively, never directly confronting her tormentors, and the school's faculty looked the other way.

Victoria Sherwood had by then transferred to a district in another part of the state, and Carly had no way of getting hold of her. She called Alan several times, thinking to confide in him, but found she didn't have the nerve. Finally she broke off the relationship with Dierdre, sank once more into depression, and went back to hanging with her old crowd. But nothing was the same; even with them she felt like an outsider.

When Eric Baer, a popular member of the student council who had always treated her kindly, asked her to their senior prom at the last minute, she saw accepting the invitation as a way to lay the rumors to rest. And it was important that they die, because, much to her disappointment, she would be forced to stay in Ellenburg for another four years; her mother had decreed that the family would pay for her college education only if she attended Case-Western Reserve University in Cleveland and lived at home. The week before the prom Mona was in Georgia, caring for her ailing mother, and Stanley was easily persuaded to allow Carly to go on the date—factors she mistakenly took as good omens.

The evening began well enough, with dinner at a pricey restaurant with two other couples, and a limo to ferry them to the country club where the prom was being held. She was a good dancer and actually enjoyed herself. When the band took a break, she and Eric went with a number of couples onto the golf course, where they shared wine and joints; as she laughed along with the others at their own wickedness, she felt they accepted her. The remainder of the evening might present problems, given the way Eric was already pawing her, but as she sailed along on a grass-and-alcohol high, Carly felt confident she could handle him.

The group returned to the ballroom as the band struck up a fanfare. Tom Clifford, class president, and Shannon Michaels, vice president, were preparing to announce the prom king and queen. Shannon, her face flushed and animated, took the microphone and, after the usual screeches and groans of the audio system subsided, spoke into it, her voice high-pitched with excitement.

"Before we announce Ellenburg High's royal couple of nineteen seventy-six, we have a special award to present. One that's well deserved. It goes to Carly McGuire, our own lesbian princess. Come on up and claim your trophy, Carly!"

She went ice-cold, her limbs numb. For a moment her vision blurred. When it cleared, she was looking at Eric, who wore a triumphant smile. The boys who had been in the group on the golf course were exchanging high-fives, and the girls were laughing and smirking. Her gaze swung to the bandstand, where Tom Clifford had produced a female mannequin with crewcut hair, dressed in overalls and a plaid shirt. A sign pinned to the overalls' bib read DIERDRE DYKE. He extended it toward her, grinning.

Not everyone was laughing, however. Some of her classmates stared at her in horror, others with startled recognition. Mr. Andrade, the principal, was white-faced and tight-lipped as he strode up to the bandstand

and snatched the mannequin from Tom's hands. The chaperones, also outraged, were close behind him.

Carly whirled and ran.

Out of the ballroom, down the hallway, across the lobby, through the front door. She smacked into the valet parking attendant, pushed him away as he tried to steady her.

"Hey, you okay?"

She started to cry, kept going.

They set me up—Eric, the whole rotten bunch of them. Why would they do that? Why? And now what am I gonna do, where am I gonna go, can't go home, that's for sure. The school will call Dad and he'll kill me, and Mom, oh, my God, Mom, can't ever go home again. . . . Dierdre—no, she said she didn't want to see me anymore after I broke it off. . . . Ms. Sherwood—I don't even have a phone number for her. . . . Alan . . .

The thought of her brother calmed her. Although she hadn't been able to tell him she was gay, she knew he wouldn't condemn her. At the end of the club's long driveway she slowed, turned right, began walking down the dark sidewalk. A few blocks ahead at Price Street was a convenience store with a phone booth. She had only a small amount of change in the little silk purse that matched the little silk dress that was de rigueur at high school proms that year, but enough to make a collect call. Alan would tell her what to do. . . .

"Call Aunt Nancy," he said.

Her mother's sister, the crazy one, who lived in New York City. "She's nuts. She can't help me."

"Nan's not nuts. She's a very well-respected partner in a major stock brokerage, is about to set up her own firm, and is on the board of a half-dozen corporations. She also feels terrible about what Mom's done to you and me."

"But Mom says she's been in and out of institutions—"

"The only institutions Nan's been in are financial ones."

"Mom lied about her own sister?"

"She lies about a lot of things, but she probably believes what she's saying. When're you gonna get it through your head that Mom's a very sick person?"

". . . You don't think I'm sick because I'm—"

"Carly, you're not. Who's sick are the assholes who did that stuff to you tonight. Call Nan; she'll help."

"Are you sure? She hardly knows me."

"Of course I'm sure! Who d'you think sent me my one-way ticket out of that hellhole four years ago? Who d'you think's been paying my tuition?"

After Aunt Nancy accepted Carly's collect call, her husky smoker's voice said, "I've been waiting years to hear from you, honey. What's wrong?"

It was difficult to tell her story to a relative stranger, and she kept breaking down, but Nan gently led her through it.

"Okay, honey," her aunt said when she'd finished, "here's the way I see it. The school's already reported what happened to your dad, and all hell's about to break loose. I love your mother, but she's never been emotionally stable, and your father . . . he's a nice man, but he's weak. I think you should come here to me."

"Come to New York? How?"

"Planes fly east from Cleveland several times a day. I

can have a ticket for the next flight waiting for you at the airport. Just go home, pack your things, and leave."

A spark of possibility warmed her. "Mom's down in Georgia with Grandma, but Dad—"

"How long will it take you to get home?"

"Maybe fifteen minutes."

"Okay, I'll call him, keep him on the phone. While I'm talking to him, you sneak in and out. Do you have enough money to get to the airport?"

She had over a hundred dollars hidden in her sweater box. "Yes."

"Good. Hurry, now."

She hesitated.

"What?" Nan asked.

"If I leave now, I won't graduate."

"Oh, yes, you will. A school district that allows a student's classmates to continually torment her—let alone do what they did tonight—owes her. And I'll see to it that they pay."

Could Aunt Nan really do that? "Mom and Dad will come after me."

"Their treatment of you for all these years is the equivalent of child abuse—or neglect, on your father's part. If they come after you, I've got a team of very good lawyers, and frankly, I'd enjoy watching them go up against Mona and Stan."

Someone wanted her. Someone cared. But . . . "Why're you willing to go to all this trouble? You don't really know me."

"I know you well enough. And you forget, your mom and I were raised in the exact same kind of household as you. There was nobody to help me when I got out, and

I wouldn't wish that kind of experience on my own flesh and blood. Life's tough enough as it is. You deserve a chance to make the most that you can of yours. But I do want something in exchange."

At the moment, Carly would have sold her soul to her. "What?"

"The same thing I asked of Alan: Be strong; do your best; contribute something; be your own person."

"Even if that person's a lesbian?"

"You know what? I don't give a rat's ass if you love a woman or a wildebeest. There're bigger issues in this world than who you sleep with, and I sense you're a person who can tackle them."

And over the next four years, under Nan's expert tutelage, she had learned the art of tackling—

The phone rang, loud in the silence. Gracie levitated as Carly lunged for the receiver, her heart pounding with the alarm that a postmidnight call always provoked. She fumbled with the talk button, answered curtly.

"Carly?"

"Lindstrom, d'you know what time it is?"

"Sorry. After I left my message on your machine, I had to go out."

"So why didn't you turn yours on—your landlady's, I mean?"

"Sam doesn't have a machine. She can barely afford a phone."

"Okay, I shouldn't've snapped at you. You said we need to talk."

"Yeah. I found out some interesting things from Sam,

and we followed up on our conversation with a visit to Meryl Travis. That led us to— Well, it's too complicated to go into on the phone. Can we come over?"

She glanced at the clock radio. Two thirty-eight, but who was sleeping? "I'll make some coffee."

"Try opening a bottle of brandy instead."

Sam D'Angelo, the woman Matt called his landlady, surprised Carly. She was twenty-five at most, thin to the point of anorexia, and her long dark hair fell limply to her shoulderblades. She wore a cheap cotton sweater and ragged jeans that were several sizes too large, and the toes that protruded from her flimsy sandals must have been freezing on this chilly night. As Lindstrom made introductions, Sam regarded her warily, clasping her hands behind her back as if to avoid a handshake. Lindstrom looked tired but keyed up—the way Carly had often felt when working on an important story. He prodded Sam forward, and they went to the kitchen, where Carly had already set out a bottle of brandy and three glasses.

"So what have you got?" she asked as she poured.

"Let us relax a little before we get into it," he said.

"I'll go first, then." She related what she'd discovered at the Talbot house.

Sam's eyes grew wide, while Matt's narrowed. When Carly finished, he said, "I can't believe she went there, let alone spent the night."

"It's occurred to me that she may have been going there all along."

"Why, for God's sake?"

"To get inspiration for her book, soak up atmosphere, commune with the dead."

"That's morbid."

"To you and me, it is. To Ard—who knows?" Carly glanced at Sam, who had leaned forward and was listening intently to the conversation.

Matt said, "That house is up for sale, right? I wonder how Ard would've explained her presence to a real estate agent."

"She had good reason for being there; she's executor of Ronnie's estate."

"You didn't mention that before."

"It didn't seem relevant. So what did you and Sam find out?"

"It's pretty confusing. Sam, why don't you tell Carly about your father?"

Sam flushed and looked down at her hands. "No, you go ahead."

Carly said to her, "If you don't mind, I'd rather hear it in your own words. I don't know what . . . John's told you, but this isn't for the newspaper. It has to do with people I love who may be in trouble."

Sam raised her eyes; they were a gold-flecked gray and very disturbed. "What I've got to say, it has to do with somebody I love, too."

"Of course."

"I . . . Dad's memory, it's all I've got. When I told John, I didn't understand that Dad might've done something wrong. . . . Oh, hell, if it's really all that bad, it'll probably come out anyway." She took a deep breath, clasped her hands on the table. "Okay, John asked if Dad had anything to do with your friends who were killed. He didn't. But he was connected with Mr. Payne, from back when he managed the mill."

"In what way?"

"He fixed things."

"At the mill? Payne's house?"

"No, it wasn't like repairing machinery or . . ." Sam shrugged and glanced at Lindstrom.

He nodded encouragingly.

"Okay. I never knew about this till two days before Dad killed himself. After he got his layoff notice, he started drinking real heavy. Didn't report to work, even though he knew we'd be needing the money. The second night, he told me that he didn't like fixing things for Mr. Payne, because it sometimes got messy, but he guessed he'd have to keep on doing it, just like Mack Travis, because where else was he going to get a job at his age? When I asked him what kind of things he fixed, he yelled at me, told me to leave him the hell alone. And the next day he shot himself."

Sam's pained, bewildered voice made Carly feel for her. She said, "I'm sorry. I know it's been rough for you."

"Thanks."

Carly turned to Matt. "So after you and Sam talked, you went to see Meryl Travis. What did she tell you?"

"That her son was a good boy who never harmed anybody. He worked hard on construction and sometimes he 'made deliveries' for Payne and Milt Rawson. Often he had to drive as far as Sacramento and be home in time for his early-morning shift."

"She say what kind of deliveries?"

"She claimed she didn't know."

"Political payoffs?"

"I suspect so."

"Well, maybe if I visit Mrs. Travis I can get more information out of her." But she doubted it. The Travis woman had been widowed in her early thirties and never remarried; when Ard had interviewed her for her book, she'd said her home in Talbot's Mills resembled a shrine to the dead husband and son. Surely she'd be averse to revealing anything negative about Mack.

Matt said, "She also mentioned a Janet Tremaine, Mack's former girlfriend. Claimed Janet could've given him an alibi for the time of the killings, but somebody 'got to her first.' So we decided to track her down. D'you know the Spyglass Roadhouse?"

"Yes." It was north, in the foothills off Spyglass Trail: a rambling log structure that featured country bands, hearty meals, and cheap drinks. Carly had only been there once, but she recalled stuffed animal heads, barstools shaped like saddles, and sawdust on the floor.

"Janet Tremaine waitresses there, so we decided to stop in for a beer. I told her I was an old army buddy of Mack's. Tremaine joined us on her break."

"What's she like?"

"Good-looking, except for her hair; it's an unnatural shade of red and chopped off like she cuts it herself without the aid of a mirror. Initially she was willing enough to talk about Mack, was surprised when I told her what his mother said about her having been gotten to before she could alibi him. Tremaine maintains she didn't see Mack the entire week before your friends were murdered."

"You believe her?"

"No. At that point she got very jumpy. So I mentioned Mack's deliveries for Payne and Rawson, to see what kind of a reaction that would provoke. Tremaine blew up at me, told me I'd better be careful about repeating what I'd just said. Claimed it could get me into bad trouble. I asked her why, and she said, 'Obviously you don't know who and what you're dealing with.' Then she got up and disappeared into the crowd on the dance floor."

"So she was angry?"

"More afraid, and using her anger to cover it."

"She said, 'who and what you're dealing with.'"

"Right."

"So we have Sam's father 'fixing things.' Mack Travis 'making deliveries.' And a warning from his former girlfriend. I'd say the *what* is something major, and Ard stumbled onto it in the course of her researching. As for the who, Rawson and Payne are the obvious choices."

Lindstrom said, "What were you arguing about with Payne at the newspaper the other day?"

"He and his partner want to buy the Talbot property by the Knob. God knows why; the Meadows hasn't turned out so well, and I hear another project on the sea north of Calvert's Landing is stalled. But they've been after Ard to sell to them, and she doesn't want to. Payne was trying to persuade me to get her to change her mind."

"Why doesn't she want to sell? I'd think she'd be glad to get that place off the estate's hands."

"She dislikes both Payne and Rawson, to put it mildly. They're homophobes and have gone out of their way to be unpleasant to both of us. Payne even went so far as to talk about asking the district attorney's office to investigate improprieties in Ard's handling of the Talbot estate. I suppose he thought that if he could have her removed, the bank's trust department would be more reasonable about selling the property."

"But he didn't act on the threat?"

"He may have talked to the D.A., but his claims are groundless. Ard's handling of the disposition of assets has been strictly accounted for."

"So then he had to come up with another game plan."

Carly's eyes met Matt's, and she could tell he was thinking the same thing she was: that the new game plan had involved an anonymous phone call to British Columbia. As she opened her mouth to speak, he shook his head and glanced warningly at Sam, who still knew him as John Crowe.

Sam had been silent, her eyes remote, since she related what her father had told her, and Carly assumed her thoughts were far away, but now she spoke. "My mother used to do housecleaning for Mr. Payne's wife. She liked Mrs. Payne, but she said he was one mean son of a bitch. Mom could be pretty mean herself, but Mr. Payne actually scared her. Maybe he scared Ms. Coleman into running away."

Carly looked at Matt. "Maybe it wasn't you after all. Maybe Payne and Rawson were the ones watching her. To tell the truth, I felt like somebody was watching me tonight. Maybe one of them, or somebody they hired, really did break into the house."

She closed her eyes, thinking back to Thursday night. At the dinner table, in front of Natalie, Ard had made her claims, and Carly had cut her off because she could see they were scaring the little girl. Later, in the living room, she and Ard had argued.

"Carly, we've got to talk about what's going on."

"No, we do not. And I never want you to mention it in front of Nat again. You frightened her."

"If something's going on, isn't it good for her to be aware of it?"

"If the something's real, yes. But I think you're on edge and overreacting."

"It is real, I tell you—"

"I don't want to discuss it!"

"But I have a plan—"

"I don't want to discuss it. What part of that sentence don't you understand?"

Ard's face had crumpled at the harsh words, and she began to weep in her eerie, silent way. God, it was unnerving when she did that! Carly would do most anything to get her to stop. So she'd comforted her, and they'd gone up to bed early.

Why didn't you listen to her, McGuire? Why didn't you pick up on that single word—"plan"?

Because you stopped really listening to her years ago, when she came home with Natalie, offering excuses for the inexcusable.

"Carly?" Matt said.

She shook her head, returned to the present. "Sorry. I was trying to remember anything that would point to Payne and Rawson as the trigger for Ard's disappearance. I'm too tired to think logically, I guess."

"Me, too." He yawned, glanced at Sam, and asked,

"What say we pack it in and grab a few hours of sleep, kiddo?"

Sam looked at her watch. "We better. I'm due at the Chicken Shack at seven. Would you believe that people actually eat Cluck 'n Egg, hash browns, and milkshakes at that hour?"

After Matt and Sam left, Carly shut off the lights and went back up to bed, where she repeatedly shifted position and punched the pillows into ever more uncomfortable shapes. Gracie had disappeared, probably into Nat's room, so she didn't even have the cat for company. Finally she got up, thinking to make a fire to warm the chill dawn, but when she set some kindling on the grate, she saw there was an unusual amount of ash, as well as a scrap of paper caught between the grate and the rear wall. She fished it out with the tongs.

It was only a fragment, burned around the edges, bearing a single handwritten line: *mine and I got the right* . . .

What? Whose? And what right?

The penmanship was crude and childlike, which went with the incorrect grammar. But that didn't necessarily mean the writer was poorly educated; for a variety of reasons, many people had bad handwriting, and she herself, editor of a Pulitzer-winning newspaper, said "I got" upon occasion.

Perhaps this was part of a letter to Ard from Matt, asking her to reconcile. Something to the effect of "You're mine and I got the right to be with you." No. That wasn't his style, and besides, she remembered his bold, well-developed handwriting from his job application.

She set the scrap on the table, curled up in her chair. So much information flooded her mind, and none of it meshed. She'd done some investigative reporting while with the L.A. *Times,* but she'd had a good deal of assistance on those stories, and none had posed such complex—or personal—questions.

Well, she'd just have to tackle them one by one.

Tackling.

It was a word that she'd heard often during the years she lived with her aunt Nancy. Nan's method of dealing with the world—and she'd elevated it to an art form. No subtlety in her game plan; she merely advanced down whatever field of endeavor she currently was playing on, knocking over all those who opposed her. But like a good lineman, she earned respect from her opponents.

During the four years Carly lived in her aunt's fashionable Sutton Place apartment while attending Columbia at Nan's expense, she'd learned quite a bit about tackling.

Business dinners for the rich and occasionally famous, during which Nan overran their objections to investing in lucrative but risky schemes. Elaborate parties designed to separate the elite from large amounts of cash for her favorite charities and political candidates. Long discussions on quiet evenings, when Carly learned that the way most people thought the world operated and the way it actually did were polar opposites. Abrasive arguments between Nan and her many lovers, which she heard through the walls; none of them, even the most powerful, was strong enough to oppose her.

Nan tackled constantly: her clients, her friends, her men, Carly herself. And Alan . . .

On the night that he died during the ice storm, Alan had been in the city visiting Nan—as was Carly, on vacation between her old job in Denver and her new one in Los Angeles. At a dinner party at the apartment, Nan had announced Alan's appointment to a full partnership in her investment firm. Although visibly stunned, he reacted graciously in the company of the guests, but later that evening, in the privacy of Nan's study, he turned the position down, berating her for announcing it without consulting him. He had the life he wanted upstate: his family, friends, good work, respect within his small community. Nan railed at him, saying he owed it to her to help carry on the firm while Carly tackled the big issues through her journalistic career. Finally Alan departed in a rage that had surely affected his judgment and led to a fatal mistake while driving.

Even in the depths of her grief, Carly couldn't completely blame Nan for Alan's death. But the circumstances under which he died made her question her aunt's desire to take control of everything and everyone. The move to L.A. proved positive, putting the necessary distance between them, and it wasn't until a year later, when Nan died of colon cancer, that Carly realized why she'd been so insistent with Alan: She'd known she had limited time left, and was afraid her firm—her own piece of immortality—would die with her unless she positioned her nephew to take over. As, of course, it had. In her will, Nan had stated that she was leaving Carly the bulk of her estate so she might "have the enjoyment in her adult life that was denied her in her childhood."

Remembering, Carly laughed, the sound loud and bitter in the empty house.

Enjoyment, Nan? Look at your little protégé now. Against her best efforts she's turned into you. She bullies her employees, buries herself in her work, ignores her friends, gives short shrift to a little girl who needs her attention. But worst of all, she can't forgive the woman she loves for a mistake she made ten years ago.

I'm you, Nan.

God help me.

A shower and a full carafe of coffee jump-started her day. Nothing to eat—her nervous stomach wouldn't permit it. She tried not to think of the leisurely weekend breakfasts she, Ard, and Nat had enjoyed. If she were to accomplish anything, she'd have to banish her memories. And tackle.

First, a call to Donna Vail, her foremost staff researcher. For a while before coming to the paper, Donna had worked for Good Connections, a service that put people in touch with those they were looking for: birth parents, adoptees, lost relatives, old loves, school classmates. As a result she had access to various databases the firm had developed. If anybody could identify Noah Estes and pinpoint his current whereabouts, Donna was the one.

"Carly!" Her employee's voice was warm. "I was just thinking about you guys. We're having a salmon roast over on the beach near Castle Rock this afternoon, and we'd love it if you could join us."

"I—we'd love to, but I'm backed up on work. I'm

having trouble with a story idea I want to assign to Sev, and I thought you might be able to help me, but if you're having a party . . ."

"A potluck, and Dan's in charge of the salmon. All I have to do is show up. What d'you need?"

"An identification, but all I have is a name—Noah Estes. There're a lot of Esteses in the county, but the phone book doesn't list a Noah."

"So this would be a local guy?"

"I think so."

"Give me twenty minutes, and I'll get back to you."

Twenty minutes dragged by like hours. Carly considered making more coffee but decided her nerves were bad enough as it was. When the phone finally rang, she snatched it up and heard Vera Craig's voice.

"Honey, you never called me back. Is everything okay?"

"I . . . yes, everything's fine."

"You sound kinda edgy."

"I'm expecting a call and—"

"Working on Sunday again? I'm gonna have to talk to you about that. It isn't good for your relationship or for Natalie."

"Vera, I've got to keep the line open." She pressed the disconnect button.

Two minutes later the phone rang again. Donna.

"Okay," she said, "I ran two searches through International Locator. First, a national name sweep. The database contains info on eighty-five to ninety percent of people in the country. There're two Noah Esteses, one in Vermont, the other in Alabama."

"Does the database give addresses and phone numbers?"

"It does, but I don't think you'll be needing those particular ones. My second search was a national death sweep. Eight Noah Esteses turned up, and one sounds like the guy you're looking for. Social Security number was issued in California. Born March sixth, eighteen eighty-three. Died November thirtieth, nineteen eighty-one. Zip code for the place he died is Santa Carla's."

"That's probably my man."

"You need anything else?"

"Your potluck . . ."

"It's hours before we have to leave. Here's a thought: Why don't you and Ard and Nat join us at the beach? See if you can't entice that sexy John Crowe to come along, too; I've got a single girlfriend I'd like him to meet. If you come, I'll give you the skinny on Noah Estes then."

". . . Ard and Nat are away this weekend. And, like I said, I'm swamped with work."

"Well, if you change your mind we'll be at Schooner Cove. Meantime, I'll get going on this."

Carly thanked Donna and ended the call. There was no way she could face a crowd of the Vails' friends today, many of whom she knew well, and who would be sure to ask after Ard and Nat. But what was she going to do for the rest of the day? Normally on weekends her time was filled with activities, but today stretched endlessly before her.

She could visit Meryl Travis and attempt to draw her out about Mack's "deliveries." She could track down Janet Tremaine and question her. She could return Sev

Quill's call and enlist his help. She could run upstairs and pull the covers over her head and scream. . . .

No, McGuire. Tackle.

The doorbell rang. Lindstrom, probably, back to re-hash what they'd talked about in the early morning hours. She moved along the hall, grateful that she'd no longer be alone. Opened the door and stared up at Garson Payne.

Payne loomed over her, eyes stony. The scar on his right cheek—a souvenir of a hunting accident, he claimed—stood out in relief against his tan, as it always did when he was angry. He said, "You didn't return my call, Carly."

"I didn't see any reason to."

He tried to move into the house, but she blocked him, her hip against the doorjamb.

"Inhospitable this morning, aren't we?"

"My home is not open to you—now or ever."

"Perhaps you'll reconsider when you hear what I have to say."

"Then say it and leave."

"Very well. Milt Rawson and I have come up with some very disturbing information about Ardis. Old but damaging information. If you'll allow me to come inside and discuss it with the two of you, I believe it will persuade her to be more reasonable in the matter of the Talbot property."

In spite of the morning sun washing over her, Carly felt a chill. It could only be one thing. How had they found out?

"Neither Ardis nor I have anything to discuss with you."

Someone was crossing the footbridge. Payne's bulk blocked her view.

He said, "Milt and I realize that you and your partner have no reason to like us, but our offer is a good one."

The footsteps slowed at the end of the bridge. Then they resumed, their sound muted as if their owner had moved off the path and onto the grass.

Carly said, "And since Ardis has rejected your offer numerous times, you've now decided to resort to blackmail."

"That's a nasty accusation, Carly."

"And you have a nasty way of doing business."

"Let's not trade insults. If we can sit down and discuss the situation rationally—"

Lindstrom's voice said, "Yes, let's do that."

Payne whirled, scowling. "Who the hell are you?"

"A friend of the family. Why are you harassing Ms. McGuire on such a lovely Sunday morning?"

"I was not harassing—"

"Was he?" Matt asked her.

"Yes, he was."

"Seems to me he'd be better off in church."

Payne said, "This doesn't concern you, whoever you are."

"He's my new staff photographer, John Crowe," Carly said. "And a good shot—both with a camera and a forty-five."

The mayor took a step backward. "Is that supposed to be funny?"

"Depends on your point of view. I find it hilarious."

"Then we'll continue this discussion later, when

you're in a more serious mood." He turned and set off at a measured pace.

Matt watched him, eyes narrowed. "Was that about the Talbot property again?"

"Yes."

"What's this I overheard about blackmail?"

Oh, God. Now is the time to go upstairs, pull the covers over my head, and scream.

"Carly?"

"I'm okay."

"No, you're not."

"Dammit, Lindstrom, I hate being told how I am, how I feel!"

"Hey, I'm not the enemy."

"Why did you have to turn up when the shit's about to rain down all over me?"

"What kind of shit?"

"None of your business."

"I'm making it my business."

"Jesus, I hate you!"

"You don't know me well enough to hate me."

"Stop being reasonable!"

"One of us has to be."

"Fuck you!"

"Carly, where's all this anger coming from?"

From years back. From the day before yesterday. From five minutes ago.

Time's up. Got to face it.

Got to tackle . . .

Matthew Lindstrom

Sunday, May 12, 2002

att followed Carly inside her house. In the days since he'd entered her office and found her sitting on her desk, she'd changed perceptibly: Her tan had faded to sallowness, and her facial skin pulled tight against the bone; her eyes were sunk in shadow.

A skull, he thought, topped by brittle, dead hair. He shook his head, pushed the image away, but he couldn't rid himself of the notion that some essential part of her was dying.

Without a word she went to the living room window. Matt followed and looked over her shoulder. Gar Payne sat behind the wheel of a green Jaguar that blocked Carly's truck, a cell phone to his ear.

"Get off my property, Payne!" she exclaimed.

As if he'd heard her, the mayor set down the phone, started the car, and drove off.

Carly expelled a long sigh. "Let's go outside, huh? It's stuffy in here. I need some air."

She led him to the patio in front of the house. It was in full sun, so she raised the umbrella between two chaise longues and they sat side by side. Matt waited for her to speak and, when she didn't, asked, "Are you ready to tell me about it?"

"I don't think you want to know. It's about Ard, and it's bad."

He didn't think he wanted to know, either. Every revelation had been bad, only to be topped by something worse. But he sensed in Carly's tone a need to tell it, as if she'd already made the decision to place it in his hands.

He said, "You may as well get on with it."

She sighed again and rested her head against the chaise's high cushion. "Payne is pushing hard now to get his hands on the Talbot property. This morning he wanted to sit down and talk about an offer with Ard and me. When I wouldn't let him in the house, he made reference to some damaging information he and Rawson have about her."

"He say what it was?"

"Didn't have to. I know."

He waited, letting her tell it in her own way.

"I told you that Ard took off for fifteen months and came back with Natalie."

"Right. She went to San Francisco."

"Well, I didn't tell you why she left. I came home one night and found her in bed—our bed—with a man. Gar

Payne. He's one of those macho homophobes who can't believe a woman can resist him. So he set out to prove it with Ard and then rub my nose in it. Apparently he hasn't grasped the concept of bisexuality."

Somehow it didn't surprise him. Maybe nothing would have the capacity to surprise him again.

Carly went on: "After I chased Gar out of here, Ard and I fought. She said she felt smothered by a monogamous relationship. She said she needed to be with both men and women. She said I was the flip side of the coin from you, but that in essence we were both the same."

"Meaning?"

"We were trying to control her, confine her to one way of life."

"She never accused me of that."

"No. Because she loved you and didn't want to hurt you. With me she always seemed to want a confrontation."

And because she'd avoided a confrontation, he'd never suspected. . . .

Or had he, on some level?

There was the night, a month or so before Gwen began talking about divorce, when he'd come home early from a wedding shoot and called out to her from the front hall. She'd come running down the stairs in her bathrobe, expressing surprise at his return. She and her friend Bonnie Vaughan had been about to color her hair.

Except Gwen never colored her hair, and Bonnie came downstairs a few minutes later, clearly uncomfortable. The dyeing project was abandoned, and after a glass of wine, Bonnie went home.

Bonnie Vaughan, Gwen's best friend. The woman

who had ended his first life with her harsh words: "You better get out of Saugatuck before somebody murders *you!*"

In light of what he'd recently learned about Gwen, it all made sense: She and Bonnie had been lovers. Whether there had been other women before Bonnie didn't matter. Gwen had loved her; Gwen had loved him. To a woman of the conservative upbringing she'd described to him, that was an untenable situation, even in the freewheeling eighties, so she'd run from both of them. And though Bonnie had initially supported Matt, eventually she'd turned her grief over losing Gwen to hatred for him—everybody's favorite scapegoat.

"Matt?" Carly said.

He didn't respond.

"Earth to Lindstrom."

"Sorry. Just remembering. So Ardis ran away, and . . . ?"

"Came back with Natalie. Came back with all her usual excuses for returning. Her love for me, her love for our home, which would be the ideal place to raise our child. She actually said that: 'our' child, as if we'd created her. But then she came to the main one, and it was a biggie."

Carly's voice had gone hard and flat.

I don't want to know. I don't.

"The man Ard was involved with in San Francisco was an abusive alcoholic and a drug user who did not want a child. One night, when they were both high and he was trying to persuade her to get an abortion, they fought. Physically. Ard grabbed a kitchen knife and stabbed him. And then she ran. After she had the baby, she came home to me.

"So that's what Gar Payne is holding over my head. Somehow he found out that Ard stabbed Natalie's father, and that I helped cover it up."

Impossible.

Or was it?

No. Nothing his former wife had done was impossible anymore.

"You say she stabbed him," he said, his own voice sounding foreign to him. "Fatally?"

"No. If that had been the case, there would've been something in the San Francisco papers. She monitored them for weeks."

"Why wouldn't the boyfriend have gone to the police?"

"Probably because he had a long arrest record, didn't want to have anything to do with the law."

"Okay, Ardis stabbed him and ran. Where?"

"Los Angeles."

"And Natalie was born there?"

"Yes."

"And when they came here, Natalie was how old?"

"Four months."

"And Ardis never heard from the boyfriend—what's his name?"

"Chase Lewis. No, she never heard from him again."

"I'm surprised he didn't appear to claim his share of the glory when the paper won the Pulitzer."

Her lips twisted in a wry smile. "I don't think

drugged-out trombonists follow the news all that closely."

"Still, he must've made some effort to find her."

"Ard's theory is that it was too much trouble for him. Of course, she said the same of me because I didn't hire a private detective every time she disappeared." Carly closed her eyes, shook her head. "God, when I look back on the past fourteen years, I wonder how I got into such a messy relationship, much less remained in it. I never considered myself the kind of woman who lets herself be victimized, but that's exactly what happened. And now I'm really in a mess."

"Well, in order to extricate yourself from said mess, first you need to find out how serious it is. Find out how much damage Gar Payne and his partner can inflict on you. While you stay here and keep working on leads to Ardis and Natalie's whereabouts, I'm going to find out what happened to Chase Lewis."

Within two hours he left for San Francisco. Highway 101 narrowed some four miles south of Talbot's Mills, widened to a freeway at Santa Carla, then narrowed again to a two-lane arterial that meandered along the bank of the Eel River. The expanse of water was swollen from the spring runoff; across it Matt glimpsed small cabins among the tall, newly leafed trees. They made him think of his own cabin overlooking Bear Rock, and he felt the strong pull of home. He was tempted to drive straight through San Francisco, turn in the Jeep at the rental car company, and use his open ticket to Vancouver. He had his camera on the seat beside him, its bag containing the films of Gwen; they would vindicate him. Let Carly McGuire solve her own problems.

But he didn't go on to the airport. Instead he took the Lombard Street exit from Doyle Drive and checked into the first motel with a vacancy sign. In the lobby he bought a city map, then went up to his room to study it.

He'd visited San Francisco once during his wandering years, but found it too dreary and expensive. In the few days he'd spent there, he'd learned it was difficult to navigate—full of one-way streets and natural obstacles that made it impossible to travel in a straight line from one point to another. After he'd refamiliarized himself with the map, he pulled the phone book from the nightstand and looked up Wild Parrots, the jazz club where Carly said Ardis had waitressed. It was still in existence, on Grant Avenue in the bohemian North Beach district. It was not the starting point he would have chosen—that was the now-closed library, with its files of old newspapers—but he decided to drive over there anyway.

Traffic in North Beach was heavy and parking spaces at a premium. Wild Parrots, shabby-looking in the early-evening light, didn't have valet service. Many blocks away he found a lot with hourly rates so high it would have been more economical merely to trade them the Jeep; then he joined the crowds on the sidewalks. The district seemed seedier than he remembered it: Barkers outside the topless clubs were more aggressive; trash littered the gutters; homeless people reclined in doorways. It was a relief to turn uphill, onto the lower slope of Telegraph Hill, where Italian bakeries and delis and esoteric shops replaced the rough-and-tumble commercialism.

The club was small, with a raised bandstand at one end and round tables scattered across the floor. A bar ran along the righthand wall, the smoky glass mirror behind it etched with a flock of colorful parrots. He recalled reading in a guidebook during his first visit to the city that such birds, once escapees from their cages but now generations in the wild, frequented Telegraph Hill.

It was early, only a little after six. A couple sat at the far end of the bar in earnest discussion, but otherwise the club was deserted. Matt took a stool at the other end and waited until a bald man in a vest whose colors matched the parrots' plumage emerged from a curtained doorway, carrying a case of Scotch. After setting it down, he approached Matt, slapping a paper cocktail napkin in front of him.

"What'll it be?"

"Sierra Nevada."

When the bartender set the bottle and glass in front of him and started to turn away, Matt added, "And some information."

"About?"

"Chase Lewis."

"What about him?"

"He used to play here."

"Yeah."

"You know him?"

"Was before my time. I know of him. They say he could've been one of the greats, but he didn't get the breaks."

"You know what happened to him?"

He shrugged. "What happens to any of them that've got the talent but don't make it? They booze, they do drugs. They're in rehab, they're outta rehab. Some of them do time. Chase Lewis, I don't know. It's been years since anybody here has seen him." He gestured at the wall beside the mirror. "That's him, the middle picture."

Matt squinted through the gloom but could make out very few details. "Would you have an address on file for him?"

The bartender's eyes narrowed. "You a cop?"

"No. I'm trying to locate a woman he was once involved with. A family member."

The suspicion in the man's eyes turned to greed. "I don't know. I'd have to check a long ways back."

"It's worth twenty bucks to me."

"I shouldn't leave the bar. Business'll be picking up pretty quick."

To Matt, it didn't look as if business would ever pick up. "Thirty bucks. Final offer."

After the bartender disappeared through the curtain, Matt got up and went to examine the photograph of Chase Lewis. It showed a slender, light-skinned black man with a small mustache and conservative Afro, smiling and cradling his trombone. A standard publicity still, and it told him nothing about the man who had fathered Ardis's child.

The man whom Ardis had stabbed and run from.

He returned to the bar, sipped his beer, waited. The couple at the far end left, and no other patrons materialized. It was nearly ten minutes before the bartender returned and slid a piece of scratch paper across to him.

"Had to get it from one of the file boxes in the storage room," he said. "Why's it that the box you want is always on the bottom of the stack?"

Matt placed thirty dollars on the bar as he read the address. "Hugo Street. Where's that?"

"Inner Sunset, a block from Golden Gate Park. Nowhere place. You'd think a guy like Chase Lewis would've lived in a more lively neighborhood."

Yeah, but I bet it was plenty lively the night Ardis stabbed him.

The apartment house was on a corner: three stories of beige stucco with bay windows, and fire escapes scaling its walls. In the arched entryway was a bank of mailboxes with buzzers beneath them, Number five was labeled with the name C. Lewis. His good luck that the man hadn't moved.

He pressed the buzzer twice but got no response. Then he rang number six, which by his reckoning would be on the same floor. No response either, but seven gave an immediate answering buzz. Matt pushed through the door into a dimly lighted lobby that smelled faintly of cat urine.

There was no elevator, so he started up the narrow staircase. A woman's voice called down, "Hey, how much do I owe you?" Her face appeared over the railing, round and eager, but it quickly turned wary. "You're not the pizza guy," she said.

"Sorry. I rang you at random. I'm looking for Chase Lewis. He doesn't answer his bell."

"The guy in five? He's not here very much. I don't really know him."

"Is there anybody else in the building who does?"

"Uh . . . Mrs. Matthews, maybe. She kind of functions as the manager—at least she's the one who calls the owners when something in the common areas needs fixing. She's lived here forever. Number two."

Matt thanked her and located the apartment at the rear of the first floor. Mrs. Matthews looked to be in her sixties, a petite blonde-haired woman in jeans and a blue sweater. "Of course I know Chase," she said. "What's he done now?"

"To tell you the truth, I've never met the man. I'm trying to locate him on behalf of a family member who was involved with him about ten years ago—Ardis Coleman."

"Ardis. Of course. Lovely girl. She didn't deserve the way Chase treated her. I was happy when she left him."

"How did he treat her?"

"Abused her, both verbally and physically. Threatened their little girl, too, and she was only a baby when they moved here."

"When was that?"

"September of ninety two."

"And Ardis left him when?"

"In November."

"What were the circumstances of her leaving?"

Mrs. Matthews looked uncomfortable. "You say Ardis is a family member. I'd think you'd know."

"She doesn't like to talk about that part of her life, but I understand there was some unpleasantness. If I'm to deal with Lewis, I think I should be prepared, don't you?"

"Well, yes. On the night Ardis left, I heard a lot of yelling and screaming up there." She motioned toward the ceiling. "More than the usual. Then it got very quiet, and someone ran out of the building. An hour later Chase came to my door reeking of alcohol, with his shoulder wrapped in a bloody towel, and asked me to drive him to the emergency service at S.F. General. He said Ardis had left him and taken the baby, and he got so upset he stabbed himself accidentally."

"Did you believe him?"

"Of course not. To me it was obvious what had happened, but it was no business of mine. And he managed to convince the emergency room personnel of his story."

"Did Chase ever try to find Ardis and the baby?"

"No. He drank even more afterwards, and I think he was using drugs as well. He kept getting fired from his jobs, but somehow he managed to support himself and keep the apartment. Then, a few years ago he got himself into a program and has been clean and sober ever since." Mrs. Matthews frowned. "Of course, he's as mean as ever, although he controls himself better. Why do you want to see him?"

"A legal matter involving the little girl. Do you have any idea when he might be coming home?"

"No, I don't. Last month he mentioned that he'd landed a long-term gig at Lake Tahoe."

"Where?"

"He didn't say." She hesitated. "When you talk to Ardis, will you tell her hello for me? She may not remember me after all these years, but just say I wish her well."

Back at the motel he paced nervously, contemplating his next move. A drink from the bottle he'd brought along failed to calm him, so finally he sat down and dialed directory assistance in the 612 area code, copied down the number he received, and called it. Seconds later, Bonnie Vaughan's soft voice answered.

"Bonnie, it's Matt Lindstrom. Don't hang up. I have good news."

"You've got a lot of nerve, calling me."

"Gwen's alive, Bonnie. She's been living in a small town in California since shortly after she disappeared. I've seen her, photographed her."

A long silence. "I don't believe you."

"It's the truth. Let me tell you how I found her." The story spilled out of him like water rushing through a sluiceway. He ended by asking, "The two of you were lovers, right?"

". . . Oh, Matt, what difference does it make?"

"It's important to me. It explains a great deal."

"All right, yes. You must've suspected. That time you nearly caught us at your house . . . She was so afraid you'd figure it out and hate her. Hate me, too. The thing was, she loved both of us, but she loved you more."

"Why d'you think that?"

"Because she stopped sleeping with me after that night. In a way, I was relieved. If there had been a scandal, I'd've lost my job. A high school principal having a lesbian affair with a married woman ... Well, you know."

"She broke it off with you, but she still asked me for a divorce."

"Because she was afraid if she stayed with you, she'd end up really hurting you. She planned to wait till the divorce was final and then leave town, claiming she'd gotten a job in another state."

"If you knew her plans, how could you think I murdered her?"

She sighed. "I didn't at first, although I thought it was strange that she disappeared before the divorce was final, without saying good-bye to either of us. But Gwen was impulsive and didn't always act rationally, so I decided something had happened to make her run. But then two years went by, and she never got in touch with me. Everybody else thought you were guilty, and I started believing it, too."

"And now?"

"It all makes sense. These disappearing acts, they're part of a lifelong pattern."

Her phrasing gave him pause. "Lifelong?"

"Well, she did run away from home in her teens. She spent a couple of years in Chicago before she came to Saugatuck. Where she got the money to attend college, I'm not sure. She didn't volunteer the information, and I guess I really didn't want to know."

"She told me her parents had died in a plane crash and that she was using their life insurance money for school. And she told me a lot about being raised by an ultraconservative grandmother in Muskegon, Michigan."

"She was raised in Muskegon, yes, but her parents are very much alive."

Yet another revelation. Why had Gwen lied to him about a thing like that? "Did she give a reason for running away from home? Was she neglected? Abused?"

"No. She said her parents and Muskegon were boring. She wanted more from life than they could offer."

"I suppose she also found Saugatuck boring. And me."

"Matt? Are you okay?"

"Yeah. I just need some time to take all this in. We'll talk again soon, Bonnie, I promise."

Carly sounded depressed when he called her an hour later, and he hated to relate news that would further deflate her spirits. As he told her the things he'd found out that evening, she listened silently.

Finally she said, "I lived with her all those years and never knew any of this. I accepted everything she told me without question. How could I be so stupid?"

"You had no reason to doubt her. Neither did I."

"She told me she stabbed Chase Lewis because he was pressuring her to have an abortion. Now it turns out she'd already had Nat. What's the sense in a lie like that? Or the lie about her parents being dead and her awful childhood with her grandmother?"

He'd thought about that as he'd nursed a drink in his dark motel room after talking with Bonnie. "I think there's some deficiency in her that makes her need drama in her life. The running away, the lies—they're all a part of that. When we were married, she would cre-

ate situations that would throw our lives into chaos: a
fire in the kitchen, ramming the car into the garage door.
Nothing major, but it got her a lot of attention."

"The same's been true with us, now that you mention
it." Carly hesitated. "So are you coming back now?"

"No. I still want to find out the details of the night
Ardis stabbed Chase Lewis. I think I'll make a run up to
Lake Tahoe in the morning."

xpensive-looking hotels that Matt didn't recall from a previous visit to Lake Tahoe hugged the shoreline, blocking views of the water. A major building boom was under way on both sides of the Nevada border; cranes rose high against the sky, the noise of piledrivers was deafening, and scaffolding covered the sidewalks. Traffic on the boulevard linking the two states crept.

By contrast, the interiors of the casinos seemed curiously deserted, even for early afternoon. The stools at the long banks of slot machines were largely empty, and many of the gaming tables were covered. The brightly lighted rooms were too quiet, too chill, too cheerless. Even the newest and most opulent of the gambling establishments seemed shabby and fouled by stale smoke. A paradox, given the near-frantic construction going on outside. Although the casinos were the victims of an economy that had never recovered from the aftermath of the horrific events of the past September 11, the developers would eventually fall victim to their own false optimism and greed.

He tried to canvass the casinos quickly but became frustrated by layouts designed to force a person to pass through most of the moneymaking attractions before arriving at a place where information could be had. Finally, while stopping for a badly needed drink at one of the bars in Caesar's Palace, he encountered a waitress who knew Chase Lewis and had heard that a group he frequently played with, the Fillmore Five, was currently engaged at the Hyatt Regency at Incline Village.

He drove north past pleasant-looking enclaves called Zephyr Cove, Cave Rock, and Glenbrook, bypassed the road to Carson City. Incline Village was near the tip of the lake, on the Nevada side, and the Hyatt Regency, some dozen stories tall, dominated the shoreline. He left the Jeep with the valet, went inside to speak with the concierge, and was directed to a smaller building on the beach, which housed a restaurant. When he stepped into its dim interior, it took a minute for his vision to adjust; then he saw wood beams, massive iron chandeliers, and a huge stone fireplace. At the far end, in a bar area, a slender black man with a receding hairline was adjusting sound equipment on a platform. Not Chase Lewis.

The man straightened and turned as Matt approached. "Sorry, man, they're not open yet."

"I'm looking for someone with the Fillmore Five."

"You found him. Dave Rand's the name."

"Can you put me in touch with Chase Lewis?"

He frowned and stepped down from the platform. "Wish I could. We'd be sounding a whole lot better if he was with us on this gig, but he pulled out at the last minute. Guy we got to replace him's pretty lame."

"Why'd he pull out?"

"Something came up. With Chase, something always comes up. He called last Monday, said we'd have to do without him."

"He say why?"

"Nope. Chase doesn't let other people know his business, especially when he's got a mad on. And from the sound of his voice I could tell he was pissed off. I'll tell you, he's a good trombone man, but as a human being"—he shook his head—"mean as a rattlesnake, and then some. Why you lookin' for him?"

"I need to settle a legal matter with him, for a family member." The lie came easily; he half believed it himself.

"Huh. You a lawyer?"

"No, just helping out."

"This family member suing him?"

"Nothing like that. I just need for him to sign some papers."

"This wouldn't have to do with Ardis?"

"Ardis Coleman? Yes."

"She and the little girl all right?"

"They're fine."

"Good. It's a goddamn shame the way Chase treated her. She was one sweet thing. Nobody was surprised when she split and took the kid—except for Chase. He's had a mad on for the whole world ever since."

"He must've loved her."

"Nope. Chase doesn't give a rat's ass for anybody but himself, but no woman's supposed to turn her back on him. Or take something from him."

Matt spotted a stack of cocktail napkins on the bar, took out a pen, and wrote Sam's phone number on one. "If you hear from Chase, will you call me?"

"Sure, but I doubt I'll be hearing. When he canceled out, I told him he'd never get another gig with us, and he knew I meant it." His eyes clouded. "You might warn Ardis that he's still gunning for her."

"You think he'd go after her if he found out where she is?"

"Damn straight he would. And she'd be one sorry mess by the time he was through with her."

Tuesday, May 14, 2002
Talbot's Mills, California

A s he approached the exit, Matt yawned widely. It was nearly one in the morning. There had been no easy way to get to Soledad County from Lake Tahoe, so he'd been forced to detour south to Sacramento and Highway 5, then take a secondary road east to Highway 101. A long trip, and he drove without pleasure, his thoughts on the puzzle that was Gwen.

A lifelong pattern of lies and running away. Parents who had presumably loved her living in limbo, never knowing what had become of their daughter. Two years as a runaway in Chicago. God knows who she'd conned there in order to get the money for college—or how she'd cast them aside after collecting. And then she'd abandoned him and Bonnie Vaughan. Abandoned Carly numerous times. Even as vile a person as Chase Lewis probably didn't deserve to be stabbed and left bleeding. God knew how many other lives she'd poisoned. . . .

The personal history that he'd learned didn't square with the woman he'd married: gentle, vulnerable, dependent, needing constant reassurance. But neither did the scene Carly had described: Ardis efficiently taking her notes at the Talbot house after she'd discovered their friends' bodies. Could such opposite components exist within one person? Apparently so.

A deer appeared in the wash of his headlights, standing by the side of the road. For a moment he feared it would leap into his path, but then it whirled and plunged into the underbrush. After that he emptied his mind and simply concentrated on driving.

Now as he pulled up to Sam's house, he saw lights in the front room. He'd phoned her from Willits and told her he'd be very late, but apparently the call hadn't kept her from worrying. But why should she worry? And why should he care if she did? She rented him a room, nothing more, although he had to admit he'd grown fond of her in a big-brotherly way.

He got out of the Jeep and mounted the porch steps. Sam must have heard him, because she had the door open before he could find his key. Carly stood in the hallway behind her, and from the look on her face, he knew something very bad had happened.

Without preamble, she said, "Chase Lewis is dead.

He was shot sometime over the weekend in a motel in Westport."

"Jesus." When the initial shock had subsided, he moved past the women, into the front room. Sank onto a butt-sprung recliner and ran his hands over his face, as if he could wash the moment away. He looked up, saw that Sam had disappeared. Carly came into the room and sat down on the sofa.

She said, "Sev Quill was routinely monitoring the sheriff's calls this morning when he heard a one-eighty-seven, code two. Homicide, urgent. He rushed over to Westport to get the story, and phoned me from there so I could tell Production to hold space on the front page. As soon as I heard the victim's name, I decided to drive over there, too."

"And?"

"I talked with Rho Swift, who's handling the investigation. Lewis checked in on Thursday night. He pretty much stayed in his room, with the Do Not Disturb sign out. Yesterday morning, Monday, the maid got concerned because she hadn't seen him, and used her passkey. Lewis was lying on the floor, fully clothed, with a gunshot wound to the head. The autopsy's not scheduled till tomorrow morning, but Rho thinks he was killed sometime on Saturday."

"Did anybody at the motel hear the shot?"

"No. He was at the far end of an isolated wing—a room he requested after looking at two others—and there weren't many other guests."

"Does Rhoda know what kind of gun he was shot with?"

"I suppose, but she didn't tell me. I do know they dug a wild-shot bullet out of the wall above the bed."

"What kind of handgun do you own?"

"Handgun?"

"When you warned me off Ardis after you found out who I was, you said you owned a handgun and weren't afraid to use it."

She looked down at the floor. "I lied."

"You don't own a gun?"

"I hate the things. I just said that to scare you."

"Does Ardis own one?"

"No."

"Are you sure?"

"It's the one thing about her I *am* sure of. She's even more afraid of guns than I am. Ronnie Talbot had a weapons collection that he inherited from his father, and she was always after him to get rid of it, even though it was stored inside locked cabinets in the library, where nobody could see it."

"Okay, did you tell Rhoda Swift about Lewis's relationship to Ardis and Natalie?"

"No."

"Carly, that's obstructing a homicide investigation."

She looked up at him, eyes agonized. "I know that. But Ard could not have done this. She could *not*."

He let it go for the moment. "So you came over here to tell me about the murder."

"I called, and Sam said you'd be back late. I decided to wait for you."

Wait for him, further involve him. He'd've been better off driving straight through San Francisco to the airport on Sunday.

He asked, "Does Sam know any of this?"

"She knows about the murder, and that I'm upset, but she thinks this is newspaper business."

He closed his eyes. Secrecy, lies, threats, fear—and now murder. What had become of the life he'd built for himself—the life that was clean, and his alone?

He said, "I think you should tell Rhoda Swift everything. Put it in her hands and let the sheriff's department deal with it."

No reply. When he looked at Carly, she had drawn her knees up to her chest and was hugging them, her face conflicted. "I found something," she said in a small voice. "In the ashes in our bedroom fireplace." She reached into the pocket of her corduroy shirt and extended a small, charred piece of paper to him.

He studied the words that were scrawled there: . . . *mine, and I got the right* . . .

"So what do you think this means?" he asked.

"I think Lewis somehow found out where Ard was and wrote her, making a claim on Natalie. She probably didn't respond, so he came up here. I think he was the person who was watching her, who had been in the house."

"But he was staying in Westport, south on the coast."

"Yes, because as a black man, he wouldn't stand out so much there. He could've been a tourist, or one of the people working in the service industry. Cyanide Wells, even Talbot's Mills, is too lily-white for him to escape notice. But Westport's not all that far from here. He must've called Ard, demanding to see their daughter, so she ran. She was probably far away when he was killed."

She wanted to believe. As he had once wanted to believe. Gently he said, "She was at the Talbot house on Friday night."

"But that was only a stopover. It was empty when I went there on Saturday."

"Yes, and Saturday's when they think Lewis was shot."

Carly stood and turned away from him. He saw her arm move as she brushed at her eyes. From behind she looked fragile, a stick figure. "Why are you doing this?" she asked.

"Because we have to face the possibility that she killed Lewis. We won't know what she did or didn't do until she chooses to come forward."

"Cold comfort to help me through the night, Lindstrom."

"I doubt I'll get through very well myself. Why don't you grab that blanket, and I'll come sit with you. We'll weather this together."

She hesitated, then took up the brightly colored throw that was folded on the back of the sofa. He moved over beside her, propping his feet on the coffee table while she turned off the overhead light. She sat, her body rigid; the throw barely covered both of them, so he gave her the larger part. Although she didn't speak, he could feel the swirl of her emotions.

"Not long till morning," he said. "Then we can do something."

"What?" Her voice was flat, bleak.

"Something," he said firmly, and tucked the throw around her shoulders.

Gradually the tension seeped out of her, and her breathing became deeper. Her head tipped to the side and rested against his upper arm. The in-and-out rhythms of her sleep soothed him, but they also brought an odd, measured clarity to his thoughts.

Bad as the aftermath of Gwen's disappearance had been, over the past years he'd built a foundation of certain things he relied upon and took to be true. He'd thought it a foundation more solid than what had sustained his previous, largely unexamined life, but apparently he'd been wrong; in the space of one anonymous phone call it had been undermined, as surely as the sea undermines a badly constructed bulkhead, and the events of the subsequent weeks had battered at it with the force of a severe winter storm.

Now it, and he, were poised to crumble.

Carly McGuire

Tuesday, May 14, 2002

arly looked down at the stack of notes in Donna Vail's neat handwriting and sighed. That morning she'd asked Vail to drop her other work and look up two items for her, but now, at close to five, she was disinclined to deal with the reporter's findings. Instead of reading them, she pushed her chair away from the desk and leaned against its high back, closed her eyes, and listened to the day winding down at the *Spectrum*.

Voices calling good-bye. Car doors slamming in the alley. Engines starting, tires crunching. The gradual cessation of phones ringing. And then . . . peace. The building, a former assay office, was solid; back here in her office, normal street noise didn't carry. Only the creaks and groans that were evidence of age intruded, and they were reassuring, reminding her that some things lasted.

She'd spent most of the day in Santa Carla—when, at twenty-four hours before press time, she should have been here tending to her newspaper—following up on the scant information Donna had found on Noah Estes. The task had been an easy one: Make contact with people; ask the right questions; give them her full attention. A good reporter's technique, and one particularly suited to a person who disliked having the focus on her. But it had also taken its toll, and now she was tired.

The information Donna had gathered about Noah Estes was bare bones: He'd died of pneumonia in a Santa Carla nursing home, Willow Creek, in 1981, his ninety-eighth year. Carly had called the home and made an appointment with the administrator, a Mr. Tompkins, claiming the paper was interested in doing an article on the Estes clan. The facility was an attractive low-rise complex on extensive landscaped grounds where a line of willow trees bordered a small stream. Inside, the usual unpleasant odors of such institutions were masked by some substance that must have been added to the air filtration system; the staff were courteous, and what few residents she saw seemed well cared for. Carly had always been biased against nursing homes, and she couldn't help but react with cynicism to Willow Creek; it was targeted to the well off—no Medi-Cal or Medicare patients need apply. But she found herself liking Mr. Tompkins, a small man with neatly manicured hands, whose puppy-dog brown eyes radiated compassion.

Instead of taking her to his office, Tompkins led her

outside to a teak bench by the side of the stream. "I knew Mr. Estes well," he told her. "His father—stepfather, actually—was one of the original cyaniders up at the Knob."

"That would be John Estes?"

"Yes. He came out from Denver at the turn of the twentieth century and later married a widow, Dora Collins. Noah was her only child by her first husband, who was killed in an accident at the mine. John was manager there until they shut down operations in the early thirties. He adopted Noah, and he and Dora had four more children of their own. They raised the family in a big house that they built out near the Knob. People who knew them claimed Noah was always John's favorite child, and possibly that's true, because his stepfather left him the Knob property when he died."

"You're something of a local historian, Mr. Tompkins."

He smiled, lines crinkling at the corners of his eyes. "Many of the people who reside here are descendants of old county families. I like to listen to and tape-record their stories; you can learn a lot from the elderly. Someday I plan to publish a volume of oral history."

"I'd enjoy reading it. This property near the Knob—is it now part of the national forest?"

Tompkins looked surprised. "You don't know? It's . . . Well, I'm getting ahead of my story. Noah Estes went to the Colorado School of Mines, like his adoptive father, and also became an engineer. He worked all over the world—South America, Australia, South Africa—but he made periodic trips back here and eventually returned for good, a wealthy man with an Australian wife and five children. They settled on the land John left him. Noah had a reputation as a gentle person with a concern for the environment—unusual in one who made his fortune in mining—and I can attest that it lasted throughout his final years."

"When did he come to Willow Creek?"

"In nineteen seventy-five, the year I started here."

"He was ninety-two then. Why didn't one of those five children, or grandchildren, take him in?"

"He wouldn't permit it. Mr. Estes was fiercely independent. He'd had a good life and didn't want to get in the way of his children and grandchildren enjoying theirs in turn. Living here didn't curtail his enthusiasms, though; he was quite active until his last two months and took great pleasure in reading—mostly about the environment—and in advising our landscapers. Much of what you see around us is due to his input."

"D'you know where I might find any close relatives of Mr. Estes?"

"They're scattered all over the county. I have an address for a granddaughter, Sadie Carpenter. She's the relative who visited him most regularly. I'll ask the receptionist to give you the information."

"One more question, Mr. Tompkins: You seem to think I should know the Estes property near the Knob. Why?"

"Well, my dear, what happened there was the basis for your paper's Pulitzer-winning series. Shortly before he moved into our facility, Noah Estes sold the land to Ronald Talbot. His son, Ronald Junior, inherited it. He, of course, was one of the men who died there."

*   *   *

Sadie Carpenter lived on Second Street, in the old part of the county seat, several blocks before the inevitable sprawl of tracts began. When Carly called to ask for an appointment, using the same excuse for wanting to talk about Noah Estes that she had with Mr. Tompkins, Mrs. Carpenter expressed pleasure at the possibility of an article on her family but said she could only see her between one-thirty and two.

"I'm a confectioner," she explained, "and my assistant and I have to turn out three large batches of chocolates today."

The house, pink clapboard with frothy white trim, was perfectly suited to a candy-making operation, but the thin, angular woman who greeted Carly didn't look as if she'd sampled many of her wares. In the fragrantly scented living room a tea service was set out, its centerpiece a two-tiered plate of chocolates. Mrs. Carpenter poured and urged Carly to partake, selecting a large nougat for herself. So much for appearances.

After sampling a truffle and pronouncing it wonderful, Carly said, "Mr. Tompkins at Willow Creek says you're the family member who visited Noah Estes most often."

"That's correct. Granddad outlived all his children— a few of his grandchildren, too. I was the only relative living here in town, although the others visited when they could. We all loved him; he was a remarkable man."

"Tell me about him."

"Well, he knew more about horticulture than anyone. He'd studied the geology and ecosystems of the area and until his mid-eighties sat on the boards of a number of environmentally concerned nonprofits. In a way, those seem strange interests for him; after all, his career was in mining. But after he retired, he regretted the destruction that most of his projects had caused, and was determined to make up for it. And living in the shadow of the Knob must have been a constant reminder of how people lay waste to the land."

"The Knob was turned over to the National Parks Service when?"

"In the fifties. Denver Precious Metals had been carrying the land as a tax write-off up to then."

"Why didn't your grandfather follow suit and donate the adjacent property, rather than sell it to Ronald Talbot?"

"Primarily because he was afraid of what might become of it, given the Nixon administration's record on the environment. And then there was Watergate and Nixon's resignation, the uncertainty of what our political climate would evolve into. Granddad felt the land was better off in the hands of an individual whose stewardship he could trust."

"And he trusted Ronald Talbot, a lumberman?"

"Definitely. Ronald Talbot was never a proponent of aggressive, destructive logging, or any logging of oldgrowth forests. He and my grandfather had worked for decades to promote responsible management of our natural resources. And Mr. Talbot was not interested in mining."

"Why was that important? I thought the veins of ore in that area were played out long ago."

Mrs. Carpenter looked at her watch, then poured more tea. "Oh, no, dear. There's a rich vein of gold in that land, one that Wells Mining never discovered and Denver Precious Metals never searched for, since their focus was only on the slag heaps and low-grade veins at the Knob. My grandfather found out about it after he moved onto the property, and he decided it would never be mined—not by him, his descendants, or future owners. Mr. Talbot agreed, and that stipulation was made one of the terms of purchase."

My God, that's what Hayward and Rawson are after. That's what Ard found out.

During a stop at the county hall of records to view the probated wills of the Talbots, Carly learned that while Ronald Senior had stipulated in his bequest to his son that the mineral rights to the Knob property were not to be sold, transferred, or otherwise exploited, Ronnie's will contained no such provision. Had he ignored or forgotten his father's agreement with Noah Estes? Had he even known about the gold under the new house he'd built there? And if he had known, would he have cared?

Ronnie had struck Carly as one who, because he'd always had enough money, didn't give it much thought. And Deke had been so deep into his art that he was oblivious to their finances. The two had lived well, but not extravagantly, and she doubted that knowing they were literally sitting on a potential gold mine would have impressed either of them.

Thoughts of her friends occupied Carly on the drive back to Cyanide Wells. She tried to remember the last time she'd seen them alive. Their annual Fourth of July barbecue? No, it had been canceled the year they were killed—something to do with having to go out of town to attend to Deke's seriously ill uncle. A dinner party? Perhaps, but there had been so many of them that they all blurred together. Their Memorial Day celebration had also been canceled, but she did remember Ronnie coming over for lunch on a Saturday early in May; Ard had fixed a crab salad, his favorite, but he had a hangover and didn't eat much. Deke had begged off, saying he needed to finish a painting.

There was one other time, in July, when she'd seen Ronnie alone. He'd appeared at her office unexpectedly on a Wednesday afternoon, when Sev Quill had offered to deliver that week's issue to the printer, leaving her at unaccustomed leisure. She and Ronnie went to Aram's Cafe and sat at a table in the backyard garden, drinking wine and talking of small things.

Natalie's getting so tall. . . . Ard's roses are wonderful this year, even if the wisteria was disappointing. . . . The rhodos out at the preserve near Deer Harbor were terrific, too. . . . We'll have to go see them next year. . . . I found a great recipe for Santa Maria barbecue. . . . That would go well with my recipe for pinto beans. . . . Last week's issue looked good, especially the photo of the mayor that made him look bloated. . . .

At one point Ronnie had held his glass up and squinted at the sunlight playing on the deep red of the merlot. "This is so nice," he said. "I wish it could go on forever."

Now she put on her glasses and reached for the notes Donna Vail had left on her desk. She'd asked the reporter to look up two of the items on Ard's list: CR-92 and moratorium 10/00. Each had continued to elude her, but as a researcher she was easily discouraged; Donna, on the other hand, was tenacious when it came to digging up information. It seemed her efforts had paid off.

Carly—there are hundreds of things that these notations could mean, but the following are the only ones that apply locally.

CR-92: Soledad County Regulation 92, enacted November 11, 1997. Stipulates that new mining may be permitted on privately held property abutting the Eel River National Forest only if mining is currently being conducted on the adjacent 20 square acres within the forest itself. The regulation was designed to prevent blasting and dredging on privately held lands that would harm the ecosystem of the forest. A bill was introduced in the legislature in October 1999 that would have made the regulation invalid, but it was defeated.

Moratorium 10/25/00: moratorium imposed by the Clinton administration on new mining in the Eel River National Forest, to prevent further damage to the ecosystem. Cancelled by Bush administration, 3/20/02. Enviro groups have major concerns about this, as there is renewed interest in the Knob area from two large mining companies. And, of course, it would open up a hell of a lot of privately held acreage abutting it to mining as well.

We really need to do a series on this, Carly. And we really need to designate someone as a reporter on environmental issues. I'm volunteering. This is scary stuff, and I don't know how we've missed it.

Donna

I know how we missed it. I've been so busy dealing with my personal problems that I've failed to pay attention to the larger issues.

Payne and Rawson started the serious pressure on Ard in March, right after the moratorium was canceled. Did Ard know or suspect their reason?

And if she did, why didn't she tell me?

"Excuse me, Carly."

Deputy Shawn Stengel filled up the doorway of her office. The armpits of his brown uniform shirt were sweat-stained, and there was a streak of dirt across his shiny forehead. Not the immaculate image he liked to project.

"Yes, what is it?" She shuffled some papers on the desk, trying to look as if he were interrupting her at an important task.

"I wonder if you'd take a ride over to the substation with me. There's something I'd like you to see."

"I'm busy, Shawn. Can't you just describe it?"

"This won't take long; I'll bring you right back."

Foreboding settled on her as she got to her feet.

*   *   *

She stood by the table in the interview room at the sub-station, staring down at Natalie's backpack.

"You dragged me over here to look at this?"

"You recognize it?"

"Of course, from the other day at the well."

"Not from before?"

"What's this about?"

"It belongs to Ms. Coleman's daughter, Natalie. We took it to the school, asked the kids if they knew whose it was. Three of her friends recognized it from this." He fingered the tear in the outside zipper compartment. "They remembered she was upset when it happened, while she was crawling under a barb-wire fence to take a shortcut."

Damn.

"You sure you don't recognize it?"

"I don't know. I guess it could be Nat's. I don't pay all that much attention to her stuff. Something's in fashion, she's got it; then it's out of fashion, and she gets rid of it. Kids . . ."

"I hear you." Stengel propped a hip on the table and folded his arms across his barrel chest. "The teacher says Natalie hasn't been to school this week, and when I stopped by the house, nobody was home."

"She and Ard . . . went out of town."

"During the school year?"

"It's an educational trip."

Stengel looked skeptical but didn't ask where they'd gone. "One other thing, Carly." He reached for a paper sack he'd carried in from his cruiser and placed it on the table next to the pack. "When I couldn't reach Ms. Coleman, I decided to search the well where the backpack

was found. There were some textbooks buried under the
rubble at the bottom. No name in them, but I noticed
something in this math workbook." He flipped its pages
and held it out.

A heart with an arrow through it. *Natalie loves
Duane.*

Well, now we know the kid's straight.

An absurd thought to pop into her mind at a time like
this. She fought off the urge to laugh, knowing she'd
sound hysterical. "I don't understand why those things
were buried."

"Me, either. You going to be talking with Ms.
Coleman?"

"Eventually."

"Will you ask her to ask Natalie about the pack?"

"Of course. I'm as curious as you are."

"Another thing: the fellow who dragged this up from
the well. You know him?"

"Yes, he's an employee at the paper. John Crowe, my
staff photographer. Why?"

"I'd like to talk with him. You have his address?"

"I can give it to you when you take me back to the office. Is that all, Shawn?"

"For now." He stood. "One thing occurred to me—
that this is a prank Natalie's friends have pulled. You
know, steal the pack, throw it down the well."

"That's probably what happened."

"What doesn't fit, though, is, I asked the kids what
kind of stuff Natalie kept in the pack. They mentioned a
Palm Pilot. Why wasn't it there?"

"She was using it when they took the pack? One of
them stole it? I don't have a clue."

"And why didn't she report the missing pack to her teacher? Or her mother?"

"Maybe she did."

"Not the teacher, anyway. I asked."

"Well, she could have told Ardis. I haven't been paying much attention to what goes on with Nat lately—work pressures, you know."

Stengel nodded in understanding. "Well, I'll run you back now. Let me know when you talk with Ms. Coleman."

If I ever talk with her again . . .

Matthew Lindstrom

Salt Point Estates, Western Soledad County
Tuesday, May 14, 2002

att had spent the morning taking photographs for next week's issue—an overturned truck at the Talbot's Mills off-ramp, and the town's most senior citizen—and then spent the rest of the day trying to track down Gar Payne. The trail led from the Meadows to the office Payne shared with Milt Rawson in Cyanide Wells, to a tract of land his secretary said he was checking out on the ridge, and finally to a new seaside housing development some twelve miles north of Calvert's Landing.

As he followed the sinuous curves of a secondary road from the ridgeline to the coast highway, he felt the temperature drop in steady increments. The afternoon was brilliantly clear, and through the redwoods he caught glimpses of the placid water. Cabins were tucked under the trees at the ends of dirt driveways; satellite TV dishes stood in clearings; dead cars, old tires, and cast-off appliances lurked under low-hanging branches. A poor section of a relatively poor county, where existence was hand-to-mouth and people wasted minimal effort on beautifying their surroundings.

At the coast road, all that changed. A wood-and-stone hotel hugged the clifftop, its grounds landscaped in purple-blossomed ice plant and twisted cypress trees, its parking lot filled with expensive vehicles. Redwood Cove Inn, obviously a popular place. He turned north past a Victorian bed-and-breakfast, a gallery, a tricked-up country store. A few miles farther, and he spotted the split-rail fence that marked the boundary of Payne and Rawson's newest development.

For the first mile and a half the land was wild and overgrown; a weathered barn stood as a monument to the tract's days as a working ranch. He turned in at the main entrance toward the lodge and restaurant, where he'd been told he could find Payne; both buildings were in the earliest stages of construction. An earthmover stood idle beside a double-wide trailer, and only one vehicle, Payne's Jag, was parked there. Matt pulled up beside it, got out of the Jeep, and knocked on the trailer's door.

"Around here," Payne's voice called.

He skirted the trailer, through knee-high weeds to the side that faced the sea. Payne was seated in a green plastic chair, a can of beer in hand. When he saw Matt, his mouth drew down in displeasure.

"What the hell're you doing here?"

"Looking to have a talk with you."

"We talked enough at Carly's on Sunday."

"I don't think so."

Payne looked at his watch. "You've got thirty seconds to get off my property."

"Or you'll . . . ?"

"Get the goddamned sheriff on your ass." He patted a cell phone clipped to his belt.

"Aren't you interested in what I have to say? I would be, if I were you." Perversely he parroted the words Payne had used in the anonymous phone call that had lured him to Soledad County.

"Okay, so say it, and get off my land."

"Fair enough. Carly McGuire asked me to deliver a message."

"Oh?" A glimmering of interest now.

"She doesn't appreciate you pressuring her partner to sell you the Talbot property. Or that you called Matt Lindstrom, Ardis's former husband, and told him where she is."

Payne was caught off guard. "Shit, how'd she find out about that? Lindstrom never showed."

"Yes, he did. He came to their house a few days after you called him. What exactly did you hope to accomplish?"

"I figured if he went public with who Ardis was, she'd be discredited. Then the bank would take over the administration of the Talbot estate, and I could deal with someone rational."

"Or maybe you hoped Lindstrom was a violent man who would do what they said he did to her all those years ago."

Payne sipped beer and looked at the sea, but a tic at the corner of his mouth gave him away.

Matt asked, "How'd you find out about Lindstrom?"

"By accident. One of those true-life TV shows when I was in the Midwest visiting relatives. You know—'This woman disappeared. Do you know where she is now?' I recognized Ardis right off. Lindstrom was harder to find, but even people who want to get lost permanently leave traces that a good private detective can follow."

Especially since he hadn't really tried to get lost. He'd simply walked away.

Payne asked, "So where's Lindstrom now?"

"Home, I suppose. They got things straightened out, and then he left. He didn't appreciate what you did, either."

"Wait a minute—how'd he know I was the one who called him?"

"Ardis and Carly suspected you because of your interest in the Talbot property. So they arranged for him to listen to your voice, and he made a positive identification. Not smart, Payne. If Carly decides to publish an account of your shenanigans, it might make people think twice about contributing to your campaign fund. And if Mack Travis and Andy D'Angelo weren't both dead, they'd be in a position to scuttle all your political aspirations."

Payne flushed, his scar turning livid. He hurled his beer can into the weeds. "For somebody who's been around— what? A week?—you've sure gotten cozy with McGuire and Coleman. You into dykes, Crowe?"

"I'm into good people, Payne. And I hate to see them pushed around by scumbags like you."

Payne growled, then struggled from his chair, staggering before he gained footing. He loomed over Matt, thrust his index finger into his face. "I want you off my property *now!* The clock is ticking."

Matt backed off, slowly. "I've delivered Carly's message. I'm going."

It wasn't more than five minutes before Payne's Jag exited the development and turned south, moving fast. Matt pulled out from under the low branches of a cypress tree and followed it to the Redwood Cove Inn. Payne left his car in a far corner of the lot and went into the lobby. Matt waited half a minute before he approached.

Inside the double glass doors he could see a large timbered room with a huge stone fireplace at one end and a bar to the right side. Leather chairs and high-backed sofas were arranged in groupings across its floor, screened from one another by bamboo in planter boxes. Payne was disappearing around one of the stands of canes, and Matt saw the outline of his tall body fold as he sat. A waiter in a white jacket moved toward him.

Two armchairs, both empty, backed up on this side of the bamboo screen, only feet from where Payne had settled.

Take a chance, Matt told himself. What're the odds he'll see me there? And if he does, so what? Man's got a right to stop in for a drink. Even the sheriff would agree with me on that point.

He walked over, sank onto the soft leather. Another waiter materialized; Matt waved him away. Behind him Payne was speaking, just loudly enough to be heard. To the waiter? No, on his phone.

"He left yet?... Damn! You think he'll call in?...
Good. When he does, tell him I'm at Redwood Cove, not
the development.... In the bar.... Thanks, Cheryl."

Cheryl, the secretary at Payne and Rawson's Cyanide
Wells office. The partner must be on his way to the coast.

Matt sat back, looked around the lobby. A number of
handsome, well-fed cats lounged on the furnishings. Outside a window wall across from the bar was a courtyard
with a lily pond; a woman sat at the pond's edge, feeding
kibble from a bucket to a family of raccoons. The mother
and two babies were so tame, they ate from her hand.
Guests wandered in and out, took seats at the bar, lounged
in front of the fireplace. After a short period of silence,
Payne began to make other calls.

"Jenny, I'm out at the cove. Something's come up, and
I'll probably stay the night. See you tomorrow."

"Ben, what the hell's the story on our interim financing?... Yeah, I know.... Okay, we'll talk in the
morning."

"Sandra, we got your Visa bill this week, and your
mother and I are seriously upset with your spending. Hold
the plastic, will you?"

"Cheryl, did he call in?... He wants what?... A double, two olives. Got it."

Next came a discussion with the waiter about a Bom-
bay gin martini to be delivered as soon as his partner arrived. Then Payne made several other calls, none of
consequence. Obviously he was an individual who
couldn't bear to be disconnected.

Fifteen minutes later a rotund, red-faced man in chinos
and a hideous lime-green shirt waddled through the entrance, paused to look around, then crossed the room

toward the sofa where Payne sat. He didn't even glance at Matt as he went by.

"So where's my drink?" he demanded.

"David's bringing it. Sit down. We've got a problem."

"The financing . . ."

"Is the least of our worries. That photographer Carly McGuire hired, John Crowe, showed up at Salt Point this afternoon. She knows about my call to Matthew Lindstrom and sent Crowe to inform me of her displeasure."

Matt listened as Payne related the gist of their conversation. "I'm afraid she's going to use it against me, ruin my political career before it gets off the ground, plus make sure we never get our hands on that property."

"Yeah, that's the sort of thing the bitch would do. The . . . other, does she know about that, too?"

"I don't think so."

"Well, even if she does, she wouldn't dare use it. Not after—"

"Here's David with your martini."

Silence. Then, "Thanks, David."

After a pause during which, Matt assumed, he was partaking of his long-awaited drink, Rawson said, "We never should've brought the second husband here. What if McGuire figures it out? We could be implicated in—"

"Get a grip, Milt. There's no way they can connect us to it. Besides, McGuire wants to protect Coleman and the kid. She's not going to make their relationship to him public."

"Speaking of them, where are they? I keep watching the house, following McGuire, and there's no sign of them."

"Maybe she sent them out of town. That's what I'd do.

And stop following McGuire. You said she almost caught you a couple of times."

"Well, I never said I trained as a private eye!"

"Dammit, keep your voice down. I don't want to broadcast our business to the entire north coast."

More silence. Then Payne stood, saying he needed the restroom.

Matt was off his chair and on the way to the door.

At a service station in Calvert's Landing he shut himself in a phone booth and got the number of the Incline Village Hyatt Regency from directory assistance. The Hyatt's operator located Dave Rand, the musician with whom he'd talked yesterday, in the restaurant. Yes, Rand said, he had time to answer a few more questions.

"Was Ardis Coleman married to Chase Lewis or just living with him?"

"They got married in September of ninety-two. Down in San Fran. I stood up for him."

"When was their baby born?"

"Their baby?"

"Natalie."

"Oh, guess I didn't make that clear. The kid wasn't Ardis's. She was Chase's, with a woman he'd been seeing a while back. I never knew that one."

So Ardis was not a mother after all, any more than Carly was. This was certainly going to surprise her.

"How'd he end up with the baby?"

"Bitch dropped her off with him right after he and Ardis got married. Was supposed to be just for the weekend, but she didn't show on Sunday like she said she would. They called the number they had for her, but it was disconnected. Nice wedding present, huh? Chase was pissed, but Ardis said she'd raise the kid as her own. But hey, how come you're askin' these things, when you're a family member?"

"It seems Ardis hasn't been completely honest with me. Did she legally adopt the baby?"

"Nope. Couldn't find the mother to get her consent."

"So when Ardis took off with the child, technically she kidnapped her."

"I suppose."

"But Chase didn't go to the police."

"Chase didn't want *nothing* to do with the cops in those days, if you know what I mean. And what the hell was he gonna do with a baby, anyway? He didn't even try to find them, just stepped up his intake of controlled substances."

Matt thanked Rand and headed across the ridgeline to Cyanide Wells.

It was clear to him what Payne and Rawson had been talking about: After their attempt to disrupt Ardis's life by summoning him hadn't worked immediately, they—or more likely their detective—had found the record of her marriage to Chase Lewis. Probably he'd also unearthed the record of Natalie's birth and pieced together what had subsequently happened. Payne and Rawson, realizing they had their hands on very damaging information, had reasoned that bringing Ardis face-to-face with Chase Lewis would make her more willing to deal.

Unfortunately, they hadn't counted on murder entering the equation.

Carly McGuire

Tuesday, May 14, 2002

he didn't know why the house near the Knob continued to draw her, but as she stood in its central hallway, door open to the cool evening breeze, she realized it no longer had the power to haunt her. It was simply a house where happy times had been lived out and a tragedy had occurred. A house that had been cleansed of all signs of that tragedy and rendered bland for sale.

She walked along the central hallway, looking into the silent rooms she knew so well. What struck her now was the lack of clutter. Ronnie had inherited a great many things from his father, a consummate collector, and all of it—books, a model railroad, stamps, coins, firearms, sculptures, animal heads, Indian artifacts, old typewriters—had found its way from the architecturally overwrought mansion where he had grown up to this new, simpler house on the land that once had belonged to Noah Estes. The things Ronnie didn't care for, such as the animal heads and firearms, were kept out of sight, but most of it had been on display. Carly supposed the real estate agent had packed it up so that the house would show better, but its absence made the house seem ordinary. The decor was nice, the curve of the staircase graceful, but the kitchen was badly designed and the rooms were too small.

No, the house—even if two people hadn't been murdered in it—was not what made this property desirable; it was the beauty of the land, the privacy. The house could be razed and another, more attractive one built. A prospective buyer would be a fool not to realize that.

So why hadn't there been offers?

Maybe there had. Maybe Ard, as executor of the Talbot estate, had turned them down. Because she knew about the vein of gold running under the property? Because she was holding out for a better offer than those, or Payne and Rawson's? An offer that would allow her to pocket some of the money?

I'm really starting to doubt her now. Whatever shreds of trust in the relationship that remained are gone.

She took hold of the banister and started up the stairs. Going to the bedroom where Ronnie and Deke died. Going to face her demons a final time.

Of course, it was no longer the room where she'd viewed their bloodied and ruined bodies. New paint, wallpaper, and carpeting had made it innocuous. But when she closed her eyes, she could picture the bodies on the bed, clad in Japanese silk robes, their features shattered by the gunshots to their heads. Blood on the pale-green sheets, the dark-green headboard, the nightstand . . .

What, McGuire? What is it?

She'd lost the image.

She moved to the center of the room, looked around. It was easily the most attractive in the house: French doors led to a balcony overlooking the pool area; window seats were tucked into alcoves on either side of them; bookcases flanked a stone fireplace. There was a large bath with a Jacuzzi tub, a huge walk-in closet.

The door to the closet was open, and out of idle curiosity she looked inside. Cardboard cartons were stacked there—probably containing the collections that had formerly cluttered the main floor. They would fetch a good price at an auction house, but apparently Ard had yet to get around to arranging for their sale. She stepped inside and followed a path through them, confirming their contents from their labels. Felt a thump on her head as it connected with the long, heavy chain that lowered the folding stairs to the attic.

Deke's studio—the one prospective buyers and the occasional interviewer or photographer were invited into—was in an outbuilding beyond the garage and greenhouse, but he'd done his actual work in the attic, under several big skylights. When Ronnie built the house, he hadn't yet met Deke, and by the time his partner declared his fondness for the attic space and had the skylights installed, it would have been prohibitively expensive to create easier access. Deke didn't mind—he was the only one who went up there, even barring Ronnie from the place where he entertained his muse. In fact, he liked to joke about entering his work space by way of a "secret passageway."

But Deke was dead, and now Carly wanted to see the studio where he'd created his paintings. She'd neglected to turn on the overhead fixture, though, and she couldn't see all that well. Craning her neck, she looked up to gauge if there was enough clearance to pull the stairs down, and saw something striped suspended from the framework of the trapdoor. A bag? Odd place to hang something—

A man's voice called out to her from downstairs.

"Detective Grossman. What are you doing here?" Nervously she ran her hand over her hair, brushing at a spiderweb that must have caught there while she'd been poking around in the closet.

"So formal, Carly." The tall gray-haired man smiled thinly. In his conservative blue suit, the recently appointed head of the Soledad County Sheriff's Department Investigations Bureau looked out of place for the countryside.

"Sorry, Ned. You startled me. Why're you here?"

"I could ask you the same."

"I, uh, received a message that the property is being shown tomorrow. Ardis is out of town, so I decided to make sure everything's in shape."

"Isn't that the real estate agent's job?"

"Well, yes, but we can't always count on her. Did you follow me here? It's not a place that you'd be driving by and decide to stop in."

"Actually, Deputy Stengel followed you and reported

your whereabouts to me. I ordered him to maintain a surveillance on you."

"For what reason?"

"We'll discuss that at headquarters in Santa Carla."

When she entered the interview room, the first person she saw was Rhoda Swift.

"Carly." Swift nodded and motioned for her to sit. Grossman shut the door and sat next to Rhoda.

Carly said, "What's this about, Rho?"

"It's come to our attention that your interest in our Westhaven homicide is more than professional."

It was what she'd feared. "I don't understand."

"I think you do. But let me fill you in on our investigation so far. In the absence of witnesses, fingerprints, and the murder weapon, we began by building a profile of the victim, Chase Lewis. Born, San Francisco. Only child—both parents deceased. Graduate, Balboa High School. Two semesters, City College. Talented trombonist, played with pickup bands while working as a security guard, and eventually turned professional musician. The lifestyle caught up with him; he was arrested several times for drug-and-alcohol-related offenses but served no serious jail time. Known to become violent when high, particularly against women. In September of nineteen ninety-two he married one Ardis Lynette Coleman in a civil ceremony at City Hall."

"*Married?*"

Rhoda nodded. "Apparently they were still married when he died."

She felt as if she'd been punched in the stomach. This news made Ard's betrayal of her complete.

"You didn't know?" Rhoda asked.

She shook her head.

"Well, there's no record of a divorce, either in California or Nevada. And another interesting thing: There's no record of Natalie's birth, at least not to Ardis. But Chase Lewis did father a child, by a woman named Marisa Wilson, in July of 'ninety-two. And the child was called Natalie."

"My God." She pressed her fingers to her lips. After a moment she asked, "This Marisa Wilson—where is she now?"

"She died of a drug overdose in San Diego eight years ago."

"Did Ardis adopt Natalie?"

"There's no record of it."

"So she has no legal right to her?"

"We'd like to question her about that—among other things."

Meaning Chase Lewis's murder.

Rhoda went on, "I understand you told Deputy Stengel that Ardis has taken Natalie out of town on an educational trip."

Carly ignored Rhoda's words and asked, "If it turns out Ardis has no legal right to Natalie, what'll become of her?"

"She'll be made a ward of the court and placed in a foster home while Social Services searches for blood relatives. If there aren't any, or they don't want her, she'll be put up for adoption."

"An older mixed-race child? She's not a very likely

candidate. Why would they take her from a perfectly viable home, one where she's loved and cared for?"

"The decision as to the viability of that home would be up to the individual judge. But to get back to the original subject: Do you know where we can reach Ardis?"

Make up something to buy time. Camping in Yosemite, maybe.

No, you've lied enough, McGuire. Don't put yourself at further risk. They think Ard—or maybe even you— killed Chase Lewis.

She said, "I want to speak to my attorney."

Matthew Lindstrom

Wednesday, May 15, 2002

att leaned across the Jeep's passenger seat and opened the door for Carly as she stepped from her attorney's car in the alley behind the *Spectrum*'s offices. She slumped in the seat, slammed the door, and stared straight ahead.

"You okay?" he asked.

A shrug.

"Talk to me, Carly."

She sighed, and then the words came—haltingly at first, but soon tumbling out so fast that it was difficult for him to understand her; several times he had to ask her to speak more slowly. When she got to the part about Rhoda Swift telling her Ardis had married Chase Lewis and later taken his child, her voice broke.

Quickly he said, "I know about that. Doesn't matter how I found out. Go on."

"They suspect either Ard or me of killing Lewis. After my attorney got there, they asked if I owned a gun, had been to the motel in Westhaven prior to the time I showed up there on Monday. Kept pressuring me to tell them where Ard is. Wanted to know if there was trouble in the relationship. That's when my attorney cut off the interview. They've got no evidence, so they can't hold me, but I'm sure they'll continue the surveillance. A car followed us from Santa Carla, and it's probably parked at the end of the alley."

"How long d'you suppose they've been watching you?"

She shook her head. "Don't know. I need you to do something for me."

"What?"

"Drive me to the house by the Knob to get my truck."

"No problem." He reached for the ignition.

She stayed his hand with her fingertips. "There's more. When I was there this afternoon, I went to the master bedroom, and I had an impression—one of those half-memories that won't quite come to the surface. Something related to what I saw the morning after the murders. I think it's important, and I need to get at it."

"Carly, under the circumstances I don't think it's wise for you to go back to that house."

"I don't, either. But you could. Do you have your camera with you?"

"My camera? Why . . . ?"

"Good. After I drive away, take it and photograph the

master bedroom from a lot of different angles. Maybe when I study the prints they'll trigger—"

"No."

"The deputies aren't interested in you. They'll follow me."

"No, Carly. I'm not breaking and entering."

"I have a key to the house. And you have my permission."

"The key was given to you by Ronnie Talbot?"

"Yes."

"He's dead, and Ardis is executor of the estate."

"So?"

"Then only she or the real estate agent, acting on her instructions, can give me permission."

"Since when're you a lawyer?"

The familiar testiness in her voice relieved rather than annoyed him; at least some measure of the old Carly remained. "I was prelaw in college and have done extensive reading in the field."

"Well, aren't you the renaissance man!"

Now she *was* pissing him off. "Look, I know you're upset, but—"

"Okay, sorry. Maybe I'd be handling the situation better if it only involved Ard and me. At this point I'd probably have no trouble saying fuck it and cooperating fully with the sheriff's department. But it also involves Nat."

"No matter what, Ardis would never hurt her."

"She's not the one I'm worried about. It's the sheriff's department." She twisted to face him, her back against the door. "In spite of people like Rho Swift and Ned Grossman, it's one of the worst in the state. The county doesn't have enough money to attract many good people, and there's still a stigma attached to the department."

"What kind of stigma?"

"You remember I said Rho Swift cracked an old case a few years back? It was a mass murder that had gone unsolved for thirteen years. Eight people, two of them children, shot to death in an isolated canyon south of Signal Port. The department mishandled it, but you can scarcely blame them; they'd simply never encountered a crime of that magnitude. By the time the feds stepped in, much of the evidence had been lost or tainted, so they weren't able to solve it, either. In the aftermath, a lot of the departmental personnel moved to other jurisdictions or got out of law enforcement entirely. The rest just became more and more demoralized."

"But you said the case was solved."

"Yes, but it takes more than a few years to build up a good department. It's getting better, but recently there have been some disturbing incidents."

"Such as?"

Carly sat up straighter, ran her fingers through her hair. "An overzealous pursuit of a speeding tourist in an SUV by a new deputy—it rolled, and the driver, his wife, and two young children were killed. A hostage situation during which an estranged husband and his five-year-old daughter were fatally shot by deputies who wouldn't wait for trained negotiators to be brought in. Another fatal shooting, this time of a ten-year-old boy whose father was using him as a decoy while stealing at a convenience store."

"Jesus."

"What I'm saying, Lindstrom, is that our deputies are not well enough trained to evaluate a situation and protect the innocents who are involved in it. Too often they shoot first and make excuses afterwards. If for some reason Ard and Nat are still in the county . . ."

"Okay, I understand. But I don't see the connection between what you half remembered in the Talbot house and the current situation."

"I just have a feeling there is one. Call it woman's intuition, if you will, but it's very strong."

Carly's expression was close to pleading; asking for this favor must be costing her a great deal. And what would it cost him to do as she asked?

Taking photographs in an empty house wasn't like knocking over a liquor store.

"Okay," he said, "I'll do it."

After the truck's taillights disappeared down the long eucalyptus-lined driveway, Matt waited, fingering the key Carly had slipped from her ring and pressed into his hand. He was sure they'd been followed here, having glimpsed a pair of headlights in the distance behind them, and a car moving slowly past after they'd turned in. Now he wanted to make sure it tailed Carly back home. After an interval of no more than thirty seconds it drove by again, more swiftly—a nondescript dark sedan. Soon the sound of its engine faded into the distance.

Matt continued to wait, listening in case another car arrived. There was no logical reason for the sheriff's department to maintain a surveillance on him; they must not yet know he was Ardis's former husband, since they hadn't mentioned him during their interview with Carly. But he decided to play it safe anyway.

Rustlings in the underbrush. Tree branches soughing. A distant howl: coyote. The wind picked up, warm, bringing with it a familiar scent. He breathed in deeply, felt a tug of emotion. Gardenias . . .

A formal affair at the faculty club in Saugatuck, in honor of some visiting dignitary whose name and field he'd long since forgotten. Near the end of the spring semester, a warm, balmy night. Men ill at ease in dinner jackets, many of them rented; women in long dresses, purchased at great strain to the academic family's budget. He and Gwen in their first public appearance as a couple, she in dark blue silk, his gardenia corsage on her wrist. An appearance of professor and student made possible by the diamond ring on her left hand.

Unsettling rumors about Matt Lindstrom and Gwen Standish had circulated through the tightly knit college community for months, so his colleagues' reactions were more relieved than surprised when he presented her as his wife-to-be. Better to marry, even unsuitably, than to burn in academic hell. The chairman of his department told her how lovely she looked and how fortunate Matt was; the president of the college took her hands and held them longer than was proper, saying she'd make a fine faculty wife.

As the party was winding down, they walked across the wide lawn to the lakeshore, where other couples stood admiring the play of the Japanese lanterns on the water. "That wasn't so bad," Gwen, who had been dreading the evening, said. "Not bad at all," Matt, who had been looking forward to showing her off, replied. "They loved you," he added. "*I* love you." As he kissed her, she put her hand on the back of his neck, the gardenias brushing his cheek, their scent becoming one that would forever take him back to that night. . . .

His face was wet. He put a hand to his eyes. Crying, for all the lost nights and lost days. For the woman he'd only imagined Gwen was.

Angrily he brushed the tears away and got out of the Jeep, turning on its headlights so he could navigate without stumbling, grabbing his camera bag. He was furious that he could still allow Gwen's memory to wound him, and fury made him careless. When a car's engine roared to life nearby, he froze, looking around.

Headlights bore down on him from the rear of the property, where Carly had said the stables, studio, and garage stood. Boxy vehicle, a van gathering speed. He threw himself to the side, sprawled down. As he tried to pull himself up, scramble out of the way, he saw Gwen behind the wheel, mouth set in a grim line, face pale in the wash of his own headlights.

She wrenched the wheel—too late. Their gazes were still locked when the van smashed into his lunging body. . . .

A hand touched his forehead, light and cool.

He tried to open his eyes. Couldn't.

Couldn't move, either.
Footsteps hurried away.

Pain. His chest, his hip, his arm.
Something draped over him. Warm.
Sleep . . .
Motion. Flashing light in his eyes.
"Get him stabilized."
"What the hell happened here?"
"Who called it in?"
"Medevac chopper's on its way."
Pricking in his arm.
Darkness . . .

"Matt?"
Carly's voice.
He opened his eyes. Winced and shut them. His head
hurt like hell.
"Matt?"
"Don't shout." The words came out a croak.
"I'm not. Here, let me give you some water."
When he opened his eyes this time, he saw her face.
Strained, tired. She looked almost as bad as he felt.
She raised his head, made him sip through a straw, but
most of the water dribbled into his beard and onto his
chest. She took the cup away, swiped at him. "Is that
better?"
"Some. Feel smithereened."
"I don't think that's a word."
"Don't care. How I feel."

"You'll mend. Nothing serious was broken in the accident."

"Accident?"

"We'll talk about it later."

"Now." He tried to grab her arm, but it hurt too much to raise his hand.

"Later. You need your rest."

Thursday, May 16, 2002
Santa Carla, California

She did this to you? That bitch! I'd like to—"

"Carly, stop."

"I will not stop! This is the absolute last straw!"

"Keep your voice down."

She compressed her lips, glancing back at the door to his hospital room and frowning.

He said, "She didn't know it was me. When she realized who I was, she tried to turn the van away, but it was too late. She covered me with a blanket, called for help."

"And cut and ran again, accepting no responsibility. Left you lying there. You could've been dying, for all she knew."

"Well, I wasn't."

"And where was Nat while Ard was running you down? Did she see the whole thing happen?"

"I don't know."

"What the hell does Ard think she's doing, skulking around the Talbot place like some demented ghost?"

"Carly, please stop. The pain medication finally kicked in, and you're making my head hurt all over again."

"This pain medication—it doesn't make you woozy?"

"I don't think so. Why?"

"Because Ned Grossman's out in the hall, waiting to speak with you. I think you should tell him the whole story."

"That I was struck by an unknown driver."

"It's too late to play these games."

"This is not a game." He grasped her arm. "There is unfinished business here. Our business, yours and mine. I want us to be the ones who conclude it."

"If the doc hadn't told me differently, I'd say you sustained brain damage along with the cracked ribs, concussion, and sprained ankle."

"Don't forget the assorted scrapes and bruises."

She glared at him.

"Lighten up, McGuire," he told her. "And get ready— we've got a job to do."

"You didn't get a look at the van's driver, and you can't identify the make or model," Detective Grossman said.

"It was dark, and the headlights blinded me."

"Perhaps we could start from the beginning. What were you doing at the Talbot property?"

He closed his eyes, took a moment to frame his reply. "My employer, Ms. McGuire, phoned me and asked that I drive her there to retrieve her truck."

"Why you and not her attorney? He drove her back to Cyanide Wells."

"I assume because he charges by the hour. Besides, she's been having difficulty with the truck—something wrong with the starter. I fixed it for her the other day, and she wanted me there in case it acted up again." An easily verifiable explanation—the story of his getting his job because of his mechanic's skills had made the rounds.

"So you drove her there. Then what?"

"The truck started right up. She drove off and . . ." Jesus, where was he going with this hastily improvised scenario?

"Mr. Crowe?"

"Could I have some water, please?"

Grossman picked up the cup on the nightstand, handed it to him. Matt thought furiously as he sipped through the straw.

"Okay," he said. "I was going to follow her, but as I started to leave, I noticed another vehicle tucked away in the shadows. Ms. McGuire had told me the property is vacant and up for sale, so I decided to investigate. I guess I frightened the occupants, because the driver started the engine and peeled off. I didn't get out of the way in time."

Grossman frowned. "Previously you said you didn't see the driver, but now you say occupants, plural."

"I had the impression of two people. Teenagers, I suppose, parking in a place where they didn't think they'd be interrupted."

"Possibly." Grossman paused, studying his fingernails. "There was an anonymous call about you to nine-one-one. Came from a pay phone at the entrance to the national forest. A woman. And someone covered you with a handwoven blanket."

"So the doctor told me."

"Do you have any recollection of them covering you?"

"No. I guess it was the people in the van."

"That was our original assumption. But one of my men found the door of the house ajar; he entered to see if anyone was hiding inside, and found a matching blanket on the back of the sofa in the living room. Then he searched the premises. There were signs of recent occupancy."

"Maybe the people in the van were using the house for a tryst?"

"If so, they had a key. There were no signs of forced entry. Is it possible that someone with access to a key had reason to lie in wait and run you down?"

"I don't know who would have a key, detective. And I've only been in Soledad County ten days. I haven't had time to offend anyone to that degree."

"Are you sure of that . . . Mr. Lindstrom?"

Hearing his real name sent shock waves along his spine; he couldn't think of a reply.

Grossman added, "When Detective Swift heard that John Crowe, the newspaper's new photographer, had been injured in a hit-and-run, she contacted me and told

me about her encounter with Matthew Lindstrom on the
highway last weekend. One of the names had to be false,
so we ran a check. The real John Crowe is running
Matthew Lindstrom's charter business in Port Regis,
British Columbia, in Lindstrom's absence.

"Matthew Lindstrom is not listed in this state's criminal files, and the FBI has no record of him. He hasn't
committed a crime—that we know of. But a man
doesn't leave a profitable business and a community
where he's liked and respected to live elsewhere under
an assumed name. Unless, of course, there is something
that draws him to that community. Something that he
wants to keep secret."

Now, Grossman, who had been standing the whole
time, pulled a chair uncomfortably close to Matt's bed,
sat, and placed his hand on the mattress. In a confiden-
tial tone he said, "I'm no world-beater, Mr. Lindstrom. I
don't make much money, have terrible luck with
women, worse luck at poker, and even my dog doesn't
much like me. But I am a good cop, and to me that
means being impartial until all the facts are in. You help
me, and I guarantee I'll do my best to help you out of
whatever trouble currently has you by the short hairs."

In the absence of a viable alternative Matt told Grossman his story—part of it, anyway. Gwen's disappearance. The suspicion that had destroyed his life. The
anonymous phone call. His decision to come to Cyanide
Wells, photograph and confront her.

"She must've seen me somewhere," he concluded,
"and was afraid I'd come here to harm her, because

she's taken her little girl out of town. Even Carly McGuire doesn't know where they've gone."

"And did you intend to harm her?"

"Emotionally, maybe. But not physically."

"Strange, you and the other husband appearing at around the same time."

"I guess one of us was to be backup, in case the other didn't show."

"And you've got no idea who your caller was?"

"I'm working on that."

"Care to share your thoughts with me?"

"Not yet."

"Fair enough. When you came here, did you know Ardis Coleman had married again?"

"No."

"Or that she was living in a lesbian relationship?"

"No."

"Do you own a gun?"

"I have a flare gun aboard my charter boat."

"No handguns? Rifles? Shotguns?"

"No. I don't care for firearms."

"Have you ever been to Westport?"

"No."

"Okay, let's talk about Carly McGuire: Did she know who you were when she hired you?"

"No."

"Does she know now?"

"Yes."

"How'd she find out?"

"Detective Swift mentioned rescuing me on the highway to Severin Quill, the police reporter. He told Carly."

"And what was Carly's reaction?"

"I'm lucky to still be alive."

Grossman smiled thinly. "Obviously the two of you have gotten past that, since she's paying your hospital bill." He got to his feet. "Okay, Mr. Lindstrom, I'll get back to you."

After the door closed behind the detective, Matt expelled his breath in a long sigh. Then he reached for the phone on the nightstand, called Carly's number, and left a detailed message about the talk with Grossman on her machine. Finally he phoned Sam at the Chicken Shack.

"John!" she exclaimed. "I went to the hospital, but you were sedated and they wouldn't let me see you. How are—"

"The doctor says they'll release me this afternoon. Can you pick me up? There's something I need to do."

Carly McGuire

Thursday, May 16, 2002

n the time it took to drive from the hospital in Santa Carla to Cyanide Wells, Carly formulated a plan. Not the best of plans, perhaps, but one that would make her feel she was doing something, plus keep her mind off what Ard had done to Matt.

When she'd been admitted to his hospital room the first time—a privilege extended to her because she was his employer and paying his bill—he'd seemed diminished, more a hurt boy than a man. His groggy confusion and the scrapes and bruises that covered his face and arms wrenched at her, and she regretted every caustic word she'd spoken to him over the past week and a half. But today she'd witnessed the return of his steadiness and strength—his quiet determination, too, as he'd insisted that the two of them would see this matter through to its conclusion. Alone she might not have attempted that, but Matt was a person she could lean on. She'd come to respect this man who had been far too good for Ardis.

Just as I was far too good for her.

Giving mental voice to the concept failed to surprise her, as it might have yesterday or the day before. For years she'd been accustomed to making excuses for Ard's actions and failings, had taken her back and forgiven her. But when Matt had said, "Ardis was driving the van that hit me," the past fourteen years' worth of abuse from her partner had become inexcusable, unforgiveable. And she'd allowed herself to see the relationship for exactly what it was.

Just like that. In an instant. Truth.

As she drove through town and headed east toward the Knob, she noticed an old brown station wagon following at a discreet distance and smiled wryly. Deputy Shawn Stengel's family car. He couldn't have maintained surveillance on her in his cruiser, but did he really think she hadn't seen him toting his brood around in that oversized machine? Either Shawn wasn't as smart as she'd thought, or he underestimated her powers of observation.

She drove past her own turnoff at Drinkwater Road and, after three quarters of a mile, signaled left onto Spyglass Trail. The two-lane blacktop snaked north into the hills, between rocky outcroppings where stubborn vegetation clung, passed through a grove of aspen, then hooked in a series of switchbacks to the west. After a mile or so, the Spyglass Roadhouse appeared.

Its central portion resembled a log cabin with a peaked roof, and jutting off it were long rough-board wings, windowless with flat roofs. On one of them sat an enormous satellite TV dish. A few cars were in the unpaved parking lot, but now, at two in the afternoon, the place had a lifeless look. Carly pulled up near the entrance and went inside, momentarily blinded by the darkness.

Two men in workshirts and jeans sat at the near end of the bar, watching a soap opera on the big screen, where a couple were cuddling in bed—the woman with perfect makeup, the man with impeccably groomed hair. The woman exclaimed, "I've never experienced anything as wonderful as last night!"

One of the watchers said to the screen, "Yeah, so where'd you and lover-boy spend it? The beauty parlor?"

Carly spotted a red-haired woman who resembled the description Matt had given her of Janet Tremaine at the far end of the bar, sitting on one of the stools, a solitaire game spread before her. As she started toward her, the waitress looked up and smiled.

"Ms. McGuire, why're you here? Nobody's shot up the place in maybe two weeks."

Carly slipped onto the stool next to her. The goddamn saddle seats were sized for men and hurt in all the wrong places. "You know who I am?" she asked.

"Sure, everybody does. Newspaper editor, important person."

"The editor of the *New York Times* is important. I'm not. Business is light today, huh?"

"Yeah." Tremaine went back to her solitaire game.

"Black ten on the red jack," Carly said.

"Huh?"

"That'll win it for you. Then I'll buy you a beer."

"I shouldn't—"

"Nonsense, it's not like you're a cop on duty. I'm having an IPA."

Tremaine swept the cards into a pile. "Well, okay. Thanks." She went behind the bar, drew drafts, and slid Carly's over to her.

Carly stood. "Let's go sit in a booth."

Tremaine's eyes grew wary.

"Come on." Carly walked toward the far side of the room. After telling the bartender she was taking a break, Tremaine followed.

"What's this about?" she asked as she sat down opposite Carly.

"Mack Travis."

"Not you, too? A so-called army buddy of his was in here asking about him the other night. Was he one of your people?"

"Uh-huh."

"I *told* him to lay off—"

"Janet, don't you think the cover-up's gone on long enough?"

"What cover-up?"

"You know. It's time you told the whole story."

"There's nothing to tell."

"Yes, there is, and you need to get it out in the open. Keeping secrets like that can damage a person."

"Secrets? What secrets?"

"You know."

"I don't!" She glanced around the room, lowered her voice. "Really, I don't."

"You told my employee that he didn't know who and what he was dealing with. You know what that says to me? It says you've been silenced by powerful people. Who are they?"

Tremaine's shoulders slumped, and she leaned forward. "Listen, I'm scared."

"Well, I'm not. And I can help you."

Silence.

"Tell me what you know, Janet."

"So you can publish it in your newspaper?"

"No, so you won't have to be afraid anymore."

". . . Oh, hell. What've I got to lose? I'll tell you."

Carly spun the truck's tires as she left the Roadhouse parking lot, sending up a spray of gravel. She vented her anger by taking the switchbacks of Spyglass Trail at a dangerous speed. Behind her, Shawn Stengel struggled to keep up in his clumsy station wagon.

Halfway down, somewhat calmer, she found a wide spot, pulled off, and waited for the deputy. Stengel was driving so fast that he almost missed seeing her. When he did, he slammed on the brakes, fishtailed to a stop, then put the car in reverse and backed onto the shoulder. As he got out and walked toward her, she called, "Hey, Shawn."

"Carly."

"Anybody ever tell you that you stick out in that big boat?"

"Anybody ever tell you it's dangerous driving like that in a truck?"

"So how come you're following me?"

"Grossman's orders. What were you doing at the Roadhouse?"

"I felt the need of a cold one." Before he could speak, she held up her hand. "That's *one,* Shawn, over more than an hour. My blood alcohol level's legal."

"I don't doubt that. But why the Roadhouse? I've never known you to go slumming."

"There're lots of things you've never known me to do. Doesn't mean I haven't done them. You planning on following me around forever?"

"Till Grossman lifts the surveillance." The deputy leaned against the truck's tailgate, arms folded across his chest. "Hell, Carly, you think I like spying on you? If you'd just tell Grossman what you know about the murder—"

"You mean tell Grossman what he wants to hear."

Stengel shrugged. "He's a good cop. If he senses he's onto something, he probably is. It's damned suspicious, Ms. Coleman disappearing at the same time her husband got killed."

"She didn't disappear. She went out of town. Before Chase Lewis was murdered."

"And without telling you where she was going?"

"That's right."

He sighed. "So where're we headed next?"

"My house. You can wait out front all night if you like. I'll even bring you a sandwich and some coffee."

"You know, I think I'll take you up on that. And do me a favor? Take it easy the rest of the way down."

*   *   *

With Stengel close behind, she drove carefully toward the flatlands, thinking over what Janet Tremaine had told her.

On the morning after Ronnie Talbot's and Deke Rutherford's murders, Janet was awakened by a banging on the door of her trailer, in a mobile home park outside of Talbot's Mills. She opened it to Mack Travis. Mack was a mess: rumpled, babbling, shaky, and drunk. Afraid her mostly old and retired neighbors would report his visit to the park manager—there had been previous complaints about him—she quickly pulled him inside. He was unsteady on his feet, so she shoved him into the armchair in front of the TV and, at his request, brought him her bottle of Southern Comfort—a liquor he hated but which he sucked down as he began talking.

Talking of bodies and blood. Of a gun and the smell of burnt powder. Of how Gar Payne and Milt Rawson would kill him. Of how he wished he were dead, too.

Over and over he mumbled and whimpered and eventually cried. Finally he passed out in the chair, and Janet, unsure whether what he'd said was real or an alcoholic delusion, left him there to sleep it off while she went to her noon-to-eight shift at the Roadhouse. But as the day wore on, every patron who came in was talking of the murders of Ronnie Talbot and Deke Rutherford.

Janet was afraid to go home. Afraid to call the sheriff's department, too, because she might be accused of harboring a killer. She solved her problem by remaining at the Roadhouse after her shift ended, drinking one shot of Southern Comfort after another, and finally spending the night on the cot in the employees' lounge. When she returned to her trailer the next morning, Mack was gone;

two days later he was arrested and confessed to the murders.

The night after Mack hanged himself in his jail cell, Gar Payne appeared at Janet's door. He knew, he said, that Mack had come there after killing Talbot and Rutherford, and wanted to know what he'd told her. Janet gave him an account of Mack's drunken ravings. Then Payne asked if Mack had left anything with her. Papers, perhaps, in a manila envelope. Janet hadn't seen any, but she offered to look and found the envelope stuffed between the chair's side and seat cushion. Payne took them, saying something about Mack's having been supposed to make a delivery for him. Then Janet made her first mistake.

Was it a delivery to Ronnie Talbot and Deke Rutherford? she asked.

Payne turned steely eyes on her. Had Mack told her that?

No, she just thought it might've been.

Payne didn't believe her. After a long pause he issued an ultimatum: She was to tell no one Mack had been there. She was to tell no one he had been there. And under no circumstances was she to tell anyone about the envelope.

And if she did?

He'd see to it that she lost her job. He'd make sure she never got another in the county. She could do jail time for harboring Travis. Or maybe her neighbors would want to testify as to her loose morals. Women who sold themselves weren't welcome in Soledad County.

Tremaine had a temper. It flared at the accusation.

Oh, no? she asked. Then what kind of women did he visit at Foxxy's up in Oilville?

Payne had a temper, too.

Women like her disappeared all the time, he said. No one would miss her if she did.

Just thinking about what Tremaine had told her made Carly's blood race. She stomped on the accelerator, leaving Shawn Stengel far behind, then eased up and told herself to think logically rather than indulge in rage. The logical conclusion, of course, was that Payne and Rawson had been after the Talbot property for quite some time; they'd probably sent Mack Travis there to deliver an offer, but somehow things had gotten out of hand and he'd killed them. Then he'd killed himself in order to escape Payne and Rawson's retaliation.

Again she stomped on the accelerator.

God, I hate people like them! Mack Travis wasn't much, but they shouldn't've used him the way they did. Janet's not much—in their eyes—but she shouldn't have had to live in fear of them for three years.

Payne and Rawson have got to be stopped. And I'm the woman to do it.

After she made Shawn the promised sandwich and delivered it to his car along with a thermos of coffee, she checked her phone messages. Calls from the office—plaintive voices begging for direction—and one from Matt. It was close to five, so newspaper business took precedence. After she'd finished with her employees, she replayed Matt's message. He'd handled Grossman well, but she knew the detective would want her to verify his story. How long before Ned came knocking on her door?

She dialed the hospital in Santa Carla, found that Matt had been discharged late that afternoon. No answer at Sam's house. Damn! Where was he? Had Grossman put a deputy on him, also?

Six-seventeen now. It wouldn't be dusk till around eight-thirty, and until then her movements would be restricted. She paced the kitchen floor, considered having a glass of wine, decided against it. A clear head was a necessity tonight. Stamina, too, so she made a sandwich and ate it standing at the counter. It tasted like cardboard, but in her present state anything would. Finally she went to her office and ran some Internet searches that turned up nothing of interest.

At eight-fifteen she went to her bedroom and changed into black jeans and a black sweater. Thick socks, a knit hat, and hiking boots completed her ensemble. From the crisper in the refrigerator she took one of the point-and-shoot flash cameras that she and Ard kept there—Ard's contention being that film lasted longer if kept cold. She put it, a small bottle of water, and a flashlight into her daypack.

In her dark living room she looked out the window. Stengel's station wagon was still parked beside her truck. She turned on a table lamp and the TV, moved conspicuously about the room for a few minutes, then drew the curtains. Slipped down the hall to the dining room, where French doors opened onto the backyard. She opened one and listened.

Night sounds. Rustling in the brush, the cries of birds, a dog barking, a car passing on the road. From somewhere nearby came the smell of a barbecue. It was so quiet, she could hear the rush and babble of the creek.

After a careful look around she stepped outside, set the lock on the door, and shut it behind her. Ran across the backyard to the shelter of an aspen grove.

Seven miles as the crow flies.

Deke had told her that the night of the big storm, when he appeared on snowshoes with candles and emergency rations. But he had known the crow's route. In her ignorance of the off-road terrain she might have to walk considerably farther.

You can do it. You have to do it.

She set out through the grove.

The houses here were on large tracts, spaced far apart, creating little light pollution. The night was dark, the moon a mere crescent. Carly took out her flashlight and aimed its beam at the ground, walking swiftly but carefully. When she came out of the trees and into the open meadow, she sighted on the towering mass of the Knob and headed toward it. Crickets fell silent as she passed, then again took up their chorus.

After about ten minutes she entered forest land. The trees were mainly pines, and their resinous smell filled her nostrils. She zigzagged through them, hands sticky where she touched their branches, and eventually realized she'd lost her bearings.

Sheer madness to think I'd find my way. I could be walking around in circles till morning.

She dug her cell phone from her pack and punched in Sam D'Angelo's number. No answer. Next she tried the newspaper on the odd chance Matt might have gone there, but only reached the machine.

Well, what would I have said to him, anyway? "I'm lost in the woods; come and rescue me"?

She put the phone away and resumed walking. After a while the trees thinned and she found herself in a clearing. Craning her neck, she located the Knob— dead ahead and closer than before. She wasn't lost after all.

She angled to the south, across the clearing, with renewed vigor. Plunged into underbrush where dead blackberry vines ripped at her clothing, and came out on a dirt road. Quickly she conjured up her mental map of the area: Drinkwater Creek, Spyglass Trail, the Knob, the Talbot house. This, then, would be the unpaved end of the trail. If she followed it to the right, it would lead her to its intersection with Highway 26, which passed through the national forest. Turn right, and within fifteen minutes or so she'd be at her destination.

She hadn't been hiking much lately, and her calf and thigh muscles ached. The boots, which weren't thoroughly broken in, pinched her toes. She ignored her discomfort and kept going. Then the growl of an engine came out of the distance. She stopped, listening to get a sense of its direction. Hazy headlights appeared behind her.

Grossman. He went to the house, found me gone, is looking for me.

The detective looking for her in this particular place made no sense, but still she ducked down and scrambled into the ditch by the roadside. It was muddy, and her boots sank deep into the muck. Moments later the vehicle passed at high speed; she raised her head, trying to glimpse it, but it was already around the bend.

Going where? Nothing out here for miles but the national forest. And Ronnie and Deke's house . . .

Ten minutes later she stood in the shelter of a stand of pines, looking at the house. No light showed. She ran across the road and angled toward it. The driveway and front parking area were clearly visible now, and vacant. The vehicle that had passed her was probably heading through the national forest toward the intersection of Highway 26 with Interstate 5 at Redding. Still, she studied the house for a few minutes more before she went over and let herself inside.

In the entry she shone the flashlight's beam around. She listened, heard only the sound of a tree branch tapping on the front window. After removing her hiking boots she climbed to the second story and went to the master bedroom. Took out her point-and-shoot, and—

"I'll do that," Lindstrom's voice said.

She whirled. His face was pale against the darkness. "Jesus! You scared me!"

"Sorry. I didn't want to show myself till I was sure it was you."

"Where've you been since you got discharged from the hospital? I've called a couple of times."

"Sam and I had dinner in Santa Carla. After we got back to Talbot's Mills, she went to her shift at the Chicken Shack and I drove here. Pulled my Jeep around back and came inside. Was setting up to take pictures when I heard you arrive."

Carly sat on the bed, took off her cap, and let her tangled hair fall to her shoulders. Her eyes had now acclimated to the darkness, and she looked around, taking in the room's shadowy outlines. When her gaze rested on the nightstand beside her, she frowned, then shone her flash on it.

"What?" Matt asked.

"That's it. I saw something there."

"When? The other day?"

"No. The morning after the murders. That was the only other time I've been in this room. But why can't I remember? Dammit!"

"Don't force it. It'll come eventually."

"Eventually isn't good enough." She closed her eyes, began employing a technique a Denver hypnotherapist whom she'd interviewed for a feature article had explained to her.

Go back to that morning. You're outside Ronnie and Deke's house. What's the weather like?

Warm. It'll get hot later.

What do you smell?

Ard's vomit. Dry grass and eucalyptus. Cape jasmine from the blue urns by the front door.

What do you hear?

Ard—she's crying. Bluejays screeching in the oak tree. A crow cawing.

Look at the house. What do you see?

Door's open.

"Carly?"

"Not now!"

Go inside the house. What's the first thing you notice?

It's cooler in here. But the temperature rises as I climb the stairs.

Go to the master bedroom. What do you see there?

I don't want to—

Look!

Ronnie and Deke are on the bed. Their heads . . . There's blood on the sheets, on the headboard. . . . I can't do this anymore.

Yes, you can. Look at the nightstand.

Okay. The nightstand. There's nothing on it, not even much blood.

Look more closely.

Well, some blood. But it's in a pattern. There're circles and a rectangle, clear and polished wood. Three small circles and a bigger one. And the rectangle's about the size of a paperback book.

She opened her eyes. "Maybe."

"Maybe what?" Matt asked.

"Come on." She stood. "It's getting late and there's somebody I need to talk with."

Dr. Arlene Hazelwood was in her sixties—a slender but strong woman with a long patrician nose, relatively unlined skin, and hair the color of old ivory. She was Carly's personal physician and one of her role models. Arlene walked in marathons to raise money for medical research, ran a program that arranged for children and pets to visit elderly patients in county nursing homes, mentored troubled teenagers, and still managed to maintain an active medical practice. An Aunt Nan without the controlling edge.

The doctor seemed unsurprised when Carly, having parted with Matt at the *Spectrum*, appeared at her door at ten-thirty that evening. She invited her into the parlor of her white Victorian on a quiet side street not far from the newspaper offices and prepared mugs of herbal tea. Then she settled into her armchair and said, "I assume this is not a social call. Are you on the trail of a hot medical story?"

"Actually I'm not. I need some information from you for personal reasons."

Arlene's blue eyes assessed her keenly. "You're not ill, although you do appear to be under considerable stress."

"I am, and it relates to the reason I'm here. You were Ronnie Talbot's and Deke Rutherford's primary care physician?"

"Yes."

"Does doctor-patient confidentiality extend beyond death?"

"It does."

"Even if the death is a homicide, and the victim's medical condition might have bearing on the reason he died?"

"What is this leading up to, Carly?"

"All right. Ronnie and Deke were close friends of Ard and me, as you probably know. A group of us—a dozen or so—celebrated various holidays together, usually at their place. Yet for at least seven months before they were killed, none of us saw Deke and seldom saw Ronnie. They didn't schedule the customary events and were frequently out of town—tending to a sick uncle of

Deke's, they claimed. But in retrospect, I remember that Deke had no family."

Arlene set down her tea and folded her hands, waiting.

Carly went on, "I suspect the reason they broke off contact was because Deke had AIDS. He was a proud man—vain, too. He wouldn't have wanted his friends to watch him waste away from the disease, so he withdrew from us at the time when he needed us most—perhaps went out of town for treatment."

"If that was true, then we should respect his wish for privacy."

"I would, except I think there's a connection between Deke's medical condition and the murders. I'm not sure what it is, but I strongly feel it exists."

"Mere intuition is a flimsy reason for you to ask me to violate my ethics."

"Would you be violating your ethics if you helped me uncover the real reason they were killed?" She leaned forward, fixing an earnest gaze on the doctor. "Recently I've learned things that indicate the murders were more than the act of a deranged individual working alone. People manipulated Mack Travis—powerful people. And tonight I remembered something significant."

Arlene cocked her head and raised her eyebrows.

"After Ard found Ronnie's and Deke's bodies, she called me, hysterical. When I got to their house, I went to their bedroom to confirm what she'd told me. There was a good deal of blood; it had sprayed on the sheets, the headboard, and a nightstand—the one on the side of the bed where Deke lay. And the pattern on that night-stand was odd. To me, it looked as if four pill bottles and a paperback book had been set there. But they must've been moved after Ronnie and Deke were shot."

"Why? And by whom?"

"I don't know why. Probably they were moved by Mack Travis. But I do know Travis was there under someone else's orders."

"Whose?"

"It's better if I don't say."

The doctor pursed her lips thoughtfully. "I've lived in Cyanide Wells my whole life, except for college and my medical training. I've observed the transitions and shifts of power. We have our good people, our worthless people, and our ruthless people. The lines are fairly well drawn, so you don't have to name names."

Carly waited as Arlene considered.

"Very well," she said, "I'll confirm what you've already figured out. Deke was dying of AIDS. After the initial diagnosis he failed at an accelerated rate. I sent him to a specialist in San Francisco, but there was little he could do for him; it was as if Deke had made up his mind not to fight. He would most likely have been dead by Christmas."

"So it was medicine bottles that made the pattern on the nightstand."

"Yes. The paperback book was probably an inspirational volume that I give to terminal patients. The last time I saw Deke, he told me he cherished it and read from it every day."

"So the presence of it and the medicines would have indicated he had AIDS?"

"Most likely."

Carly paused, full of fresh grief for her friend. "How did Ronnie handle Deke's illness?"

"Admirably. He was a rock, even when I had to tell him his own blood test was HIV-positive."

Oh, Ronnie . . . "When was that?"

"July twenty-second, shortly before they were killed."

July twenty-second. Wednesday afternoon.

"This is so nice. I wish it could go on forever."

Ronnie had said that to her as they sat drinking wine in the backyard garden of Aram's Cafe. But he hadn't been talking about the moment, as she'd assumed. He'd been talking about his life. And Deke's.

"Carly?"

"I'm sorry. I was just . . . missing them."

"I miss them, too. Miss all the patients I've lost. I've dealt with death my whole career, but I've never been able to inure myself to it." Arlene looked away for a moment, then said briskly, "Now, is there anything else you need to know?"

"One thing: Why wasn't AIDS mentioned in the autopsy reports?"

"There was no need to mention it; it had no bearing on the way they died. And the county medical examiner is a dear friend of mine."

"You asked him to suppress information?"

"It was a mutual decision. I warned him of their condition so he would take extra precautions while performing the autopsies. He, in turn, urged the investigating officers and EMTs to be tested yearly— just routine, he told them, since the victims were homosexual. So far, none has come up HIV-positive."

"What if they hadn't bothered to be tested?"

"Then he and I would have gone to the authorities and divulged everything. Doctor-patient confidentiality is sacred to us, but nothing is more sacred than protecting innocent lives."

"So why did Mack Travis think he needed to conceal Deke's illness?"

Carly looked at Matt and shrugged, lowered her head, and stared at her crossed ankles. They were in her office at the *Spectrum,* where he'd been waiting for her while she talked with Dr. Hazlewood. She was sitting in the center of her desk, he in her chair with his feet propped up in front of her.

"Tired?" he asked.

"Yeah. I didn't tell you before, but on my hike to Ronnie and Deke's house I got lost. In a pine forest. I tried to call you on my cell phone."

"And what did you expect me to do?"

"That's what I wondered after you didn't answer."

"Well, if I had answered, I'd've done something."

"Like?"

"Send out a carrier pigeon with a map. Set the Talbot house on fire to guide you. Steal the sheriff's department helicopter and fly low over all the pine trees in the county, bellowing for you on a bullhorn."

She looked up, smiling. "You know, Matt, you almost make me wish I was hetero."

"Oh, yeah?"

"I said *almost.*"

"Just as well. I'm not sure this simple boy from Minnesota could handle becoming romantically involved with his ex-wife's former lover."

"Probably not, but I doubt there's anything simple about you."

"You, either. Maybe that's why we're friends."

Friends.

It wasn't a word—or a concept—she took lightly. But they had become just that.

"Maybe," she said. "We both know what it's like to be outcasts. We both know how it feels to be unfairly attacked. And"—she raised her hand dramatically—"we have both suffered the slings and arrows of outrageous Ardis."

He rolled his eyes, took his feet off the desk, and stood. "That declaration tells me you need at least twelve hours' sleep."

"I do, but where? I'm too damned tired to slink through the countryside to my back door. And if you deliver me to the front, that damn Shawn Stengel—"

"I know a place in Talbot's Mills where there's a lumpy sofa. I might even trade you my bed for it."

Matthew Lindstrom

Friday, May 17, 2002

t ten in the morning Carly was still asleep in Matt's room. He stole in for some clothes, showered and dressed, left her a note on the kitchen table, and departed quietly, heading for Cyanide Wells and the *Spectrum*.

Shortly before he was discharged from the hospital the previous afternoon, he'd received a call from the paper's production manager, asking somewhat wistfully if he'd be able to develop the film he'd shot on Tuesday in time for next week's issue. Matt felt he ought to fulfill his obligations to the paper while Carly was unable to fulfill hers, so he told the manager he'd have the photos on his desk this afternoon.

The newsroom was empty when he arrived, but Brandi Webster sat at the reception desk, glaring at her computer screen. Her usually perky features were drawn, her voice curiously flat as she expressed dismay over his accident and asked how he was mending.

"I'm not too bad, if I don't make any sudden moves. At least I'm not muddleheaded anymore."

"Well, I'm glad it wasn't any worse. What kind of a person does a thing like that, anyway? The sheriff's people have been working overtime to find them. They were in here yesterday asking a lot of questions."

"Oh? About?"

"Stuff like how well do we know you and do you have any enemies. Nobody could tell them much, since you just started." She turned back to her computer. "This damn thing's so slow. I wish I had a better one."

"What're you doing?"

"Updating the subscriber lists, and I'm way behind. I haven't gotten much done this week, and neither has anybody else, because Carly hasn't been around. We all complain when she is, because she can be such a bitch, but her bitchiness kind of puts an edge on that energizes us. What's with her, anyway?"

"I don't know, Brandi." He made a hasty exit before she could ask him anything else.

In the darkroom he wound film onto the spool for developing and, after a few minutes, found himself enjoying the quiet, dim atmosphere under the glow of the safelight. As he busied himself with the exacting processes of drying, enlarging, shading, and printing, he realized how wrong he'd been to give up photography. Although it wasn't a viable way to make a living in Port Regis, it could again be a pleasurable pursuit, maybe even a sideline. When he went back, he'd set up a darkroom.

The pictures of the overturned hopper truck, its load of artichokes spilling down the slope at the Talbot's Mills off-ramp, appeared ordinary at first, but when he examined them more closely, he saw a man and a woman who had pulled up their sweatshirts to form baskets and were filling them with the bounty. He made another print, emphasizing the enterprising couple. His portrait of Cyanide Wells's most senior citizen—101-year-old Elsa Turner, who still tended a vegetable garden, canned, and had recently published a first volume of poetry—had turned out well, speaking of vital old age and indomitable spirit. When all the prints were out of the dryer and on the production manager's desk, Matt found himself reluctant to put the darkroom in order and leave.

Well, what about his personal films, the ones he'd taken in order to vindicate himself? He dug the canisters out of his camera bag and set to work.

Ardis and Natalie arriving after grocery shopping. The images created an ache under his breastbone. Ardis—once his Gwen—so lovely in spite of the years' passage. Sunlight caught in the wind-tangled strands of her hair; love glowed in her eyes as she smiled down at the little girl. And Natalie: laughing, innocent, trusting. A child taking pleasure in something as small as Ardis's hand on her shoulder as they crossed the footbridge.

For a moment thoughts of what might have been had he and Gwen had a child threatened to take hold of him. Then reality pushed them aside.

The pictures that he'd taken the next morning of the

property and its surroundings were pedestrian—mere documentation. The SUV in the parking area, its license plate, the mailbox, footbridge, trees to either side.

But what was that?

He picked up a loup, peered at the contact sheet. Took it outside the darkroom and examined it under the neon light. Went back inside and put the negative in the enlarger. Studied the image again.

A man was standing in the trees to the left of the footbridge. No, not standing—he was walking toward it. A slender man with dark, curly hair.

He went back into the darkroom, positioned the negative, and enlarged it. The man's features were dappled by sunlight but recognizable from the publicity still Matt had seen at Wild Parrots.

Chase Lewis, about to pay a call on the woman who had left him and taken his child.

"I don't understand." Carly was sitting on Sam's sofa, a mug of coffee clutched in both hands. Matt noticed that she'd appropriated one of his T-shirts.

Although he knew she wasn't fully functional— she'd gotten up only half an hour before he returned— he had little patience with her. "Look at the print." He waved the eight-by-ten at her. "Look at the man in the trees by your footbridge."

"I see him. Are you sure it's Chase Lewis?"

"Positive. I took this shot on the morning of Thursday, the ninth, around ten-thirty. Ardis was home; her SUV was there. Lewis paid her a visit the day before she staged her disappearance."

Carly frowned at the photographs. "But why didn't she tell me he'd been there? That night all she said was that she thought someone was watching her and had been in the house."

"She didn't tell you, because she didn't want you to find out she'd married him and stolen his child. My guess is, she was setting you up to take her disappearance seriously."

Carly's fingers gripped the mug harder, and coffee sloshed onto her bare thighs. Matt took the mug from her and set it on the table.

"Scenario," he said. "Gar Payne calls Lewis, tells him where to find Ardis and Natalie. First Lewis writes to her; that scrap of paper that you found in the fireplace—'. . . mine and I got the right . . .'—was what was left of the letter. Then, when he doesn't get a reply, he drives up to Cyanide Wells and goes to the house, demands his daughter. What would Ardis have done?"

"She wouldn't have argued with him. He'd been violent with her before. And she knew she was in an indefensible position. Lewis could've gone to the sheriff's department, had her arrested for kidnapping. But she wouldn't have agreed to let him have Nat."

"So what alternative did she have?"

"I think she probably agreed to bring Nat to him, set a date and a time. Sent him to the motel in Westport, since she couldn't chance them being seen together here, and staged the disappearance, including the backpack in the well. She thought I'd report it, and Lewis would be afraid he'd be blamed and go back where he came from. Then, after a while she'd surface and reclaim her life."

"Or begin a new life elsewhere."

Carly compressed her lips, looked away from him.

Quickly he went on, "The plan was hastily conceived; she only had from Thursday morning to Friday evening. And she made mistakes, like leaving the bloody bowl in the sink and the meat in the garbage cans. When there were no reports on TV or radio about their disappearance, she knew she'd screwed up."

Carly closed her eyes. Matt knew she was fighting the inevitable conclusion, searching inside herself for some shred of doubt. He'd done similar soul-searching in the darkroom after he'd recognized Lewis in his photographs.

After a moment she said, "I don't know where she stashed Nat after they left the Talbot house, but I do know she went to Lewis's motel on Saturday. I don't know where she got the gun; maybe it was his. He might've threatened her with it, and somehow she got it away from him. But I do know she killed him."

When she opened her eyes, they were bleak and lusterless. Seldom in his life had he seen such sadness.

While Carly showered and dressed, Matt paced the small living room. Perhaps now that she accepted the idea that Ardis had killed Chase Lewis, he could persuade her to tell the sheriff's investigators what they knew. Because of Natalie, the department could call in the FBI, and with their resources she'd soon be delivered to safety. It would be Ardis's business to explain herself to the authorities, and he and Carly could free themselves from this mess and get on with their lives.

Carly returned, looking fresher but red-eyed, as if she'd been crying in the shower. He didn't comment, simply outlined his thoughts to her. She listened quietly but surprised him with her reaction.

"What makes you think this is a matter for the FBI?"

"A kidnapped child who's probably been taken across the state line by now? I'd say that qualifies."

"I don't know if there's a statute of limitations on kidnapping, but Ard took Nat a long time ago, and she's been happy with us. Besides, I'm not so sure they've even left the county."

"If you'd murdered someone, wouldn't you put as much distance as possible between yourself and the crime scene?"

"I would, but . . ." She sat on the sofa, drew her legs up, wrapped her arms around them. "Ard knows a fair amount about police work and what kinds of information the authorities can access, but she doesn't respect our sheriff's department. And she can be naive. She probably thinks she's covered her past well; maybe she thinks Lewis finding her was a fluke. She was at the Talbot house two days ago; something kept her here."

"What? What's so important that she'd risk arrest for it?"

"Natalie, of course."

"But wouldn't she think it best for Natalie if they went far away?"

"I can't fathom what she would or wouldn't think anymore. I feel as if you and I are operating in a vacuum. I wish we knew what the sheriff's investigators have found out so far."

"Well, since they suspect you of being an accessory,

if not a murderer, I don't think they'll be forthcoming if you ask."

She studied him thoughtfully. "No, they're not about to share with me. But you . . ."

"Oh, no. Don't go there."

"From what you told me about your talk with Grossman yesterday, you handled him very well. You could go see him."

"On what pretext?"

"You could tell him you need to go home to B.C. Ask his permission; then get him talking about the case."

"He doesn't strike me as the garrulous type."

"But he is—at times. I've heard rumors about him: He's a lonely man and likes his Scotch. He's particularly fond of single-malt."

"Oh, yeah, I'm supposed to walk into the station carrying a fifth—"

"I happen to have his home address."

"You're insane. It'd never work."

"It might. I think Ned cares more about the truth than his clearance rate. He's one of the good guys. So are you, Matt."

He stared at her face, which wore a pleading little look. Noted the slyness underlying it. "Did you learn this from Ardis?"

Wide-eyed innocence now. "Learn what?"

"The art of getting your own way."

She laughed—hooted, actually—stripped of her guileless mask. "I learned at the knee of my late aunt Nancy. Compared to her, Ard is a mere novice."

"Then your aunt must've been a truly frightening woman." He fell silent, considering the situation. The detective hadn't believed he'd told him his full story during their interview at the hospital; perhaps his distrust could be worked to an advantage.

"Okay," he said, "I'll go try to bond with Grossman."

The detective lived in Santa Carla on a narrow, tree-lined street whose small stucco bungalows differed only in their colors. In that area, however, diversity ruled: standard white, cream, gray, and beige intermixed with garish turquoise, orange, lime, and fuchsia. What was it about stucco, Matt wondered, that inspired some people to excess?

Grossman's house was in the more subdued camp: cream, with a tidy patch of grass inside a chain-link fence. An enormously fat black-and-white spotted dog of indeterminate breed sprawled on the concrete path; at first Matt hesitated to open the gate, but then the animal looked up and yawned, revealing a largely toothless mouth. Matt entered, said, "Hi, dog," and went up to the door. The dog heaved itself to its feet and followed, snuffling at his shoes as if it thought they might be good to eat.

Grossman, clad in a pullover, jeans, and moccasins, opened the door and raised his eyebrows. "Mr. Lindstrom, what brings you here?"

"I'd like to talk with you." He held up the bottle he carried. "And I've brought refreshment."

The detective smiled thinly. "Attempting to bribe an officer of the law, are you?"

"Not really, but I heard you like single-malt. It's also

a personal favorite of mine, and I don't like to drink alone."

"Neither do I, Mr. Lindstrom."

"Matt, please."

"Ned." He opened the door wider and admitted Matt to a small room where a TV was turned to a golf game, the sound muted. The dog entered, too, wheezing.

"That's Everett," Grossman said, switching off the TV. "The critter who I told you doesn't much like me. Frankly, the feeling's mutual. He's a canine garbage can. Scarfs down stuff even I wouldn't eat. Take a seat; I'll get us glasses. No ice, right?"

"No ice."

"Good man."

He sat on the sofa, and Everett followed on his owner's heels, probably hoping for a snack. In their absence Matt studied the room. A diploma from Humboldt State University and a number of framed certificates hung on the wall behind the TV. A couple of bowling trophies sat atop a bookcase full of thick volumes, most of them dealing with police science. No personal photographs, nothing that revealed the inner man. The room smelled stale, as if it were uninhabited a great deal of the time, and a thin film of dust overlay everything.

Grossman returned, shadowed closely by Everett, whose hopes of a snack apparently had been fulfilled, since he was licking his chops in an extremely satisfied manner. After pouring a round, the detective settled into an armchair that faced the TV. As he swiveled it toward Matt, the dog sat at his feet and rested its head on his knee; Grossman began rubbing the floppy ears.

Sure the two of you don't much like each other. Matt raised his glass in a toast, sipped.

Grossman followed suit, smiling in appreciation. "Whatever you want to talk about must be damned important. This is quite a bribe."

"It's important, all right. I need to get back to British Columbia. I'm concerned about my charter business. You didn't tell me not to leave the county, but I thought I should ask your permission."

"A problem up there?"

"Nothing serious, but we're getting into our peak season now, and my deckhand's not going to be able to handle the volume of business."

"I understand. My grandfather was a commercial fisherman, out of Calvert's Landing. When the fish were running, he needed all the hands he could get—mine included. I imagine it's the same with tourists."

Everett farted noisily. Grossman wrinkled his nose and glared at him but went on rubbing his ears. "How close are you to Carly McGuire, Matt?"

"Carly? Why?"

"Just wondering. You do have something in common—Ardis Coleman."

"Does she strike you as a good reason for closeness?"

Grossman shrugged. "You were with Carly when Natalie's backpack turned up in the well—retrieved it, in fact. You drove her to the Talbot house Tuesday night, even though her attorney could just as easily have done so."

"I told you she was having trouble with her truck—"

"Yes, she was, until you disarmed the alarm the week before. She's had no problems with it since, according to the folks at the paper. And in addition, she paid your hospital bill."

"She felt she ought to, since I was injured while doing her a favor. My health insurance—"

"And after she eluded our surveillance last night, she slept at Sam D'Angleo's house, where you rent a room."

"How d'you know that?"

"Deputy Stengel went to the door around two-thirty this morning to ask her to refill the thermos of coffee she'd given him. The lights and TV were on in the living room, but Carly didn't answer the bell. He was mightily disgruntled about that when he reported in this morning—Shawn likes his creature comforts—and it made me wonder if she'd slipped out on him, and if so, where she'd gone. So I asked myself, 'Who's she been hanging around with lately?' Your name came up high on the list."

"That doesn't prove—"

"Later I talked with a neighbor of Ms. D'Angelo's, who said she'd looked out her bathroom window and seen the two of you arriving. She recognized Carly because she used to houseclean for her and Ardis."

"So what is it you think? That I'm having an affair with Carly?"

"Hardly. But I'm curious as to what the involvement between the two of you is."

"We're friends, that's all."

"And where does Ardis Coleman fit in?"

"She doesn't. She's left Carly."

"Then this story of the educational trip . . . ?"

"Face-saving on Carly's part."

"Face-saving, in spite of the fact that Ardis's husband was just murdered?"

"Carly's confused and fragile right now. And naturally she doesn't want to believe that her partner—former partner—could murder someone."

Grossman stood and poured them another round, sat down, and fixed Matt with a flat, knowing stare.

"Okay, Matt," he said, "you want to go back to British Columbia? Well, I've got a proposition for you."

As he drove north from Santa Carla, Matt felt like a double agent. Or maybe a triple agent. Which one, he wasn't sure. He'd read spy novels with pleasure but had never been fully able to comprehend the twists and turns of their plots. Who was on which side? Who was on both? Who was acting strictly on his own? And now he couldn't fully comprehend his present situation. Whose side was he on? Carly's? Grossman's? Both? His own?

The proposition the detective had offered him was simple: The surveillance on Carly would be lifted, and over the course of the next few days Grossman would feed Matt bits of information about the Lewis investigation. He, in turn, would pass them along to Carly and observe her reactions, which he would then report to Grossman.

"You're going to have to let go of this misplaced loyalty to Carly, unless you want to be charged as an accessory in the Lewis murder," the detective had told him. "She knows a great deal more than she's letting on, and the information I give you may trigger a telling response that will help us solve it."

What he offered Matt in exchange for his cooperation was also simple: He would be allowed to leave the country by the following weekend. In addition, Grossman would personally inform the authorities in Sweetwater County, Nebraska, and Saugatuck, Minnesota, that Gwen Lindstrom was alive and had been living in his jurisdiction for the past fourteen years. And when the Lewis investigation was closed, he would make sure that the solution to her disappearance received national publicity.

"Maybe then," Grossman said, "you'll feel free to return to your home and your people."

Matt shook his head. "Port Regis is my home. I have no people."

No people. No real friends, either.

Except for Carly.

When she let him into her house at a little before ten that evening, he stepped into chaos. A heap of clothing lay in the entry, and cardboard cartons filled with cosmetics, underwear, shoes, and books stood by the door. Gracie, the little white cat, cowered just inside the living room. Carly held a black-and-red lacquered jewelry box, which she dumped on the floor.

"What's all this?" he asked.

"Housecleaning. I'm getting rid of Ard's shit." She swept her arm at the accumulation. "She's dead to me. When people're dead, you clear out their stuff."

He was silent, staring at the things his former wife had left behind.

"Why're you pulling that long face?" Carly demanded. "Isn't this what you did when she disappeared?"

"Not exactly. When the lease ran out on her apartment, I asked a friend to do it." Bonnie Vaughan. Later she'd told him she cried the whole time.

"Not nearly as satisfying." Carly started for the hallway to the bedrooms.

"Don't you find it sad?"

"No. I'm too pissed off."

"Maybe you should wait till you can feel something other than anger."

She paused, turning. "Why?"

"Because I didn't, and I regret it. Before our friend cleaned out Gwen's apartment, I went over there. Tore it up in a rage, looking for clues to what happened to her. And all I came away with was a bitter taste and the realization of how completely she'd banished me from her life. There were photograph albums, you see. Pictures of the two of us. Our wedding photos. She'd spent a lot of time putting the albums together, so when we split, it was natural she should have them. But apparently the only reason she wanted them was to destroy them."

"Oh, Matt, no." Carly shook her head. "Go into the kitchen; pour us some wine. There's a bottle next to the cooktop. I'll be right back."

He did as she told him. Apparently household items belonging to Ardis were also being ousted: dishes and vases and a pasta maker sat on the floor; the table by the window was covered with pots, pans, and small appliances. A calendar of famous rose gardens that he'd seen on the wall lay beside them. But Natalie's drawings remained on the refrigerator door.

He poured wine from the open bottle of merlot. Carly entered, carrying a manila envelope, and held it out to him.

"I found this at the back of her closet," she said. "I never knew it was there."

The envelope was stuffed full of photographs: their wedding, holidays, the two of them on his father's boat. Gwen stood in front of him, and he had his arms wrapped around her, his chin resting on the top of her head. A happy young couple, their whole lives ahead of them . . .

"I can't deal with this, Carly. Get rid of them."

"No, I'll put them away for you. Just like I'll keep her stuff—for now."

He was sitting at the table when she came back, his eyes closed. Her hand touched his shoulder briefly; then she sat and picked up her glass. "How did it go with Grossman?"

On the drive back he'd realized he could hold nothing back from her. She was his friend, and besides, he was the one who had insisted that they, and they alone, should bring the situation to its conclusion.

"He wants me to spy on you. Here's the deal."

"Okay," Carly said when he'd finished, "I don't blame him for using whatever means he can to work his case. In fact, I think it's damned clever of him. What information did he feed you?"

"Ballistics. And you're not going to like what you hear. The bullets they took out of Chase Lewis and his motel room wall were unusual. Short thirty-two caliber, copper-jacketed, of a type not manufactured in this country. The lab technician thought he'd encountered something similar before, so he accessed past records for county homicides. The bullets were a match for those that killed Ronnie and Deke."

"I never heard anything about the bullets that killed them being unusual."

"It was never revealed by the department, even after Mack Travis killed himself and they closed out the case. Grossman said the sheriff never believed in Travis's guilt."

"Then Ard didn't kill Lewis, after all. Whoever killed Ronnie and Deke did."

"Possibly."

"Gar Payne? Milt Rawson?"

He shrugged.

"I'm afraid I don't know much about ballistics. Could they tell what kind of gun the bullets were fired from?"

"Not the exact make, but from the bullet, the tech thinks it's an older gun, perhaps a collector's item."

Carly swirled her wine, stared into its depths. Matt could tell that the information had disturbed her.

"The technician couldn't be wrong?" she asked.

"Grossman said that kind of evidence, like fingerprints or DNA, doesn't lie."

She nodded, still staring down. When she finally looked up, her face was pale.

She said, "Let's go, Matt. There's something I need to check out."

*   *   *

He shut off the Jeep's engine and lights. The night was oppressively dark, the Talbot house a black hole before him. Carly slid out and slammed her door, then looked back through the open window and said, "You coming?"

"Yeah." He unlatched his seat belt, took his time. Easing into it. All the way here she'd been silent, refusing to answer his questions, her tension palpable. He knew without a doubt that whatever her reason for coming back to the house, it would lead to yet another unpleasant revelation—perhaps the most unpleasant of all.

By the time he caught up with her, she was through the door and taking a flashlight from her daypack. He followed as she switched it on and moved along the hallway to an open door about halfway down. Inside was an office with a row of file cabinets and a computer workstation that was at odds with a handsome rolltop desk. She went to the desk, opened it, shone the light around.

"Carly, what . . . ?"

"In a minute." Her voice was grim. She fumbled with an ornately carved panel, pressing it in several places till it popped open, then took out a set of keys that were its only contents. "Come on." She led him across the hall to a facing door.

The room was a library, furnished in leather, with bookcases built into the walls. Below the heavily laden shelves were carved wooden doors with brass fittings. Carly went to one of them, squatted down, and slipped a key into the lock. It wouldn't turn, so she tried another and then another until one did.

Matt moved closer. She was removing a glass-fronted

display tray, one of several that were stacked inside the cabinet. "Help me with this, would you?" she asked.

He grasped one end, and they lowered it to the floor. She turned the flashlight's beam on it.

Handguns. Sunk into velvet-lined indentations specially contoured for them. Each depression had an engraved brass plate positioned below it.

And one was vacant.

Carly made a sound close to a sob.

Matt read the label: "Austrian Rast and Gasser Army Revolver, Manufactured eighteen ninety-eight."

Carly said, "Ronnie's father's collection. The missing gun is probably the one Ard used to kill Chase Lewis. And Ronnie. And Deke." Her voice shook.

"Not them, too! My God, Carly. Killing off a man who abused her and was threatening to take Natalie away is one thing, but Ronnie and Deke were her friends."

She was silent.

Still not believing it, he asked, "Where would she get ammunition for that kind of gun?"

"The collection includes it." She motioned at spaces for cartridges—eight of them, all empty.

He took the flashlight from her hand, shone it upward at her face, and had a sudden vision of how she would look as an old woman.

She shaded her eyes and said, "Ard has known for years that these guns are here. And she's also known where the keys to the cabinets are kept."

"But so do you. And probably any number of people. Mack Travis—"

"Would have had no way of knowing about them.

Ronnie didn't like the guns, locked them up, but kept them out of sentiment—or guilt. He couldn't get rid of any of his father's stuff, because while he loved him, they didn't get along. His father was always after him to give up on the lifestyle he'd 'chosen.' As if he'd gotten up one morning and said, 'I think I'll turn gay now.'"

"What about Gar Payne? Or Milt Rawson? They might've known."

"No, I'm sure neither of them has ever been in this house."

"Other friends of yours?"

"Some of them may have known about the collection, although not many. Ronnie didn't talk about it much; that would've been dangerous. Burglars go after firearms, particularly old and valuable ones. And I seriously doubt that anybody knew where the keys were kept. The only reason Ard and I found out was that during the last Christmas party here we were wrapping gifts in the office. Ronnie came in to get the keys because an old friend of his father's had stopped by and wanted to look at the collection, thinking he might buy it."

"Was the friend with him?"

"No. Ronnie was even uncomfortable that Ard and I saw him get the keys."

Though it was cool in the library, Matt's face was filmed with sweat. He got up, felt his way across the room, and sank into one of the leather chairs. When he spoke, he barely recognized his own voice.

"Why would Ardis kill Ronnie and Deke?"

"Well, she did get a great series of stories out of their deaths."

"No one kills a friend to score a journalistic coup."

"Try this one, then: a rich vein of gold running under a house whose owner has just made you executor of his will."

All the way back to Carly's house they argued about taking what they knew to Grossman.

"Her killing Chase Lewis I can somewhat understand," he said. "But this other—you can't be willing to risk her getting away with it."

"I need time—just overnight, that's all."

"Christ, Carly, you don't know what else she's done. Or what she might do next."

"Will ten or twelve hours make a difference?"

"It might."

"She's not some crazed serial killer. Besides, they issued a be-on-the-lookout order for her days ago. What more can they do in the middle of the night?"

She had a point. "All right, but we're going to see Grossman first thing tomorrow."

"Agreed, Why don't you come over at eight? We'll drive down to Santa Carla together."

After he dropped Carly at her footbridge, he sped off, turning on the Jeep's radio in the hope that some music would calm him. The only station that came in clearly was KSOL, easy listening out of the county seat. Not his first choice, but in his present frame of mind, anything would do. He'd just arrived at Sam's when the announcer's voice broke in; he left the Jeep running and turned up the volume.

"This just in: Acting on an anonymous tip, Soledad County sheriff's deputies stopped a car driven by Cyanide Wells Mayor Garson Payne and, in the process of investigating a routine traffic violation, seized a handgun from the glove box. Although ballistics experts have yet to confirm it, a department spokesman says they are 'ninety-nine percent certain' that the weapon, an old Austrian army revolver, was used to kill San Francisco musician Chase Lewis in his Westport motel room last weekend. In a related development, the spokesman said that technicians have matched the bullet that killed Lewis with those used in the three-year-old fatal shootings of prominent Cyanide Wells residents Ronald Talbot Junior and Deke Rutherford. Interviewed outside the Talbot's Mills sheriff's department substation, where Payne is being held pending arraignment, the mayor's attorney, James Griffin, stated that his client has no idea how the gun came to be in his car. The case against the mayor will be thrown out of court upon arraignment, Griffin contends, because of the 'illegal nature' of the search . . ."

Matt put the Jeep into a fast U-turn.

Carly McGuire

Saturday, May 18, 2002

hen she'd entered the house after Matt dropped her off, Carly had taken grim satisfaction at the sight of Ard's stacked and strewn possessions. Earlier she'd allowed him to sway her about immediately disposing of them, but on Monday they were headed for the Salvation Army. Or maybe the county dump. She didn't want to saddle anyone, no matter how needy, with the accumulation of Ard's lying, cheating, murderous life.

In the postmidnight hour she moved through the empty house. It felt as it had the night she'd moved in, a lonely twenty-eight-year-old who feared she'd made the biggest mistake of her life. How could she, who had lived in crowded, noisy cities since her late teens, adapt to such isolation and silence? What had possessed her to think she could grasp the reins of a failing country weekly and guide it to success?

Well, you adapted, grasped, and guided. You created a successful life for yourself. You would've been fine if Ard hadn't come into it. Moral: Never pick up hitchhikers.

But for years the hitchhiker, and later her daughter, had brought joy to this house. In spite of the fights and Ard's penchant for fleeing, there had been many good times.

All behind you now, McGuire, the good and the bad.

But can you ever really put that big a part of your life behind you?

She tried to reconcile the woman she'd thought she knew with the woman who had killed their friends, but couldn't. She thought back to the night they'd died, trying to find a shred of evidence that would prove Ard innocent. The coroner had put the time of death at around three in the morning. Ard was supposedly in bed beside her at that hour. But they'd had an argument, and Carly had taken a sleeping pill. Still, wouldn't she have noticed if Ard had left for any appreciable length of time? Maybe, maybe not. And Ard was the only person besides her who had access to Ronnie's gun collection. . . .

Suicide.

The word loomed suddenly in her mind. Odd that the two men who had fixed things for Payne and Rawson had killed themselves. Could there be a connection . . . ?

The phone rang, shrill in the silence. She started, then rushed to the kitchen to pick up.

"Carly?"

The sound of her name, spoken in the old familiar

way, jolted her. She drew in her breath, a combination of surprise and anger threatening to choke her. It was a moment before she could respond.

"Ard. Where are you? Where's Natalie?"

"Carly, I need your help. Chase . . . It's been on the news. Everybody thinks I did it."

Get her back here, McGuire. Make her turn Nat over to you.

"Look, Ard, why don't you and Nat come home? I'll hire a good attorney; we'll get through this together."

"I can't. It's over between you and me. It's been over for a long time. But Nat . . . she's sick. She caught cold and then her asthma flared up, and now she's out of medication, but I don't dare go to the pharmacy for a refill. And I think the cold's turning into pneumonia. I want her to be with you, where she belongs. Our . . . your place is the only home she's ever known."

"Of course I'll take her. I'll see she gets what she needs."

"Thank you. I can't be responsible for her anymore. She's been sick for a week—so sick I haven't been able to move her—and it's all my fault."

"Then bring her here right away."

"No, I can't come there. It's the first place the sheriff's department will expect me to show up. They're probably watching the house."

"They were, but not anymore."

"Look, will you quit talking and come get her?"

"Okay—where?"

"At the Knob. We've been camping out in my rental van near that lookout point—the one Ronnie showed us."

"I can be there in half an hour."

"Good. And one other thing . . . could you bring me some money? My credit cards're maxed out, and I've run through all my cash."

Demanding a ransom, are you?

"How much do you need?"

"A few thousand. Whatever's in your emergency stash."

Nearly three thousand dollars in a Jiffy bag in the office-supply cabinet. Ard must've snooped. She'd never respected anyone's privacy.

"I'll bring it."

"Oh, Carly, thank you. I know you'll take good care of my little girl."

Chase Lewis's little girl, who has now become excess baggage.

"Half an hour," she said, and replaced the receiver.

Carly pulled her truck into the parking area at the trail-head and got out. The national forest was an eerie place at night: chill even after the hottest of days; silent but full of dangerous, prowling life. She took out her flash-light and began walking along a familiar path that was altered by darkness, keeping a wary ear out for sounds in the underbrush. A dry winter had brought mountain lions and bears down from the higher elevations in search of food and water; coyotes and wild pigs also in-habited these foothills.

She followed the trail slowly and cautiously, but her thoughts moved at a furious pace. Something had occurred to her before Ard's call, and she was now linking previously unrelated bits and pieces of information, discarding others. If she could only make the final connections—

A thrashing overhead, then a scurrying in the underbrush. The scream of a small victim.

Owl, probably a great horned, catching his dinner. I hate that sound.

She was nearing the Knob now, but still there was no sign of Ard's rented van. She'd probably driven in on the fire trail to the far side. How she'd eluded the forest rangers while camping in territory that was closed to all but official vehicles, Carly couldn't imagine. Or why, after Nat fell ill a week ago, she'd continued to stay here, where nighttime temperatures were always frigid. Her treatment of the child had become criminally negligent.

The trail began angling uphill, around boulders and over rocky ledges. Soon she spotted the ramshackle building that had once held the cyaniders' equipment. Slag heaps rose to either side, and where the trail split, her flashlight picked out the boarded-up entrance to the old mine, now covered in a wild pattern of graffiti. She turned to the left and started around toward the lookout point.

The terrain was rougher now, and bulky shapes lurked in the darkness—a dumping ground of broken equipment and metal drums that had once contained cyanide, abandoned by the mining company and allowed to remain by the forest service as a memorial to the place's history. Some people thought the area should be cleared, but Carly preferred it this way; to beautify and sanitize it would be denying the reality of what had occurred here. . . .

She stopped, staring at the shapes without really seeing them.

As a memorial . . .

Reality's starting to interfere with the writing. . . .

He was a proud man . . .

This is so nice. I wish it could go on forever. . . .

Suicide . . .

The connections were made.

She began walking faster.

"You're ten minutes late. I thought you weren't coming or had called the cops. So I hid up here."

Ard's voice came from a ledge above her. Carly shone the flashlight upward; she stood with her arms folded, legs planted wide, wearing jeans and a sweatshirt that were insubstantial for the chill night. Even at a distance she looked tired and unkempt. There was no sign of Natalie.

"You know I wouldn't do that to you."

"Did you bring the money?"

"Yes. Where's Nat?"

"In the van. Leave the money there on the ground where I can see it. Drive back to the entrance, and I'll deliver her to you."

"You're not getting the money till Nat's safe with me."

Ard was silent for a moment. "Well, it seems we're at an impasse. If I don't get the money, you don't get the kid. If you don't get the kid, I don't get the money. How're we going to work this out?"

"Maybe we can strike a deal."

"What?"

"You answer a few of my questions—truthfully, for a change—then the money is yours."

"Done."

"First question: When you got to Ronnie and Deke's that morning"—no need to explain which—"what did you find?"

"Jesus, Carly, can't you think of anything better to ask? You know what I found: our friends murdered in their bed."

"I don't think so. You found Deke murdered in their bed, but not Ronnie. He killed himself. It was a murder-suicide pact."

Ard was silent.

"Second question: What did you do then?"

No reply.

"All right, let me tell you what you did. You removed the gun from wherever it was and replaced it in its case in the library cabinet—where it stayed until you took it out to kill Chase. You removed Deke's medications and inspirational book from the nightstand so no one would know he had AIDS. And you probably removed their suicide note from wherever they'd left it."

"There wasn't any note—" She broke off, realizing her mistake.

"Is that a yes?"

Silence.

"A *yes?*"

"All right! It's a yes!"

Carly crossed her arms, gripped her elbows with iron fingers. "And then what did you do?"

More silence.

"What did you do to their bodies, Ard?"

Ard continued to hesitate. Carly sensed what was going on with her: the trembling lips, the filling eyes, the silent weeping.

After all she's done, she still thinks that will work with me.

"What did you do to their bodies?"

"Carly, it was awful. They were wearing their fancy Japanese kimonos, and they'd been drinking champagne, and I guess they thought they'd look peaceful and released from all of it, but they didn't. Neither of them knew what gunshot wounds to the head can do, but Ronnie found out and— God, I don't even want to think about how it must've been for him. Still, even our inept sheriff's deputies would've been able to figure out it was a suicide pact, so I had to kind of . . . rearrange things. That was the really horrible part—touching them."

Carly was shaking now—sickened and enraged both by how Ard had desecrated their friends' deathbed scene and by her self-pitying whine. She said, "Last question: Why? Why did you do those things?"

"I didn't want anyone to know about the AIDS. Ronnie only told me about it when he gave me my copy of his will. He and Deke were so private—"

"Bullshit. You wanted a story. The murder-suicide of a gay couple was good but not great copy. An unsolved murder of a gay couple was. You did those horrible things for a *story*."

In the flashlight's beam Carly saw Ard's eyes narrow and her mouth firm. "All right, so what if I did? You're a newspaperwoman. You ought to understand. Besides, why should you complain? It was your paper that got the Pulitzer, not me!"

"And you resent me for that?"

"For that and a whole lot of other things. You ordered me around at work from day one; you were so convinced you were the better journalist. And at home it was always *your* house that we lived in, *your* money that put food on the table. You even tried to tell me how to raise Natalie. It's always been about you, you, you. That morning I saw my chance to have something of my own, make a name for myself—but then *your* paper won the Pulitzer."

Carly stared up at her, unable to believe the depth of the woman's anger. Had she really treated her so badly? And if so, why hadn't Ard confronted her at the time rather than let her resentment fester?

"Then I got my book deal," Ard went on, "but I couldn't write the damn thing. That morning at Ronnie and Deke's had finally caught up with me, and I just couldn't get past it. And then Chase showed up, claiming he wanted Natalie, even though he didn't give a shit about her. All he wanted was money to keep him from going to the cops about me kidnapping her. Kidnapping! I saved her life. At best she'd've become his punching bag; at worst . . . But I didn't have any money; I'd spent the whole advance for the book."

"You could've come to me for the money. You didn't have to kill him."

"Oh, sure, I could've come to you. And spent the rest of my life enduring your holier-than-thou attitude."

Am I really that bad a person?

No, I'm not perfect, but I'm not the monster she

makes me out to be. I've taken measure of myself in the past ten days, and I can live with what I've seen.

I can do good things—especially for Natalie.

She said, "That's enough, Ard. Come down from there and take me to Nat."

"Look, this stalemate isn't doing Nat or me any good. She's sick, she needs help. And I've bought some time, but not much."

"What do you mean?"

"Gar Payne was arrested tonight. Seems the gun that killed Chase, Ronnie, and Deke was in the glovebox of his car."

"You planted it there. And made an anonymous call to the sheriff's department."

"What if I did? It'll keep them busy till I can get out of the county."

Was there no end to what Ard would do? "Maybe the charge against Payne will stick. Then you could stay here. You'd still have control of the Talbot estate—and the gold."

"Gold? What gold? The mine's not part of the estate. Anyway, there hadn't been any gold there since the thirties."

Faking, or does she really not know?

Carly said, "Gold is the reason Payne and Rawson want that land. A rich vein of it runs through there."

" . . . You're lying. They want it for a development."

She doesn't know. But what about her notes on Noah Estes, Denver Precious Metals. Wells Mining?

Of course—simple reminders to research the history of the area where the murders took place. She's always been big on history.

"I'm not lying. If you'd done your homework, you'd've known."

Ard stood, hands loose at her sides, perplexed. Then she shook her head. "Well, gold, whatever—none of that matters now. Payne will wriggle out of the charges, and then they'll be looking for me again. I've got to get out of here. Just give me the money, will you?"

"No."

"But you said if I answered your questions—"

"I'm not the only one who can lie."

Ard's fists balled, and her face twisted with rage. "Then you won't get Nat! I never intended for you to have her, anyway. She's not in the van. You'll never see her again!"

She whirled and disappeared from the ledge.

For a moment Carly stood stunned; then she began to run—around the Knob toward its northeast side, where the fire trail ended. She had a head start on Ard, who would have to make the long climb down. If she could find the van, she might also find Natalie; not having her along was probably another of Ard's lies.

The ground was steep and treacherous. She skidded on stones, tripped over unseen obstacles. Fell once to her knees and dropped the flashlight, pawed for it, got up, and ran again. The terrain finally leveled off, and she caught a glimpse of the fire trail dead ahead of her. At its end she stopped and shone her light in a circle. Walked on a ways, and shone it around again.

A boxy shape was wedged into a stand of aspens to her right. The van. She moved cautiously toward it, tried the door. Locked. She aimed the flashlight through the windows. Empty. Dammit, Ard hadn't been lying after all.

Circling, she tried all the doors. Also locked. She pressed the hood release, thinking to disable the engine, but it wouldn't move. Finally she shut off her light and listened for Ard's footsteps, but heard nothing.

Hiding. Staying still. But she knows where I am. The slightest sound carries for miles out here. No way I'll find her.

She circled the van again, shining her light through the windows one more time. Its rear compartment was loaded with Ard's and Nat's luggage, a collapsed air mattress, a cooler, a familiar-looking Indian-weave blanket, a striped bag . . .

She went up on her tiptoes, staring intently. She'd seen that bag before, suspended from the ceiling of the walk-in closet off Ronnie and Deke's bedroom. Caught in the pull-down stairs to Deke's attic studio. It wasn't a bag at all. It was a pillowcase, now stuffed with matching sheets from a set that fit Nat's bed at home. And the blanket—it used to lie on a hassock in Ronnie and Deke's living room.

Now she knew where Natalie was.

As she sped along in her truck, Carly used her cell phone to call the sheriff's department central dispatch and ask them to send cruisers to the Talbot house. As she disconnected, she lost control and skidded on loose gravel. Stones flew up and bounced off the undercarriage; the truck pulled to the right, as if one of its tires was going flat.

Not now, dammit!

She wrenched the truck to the left, glanced in the rearview mirror. No headlights behind her. No taillights ahead. She slowed for the last curve and the turn into the Talbot driveway.

No van, and the house was dark.

She stopped the truck near the front door, stalled the engine, and jumped out, almost forgetting her key ring. When she got to the door her trembling fingers wouldn't connect the key with the lock. She took a calming breath, then let herself in.

Her flashlight's batteries were dying. When she tried the wall switch, nothing happened. The power was off. What a horror it must've been for Nat, who feared total darkness and always slept with a nightlight, to camp out here. She trained the flash's fading beam on the stairs and moved quickly toward them.

"Stop, Carly," Ard's voice said.

Astonished, she froze. Ard was behind her, near the exercise room. She'd beaten her here somehow, hid the van out back.

She turned slowly, bringing the light around on her. Ard stood several feet away, pointing a small handgun at her—another from the collection, she supposed.

Ard said, "I saw you at the van. I wasn't far behind. There's a shortcut from the fire trail to the main road, so I got here first."

Fear was making Carly's mouth dry, her palms wet. "Ard, I'll give you the money if you let Nat come home with me."

"You can't buy my child."

Carly made an involuntary move, and Ard brought the gun higher. "Stay where you are," she told her.

"All right. What happens now?"

"You give me the money."

"And then?"

In the silence that followed her question, she stared at Ard's face. The flash's dim light showed it was composed, devoid of emotion.

She's going to kill me. And it'll be easy for her. She's like an animal that, once it's tasted first blood, is compelled to kill again and again.

"I've called the sheriff's department, Ard. They're coming here. Even if you get away before they arrive, they have a description and the license plate number of the van."

"Give me the keys to your truck, then."

"They're in the ignition."

"Bullshit! The key to this house is on your ring, and you used it to let yourself in."

"I haven't carried that key on my ring since—"

The sound of a car's engine. Headlights turning into the drive, washing over the house.

"That's the law now," Carly said.

Ard turned her head but kept the gun aimed at her.

In that instant Carly snapped off the flashlight, sidestepped, and ducked down by the wall.

Ard fired, but the shot went wild, smashing into the wall above Carly's head. Carly crouched lower, ears ringing, as Ard ran toward the door.

Before she reached it, the door opened and Matt's dark form, backlit by the headlight glare, came running through. Ard fired wildly again, and he grabbed her; then Carly heard the gun clatter on the floor. Ard fought him, screaming. Before he was able to spin her around and pin her arms behind her, she bit his shoulder. Then she doubled over and suddenly went limp.

Carly rose on wobbly legs. The hallway was silent except for Matt's and Ard's labored breathing.

Then Ard said in a small, trembly voice, "I didn't mean for any of this to happen, Carly. Please tell him to let me go. You can have Natalie. I don't even want the money."

Carly turned on the flash and moved its beam to Ard's face. It was twisted, tear-streaked, and her eyes blinked at the sudden light.

"Please!" she said.

She's pleading for her life, and I don't feel anything.

She looked from Ard to Matt. He nodded, face grim.

He doesn't feel anything either.

We're both free.

"Mom?" the voice that came from Deke's attic studio was weak and frightened.

"No, honey, it's Carly. Your mom . . . sent me to bring you home." She scrambled up the steep pull-down stairs at the back of the master bedroom closet.

"What was that noise that woke me up?"

"Just my truck backfiring."

In the moonlight shining through the skylights she saw Natalie sitting up in a bed improvised from blankets, a sleeping bag, and an air mattress. She went over, squatted, and enfolded her in her arms. Even though it was cold in the room, Nat felt hot and sweaty.

"I can't go home," she said. "There's this man. . . ."

"Don't worry about him. He's . . . gone away."

"Are you sure? Mom said he never would. . . ."

"She was wrong."

From outside, Carly heard the rumble of sheriff's department cruisers, the chatter of their radios.

"Where is Mom? Why didn't she come for me, too?"

"She . . . She had something she had to do, so I volunteered to bring you home."

"I don't feel good."

"I know. We'll get you to a doctor."

Nat tensed suddenly, staring over Carly's shoulder. She glanced behind her and saw that Matt had come up the stairs and was standing at their top. "It's okay," she told Nat. "This is my friend Matthew."

The little girl relaxed some but continued to look suspiciously at Matt. He stayed where he was and said, "Hello, Natalie. Carly's told me a lot about you."

Nat didn't reply.

Carly said, "Have you been staying here the whole time since you and your mom left home?"

"Except for the night we went to Westhaven. We stayed in a cruddy motel, and that's when I got sick. Mom decided we should come back here till I got better, but we had to be very quiet and hide from that man. Mom said he was here in the house. A couple of times I heard him."

She heard me. I could've found her, brought her home sooner.

Carly stood and eased Nat to her feet. She was fully

clothed in jeans and a heavy wool sweater. "Can you walk?"

"I don't know." As she spoke, she swayed and stumbled.

"Matt," Carly said, "maybe you could carry her downstairs."

"Is that okay, Natalie? May I carry you?"

"I guess."

He scooped her up, and they descended the steep staircase. In the bedroom Carly motioned for him to hold back and went to look down into the hallway. No one was there, but garish red-and-blue lights bounced off its walls.

She ran down the stairs and outside. Ard was being guided by a deputy into the backseat of one of the cruisers, her head sagging on her long neck like a flower on a broken stalk.

Carly turned away and went back to Matt and Natalie.

After the doctor at the emergency room in Santa Carla assured them that Nat would fully recover and was resting comfortably, Carly led Matt outside. The sky over the mountains to the east was tinged with pink and gold, but above them it was still midnight blue. She raised her face to it, breathed in the scents of the springtime dawn.

"So how'd you find me?" she asked.

"I went to your house after I heard a bulletin about Gar Payne's arrest on the radio. I figured Ardis had planted the gun. When I found your lights on and the door unlocked, I got alarmed and called Grossman. He called me back after you alerted the dispatcher, and told me where you were headed. I was close by, so . . . Well, that's me: Lindstrom to the rescue. Some rescue. I almost got myself shot."

"Thank God she missed you, too."

He glanced back at the hospital. "What d'you suppose will happen to Natalie?"

"I don't know, but she wants to come home. The courts usually take the wishes of a child her age into consideration. And Ard won't have any say in it; she's admitted to child stealing and murder."

"But it's your word against hers. Once she gets a lawyer, she'll probably manipulate her way out of it."

"Nope. Not this time." Carly reached into her pocket and took out her small voice-activated tape recorder. "It's all on here. Old reporter's trick: Never leave home without it."

Matthew Lindstrom

Friday, May 24, 2002

hen Matt crossed the footbridge, he saw Carly sitting on one of the chaise longues on her patio, and Natalie at the nearby table, drawing on a sketch pad. Carly set aside the book she was reading, pushed her glasses atop her head, and came to meet him.

"I just dropped by to say good-bye." He waved at Natalie, who had looked up and was regarding him solemnly. She nodded and went back to her drawing. "We're heading out now," he added.

"We?" Carly looked past him to where Sam sat in the Jeep, examining her image in the mirror on the visor. "Hmmm."

"Not what you think, McGuire. The kid needs to get away from here, so I've signed her on as a deckhand.

Johnny Crowe says business is booming, but I want to spend more time on my photography. Sam's a hard worker, and I think she and Johnny'll hit it off."

"And what about you?"

"I don't understand."

"Are you going to open up and hit it off with somebody?"

He smiled. "Maybe. I'm sure there'll be no shortage of possibilities. Millie Bertram is always throwing eligible women at me."

"So catch one, why don't you?"

"I just might do that, now that I'm no longer haunted by a ghost." His gaze moved to Natalie. "How is she?"

"Subdued. She hasn't fully comprehended what's happened to Ard. Thinks she's ill—which she is, at least according to her lawyer. The psychologist I took Nat to agrees she doesn't need to know everything till she's made significant progress. I received temporary custody yesterday, and after a family court evaluation, that may become permanent. I like the judge; she says better the home where Nat's been living than foster care.

"Are you going to be okay with that—raising a little girl alone?"

"It's more likely to be a case of Nat and I raising each other."

He stepped forward and hugged her. Then he broke away and strode across the footbridge toward the Jeep. At its end he turned and called, "Keep in touch. The two of you come see me, okay?"

She nodded and waved.

He slid into the Jeep and said to Sam, "Quit staring at

yourself. You're a pretty woman, and you'll sweep the Port Regis guys off their feet."

Then he started the engine and drove on, into his fifth and final life.

Carly McGuire

Friday, May 24, 2002

Warmed by her brief talk with Matt, Carly returned to the patio. Nat was still drawing, the tip of her tongue caught between her teeth.

"May I see?" Carly asked.

Nat hesitated, then handed over the sketch pad.

The delicate, precise pencil strokes depicted a garden scene, and at the center of it, working the soil beneath a rose bush, was a surprisingly realistic portrait of Ard.

In a low voice Nat said, "She's never coming back, is she?"

Point number one from the psychologist: Don't lie to her. If she asks, she's ready to hear.

"No, she's not."

"I didn't think so. She was so weird all the time we

were hiding in Uncle Deke's studio. I mean, she didn't talk or read or anything like she used to. She just sat, staring at me or the wall. It was really scary."

"And you'll always remember that. I'm sorry to say, bad memories don't go away. But after a while they fade. Try to remember your mom like she is in your drawing."

Nat nodded and reached for it.

"You know," Carly said, "you're really a good artist, honey. Maybe we should sign you up for some lessons."

"That'd be great. But will you stop calling me 'honey'? You've been doing that all week, and I hate it. It sounds like you feel sorry for me. I don't like *anybody* to feel sorry for me—not even you."

This child has just captured my heart.

"I promise I will never feel sorry for you or call you 'honey' again. So what *shall* I call you?"

"Natalie or Nat, like you used to. Those're my names."

"Okay, Nat. I'll check into those art lessons."

We've got a long road ahead of us, kid, but we'll tough it out—the two of us, together.

More
Marcia Muller!

Please turn this page
for a preview of

THE
DANGEROUS HOUR

available
wherever books are sold.

I dropped the legal pad full of notes on my office desk, went to the high, arching window that overlooked San Francisco Bay, and waved exuberantly at the pilot of a passing tugboat. He stared, probably thinking me demented, then waved back.

The reason for my impulsive gesture was that I'd just come from a midafternoon meeting with my entire staff in our newly refurbished conference room—a let-the-phones-go-on-the-machine, everybody-must-attend gathering, during which we'd discussed McCone Investigations' present healthy state and bright future prospects. When the session broke up, the others were as high-spirited as I.

During the past two years our business had tripled. Last year we'd taken over all the offices fronting on the north-side second-story catwalk at Pier 24½. My nephew, Mick Savage, now headed up our new computer forensics department and was about to hire another specialist in that area. His live-in love, Charlotte Keim, was overwhelmed with her financial investigations—locating hidden assets, tracing employees who had absconded with company funds, exposing other corporate wrongdoing—and I'd authorized her to begin interviewing for two assistants. Craig Morland, a former FBI agent, was invaluable on governmental affairs, as well as a damn good man in the field; and my newest hire, Julia

Rafael, had shaped up into a fine all-around operative. I didn't see any reason why either wouldn't eventually supervise his or her own department. Of course, my office manager, Ted Smalley, had yet to settle on an assistant who lived up to his exacting standards of efficiency—so many had passed through his office that I'd stopped trying to remember their last names—but I had no doubt that in time the individual whom he called "a paragon of the paper clips" would appear, résumé in hand.

Not a bad situation for a woman who once worked out of a converted closet at a poverty law firm.

Still, sometimes I missed those days when my generation had held the firm conviction that we could change the world. Which was why the ratty old armchair where I'd done some of my best thinking inside that closet now sat under my schefflera plant by the window of this spacious office at the pier—covered, of course, by a tasteful handwoven throw. I flopped into it to savor my professional good fortune.

I'd basked in the afterglow of the meeting for only a few minutes, while conveniently ignoring a couple of personal issues that had been nagging at me, when the phone buzzed. I went to the desk and picked up.

Ted. "You'd better get out here fast!"

Something wrong. Really wrong. So much for basking.

I dropped the receiver into the cradle. As I hurried onto the catwalk, I heard the words ". . . silent. Anything you say can and will be used against you in a court of law."

Two men near the top of the stairway. Plainclothes police officers; I recognized one. He stood poised to assist as his partner struggled with Julia Rafael, attempting to handcuff her. She bent over, kicking backward at his shins, trying to break his grasp. Beyond them Ted and Mick stood, looking confused and helpless.

"You have the right to speak to an attorney . . ."

Confusion gripped me, too. "What the hell's going on here?" I demanded.

Before either man could reply, Julia screamed, "Help me, Shar! I didn't do anything!" Then the fight went out of her, and she collapsed, nearly taking down the officer.

He steadied himself, went on, "And to have an attorney present . . ."

He finished Mirandizing Julia and yanked her upright by the cuffs. She cried out in pain, and I warned, "Careful. You've got witnesses."

He ignored me.

I turned to the other officer. August Williams, an inspector on the SFPD Fraud detail. On several occasions I'd supplied him with leads that I'd stumbled across. "What's the charge, Augie?" I asked.

"Ms. Rafael has been accused of grand theft," he replied. "Specifically, stealing and making purchases with a Master-Card belonging to—"

"I'll take her downstairs," his partner said.

I looked at Julia. Now she stood erect, dwarfing the arresting officer by some two inches. Her severe features were stony, her dark eyes blank. She didn't meet my eyes.

She'd been in this situation before, as a juvenile, and knew the drill.

I said, "Go with him, Jules. I'll call Glenn Solomon."

At my mention of the city's top criminal-defense attorney, the inspector who was ushering Julia toward the stairway paused, then glared at me. Great—a hard case, one of the type that the department was attracting, and eventually having to discipline, in increasing numbers. Thank God he was partnered with Williams, an even-tempered and by-the-book cop.

As his partner ushered Julia down the stairway, I touched Williams's arm. "Augie," I said, "make him go easy."

He nodded, his jaw set.

"As you started to say," I added, "a MasterCard belonging to . . . ?"

He looked down at me—a big, handsome man with rich brown skin, close-cropped gray hair, and concerned eyes that were pouched from lack of sleep. For a good cop, sleep is always in short supply.

"A credit card belonging to Supervisor Alex Aguilar. He alleges she stole it from his wallet after he rejected her sexual advances last month, and has used it to run up over five thousand dollars' worth of purchases."

Alex Aguilar. Founder and director of TRABAJO POR TODOS—WORK FOR ALL—a Mission-district job-training program designed to bring the city's disadvantaged Hispanics into the mainstream. Two-term member of the city's board of supervisors. Rumored to be positioning himself to become our first Hispanic mayor.

Alex Aguilar—our former client. He'd hired us to investigate a series of thefts from the job-training center. I'd assigned Julia, since she was my only Hispanic operative. When I called Aguilar after she'd brought the investigation to a satisfactory conclusion, he said he was pleased and would recommend our services to others.

Now he was accusing her of grand theft.

"I don't believe it," I said.

Williams shrugged. "I'm sorry, Sharon, but there's more. I have a warrant to search any part of your offices that Ms. Rafael has access to."

I took the document he held out as a pair of uniformed officers came up the stairway. It specified packages and merchandise from Amazon.com, Lands' End, J. Jill, Coldwater Creek, Sundance, Nordstrom, Bloomingdale's, and

The Peruvian Connection, as well as a MasterCard in the name of A. Aguilar.

The warrant was in order.

"Go ahead and search," I said.

I accompanied Williams and his men to the office Julia shared with Craig Morland. Craig wasn't there, and neither were any of the items listed on the warrant. When they finished, Augie asked, "What other areas does she have access to?"

"All of them. I trust my employees and don't restrict them."

But was I wrong to put my trust in Julia? Given her history?

I pushed the doubts aside and added, "We'll start with my own office."

After Williams and the uniforms had left empty-handed, I said to Ted, "Get Glenn Solomon on the phone for me, please."

Ted hesitated, looking at Mick, who had remained on the catwalk with him. "May we speak privately?"

"Of course."

We went inside his office, and he shut the door. "You didn't tell them about the mail room," he said.

". . . It slipped my mind."

"Nothing like that slips your mind. You deliberately didn't tell them. Does that mean you think Jules is guilty?"

"I don't know what to think. They must have some pretty compelling evidence, to walk in here and arrest her without first asking her to come in for questioning."

Ted crossed his arms, leaning against his desk, and shook his shaggy mane of gray-black hair. He'd been growing it long—always the prelude to some change in fashion statement—and it was at the unruly stage. "I can't believe you don't have more faith in her. After all, you hired her in spite of her juvenile record. You're the one who keeps praising her for the way she's turned her life around."

His implied accusation made me feel small, disloyal to an employee who had, up until now, given me no reason to doubt her. But doubt still nagged at me. Ted saw I was conflicted and let me off the hook. "I'll get Glenn on the phone now."

"Thanks. And then will you please print me out a copy of the Aguilar file?"

I went back to my office and flopped onto my desk chair, numb. All the good feelings I'd been reveling in were gone now. Once again life had reminded me that things are never as secure as they seem. That none of us is immune to the sudden, vicious blow that can descend at any time and place.

Ted put Glenn through a few minutes later.

"This is bad news, my friend," he said when I finished explaining the situation.

"You don't need to tell me that."

"Julia Rafael—she's the big one, right? Five-eleven or six feet, bodybuilder's shoulders? Standoffish?"

"She's shy. She came up the hard way, and she's not comfortable with people outside her own sphere yet."

"I wasn't putting her down. That's how I acted when I first enrolled at Stanford. Down there on the Farm with all the rich kids, a scholarship student whose father was a grocery-store keeper in Duluth, and Jewish to boot. The one time I met your Ms. Rafael, she interested me. Any chance she might've done what Aguilar alleges?"

"I can't imagine her coming on to him. Or stealing his credit card in retaliation. But sometimes she does display a curious pattern of behavior."

"How so?"

"First, there's the shyness, which, as you say, comes off as standoffishness. On the other hand, in a professional situation she can be cool and assertive. But if someone says or does something—no matter how innocent—that she interprets as an ethnic, class, or gender slur, she'll lash out. I've had to warn her about that several times."

"Passive-aggressive," Glenn said.

"With a wide swath of middle ground."

"Quite interesting."

"As a case study, maybe, but not when my agency and career are threatened. If Aguilar goes to the Department of Consumer Affairs and lodges a complaint against us, it'll be expensive at best, disastrous at worst."

"DCA licenses you. And Julia."

"Only me. She's a trainee, hasn't put in the requisite number of hours to take the test."

"So you're the liable party."

"If they can prove I had knowledge of what she did."

"Which you didn't."

"No, but . . . Jesus, Glenn, you never know which way one of their hearings may go. I've heard horror stories. Their investigators just show up at your office—and not to ask if you're having a good day. They question you extensively and demand to see your files on the particular case, and if you resist turning them over, they return armed with a subpoena and the firm conviction that you must be guilty. Sometimes they even perform a general audit. If BSIS—Bureau of Security and Investigative Services, the people who control the licensing process—then deem the complaint valid, there's a hearing, whose results can range from a dismissal to the temporary or permanent loss of your license. Even if the complaint is dismissed, it's an all-around expensive proposition, involving lawyers' fees and court costs, to say nothing of damage to your reputation."

"Have you ever been involved in such proceedings?"

"No. During my early years in the business, when I was brash and took foolish risks, any number of complaints probably should've been lodged against me. But I was lucky. Now I keep to the straight and narrow, mostly, and insist my operatives do the same."

"Well, we'll worry about DCA later—if Aguilar even bothers to file a complaint. In the meantime, I'd better take myself down to the Hall of Justice."

"You think you can get Julia out of custody?"

"I doubt it. It's unlikely there'll be a duty judge on the weekend. But at least I can hear her side of the story, try to nose out what kind of evidence they have. Where will you be?"

"Here at the pier, I guess. I've got a lot of paperwork to finish up before the weekend."

"I'll see you there later, then."

After I replaced the receiver, I looked at my watch. It was five-fifteen, the time when Julia, a single mother, would normally be heading home to her young son, Tonio, or calling her sister, Sophia Cruz, to ask her to care for him. I should get in touch with Sophia, alert her to the situation.

I called the flat that Sophia and Julia rented together on Shotwell Street in the Mission district. The phone rang four times before Sophia picked up, sounding distraught.

"Sharon! Thank God!" she said. "I've been trying to get through to Jules for hours. All I got was the machine at the office, and her cell's not working."

Julia, like me, had a bad habit of forgetting to turn on her cellular, but why hadn't Ted or someone else picked up? "When did you call the office?"

"Around three-thirty, when the police came with the search warrant."

We'd all been in the meeting then, phones on the machine. "Did you leave a message?"

"No, I was too upset. The warrant, it was for the apartment and our storage bin. I had to let the police in, and they took a bunch of stuff away from the bin, gave me a receipt. All this stuff that I didn't even know was there, and I can't believe—"

Her words were spilling out breathlessly. I said, "Slow down, Sophia. What kind of stuff?"

"Unopened packages from mail-order places. Amazon. Lands' End. Nordstrom's. Packages that had been opened, too. Computer stuff. Fancy outfits."

All items that could easily be bought with a stolen credit card.

"What's going on, Sharon?"

"You'd better brace yourself. Julia's been arrested." I told her what I knew of the charges.

Sophia was silent for a moment. Then she said, "She told you she didn't do it?"

"She told me she didn't know why she was being arrested."

More silence. Apparently I wasn't the only one who was having doubts about Julia's honesty. Now I felt the same reproach toward Sophia that Ted had displayed toward me.

"What?" I said. "You think she's guilty?"

"I don't want to think so. And the stealing isn't like Jules. Even when she was a teenager, turning tricks and dealing, she didn't steal. But the sex thing, coming on to the guy . . . For months now, since she and that Johnny broke up, Jules has been kind of down and sticking close to home. Then a few weeks ago she's off to the clubs, hot to trot and find herself another loser."

Julia had perfectly terrible taste in men, and Sophia

rejoiced at the departure of each, while dreading the appearance of his replacement.

I said, "So you're suggesting she set her sights on Alex Aguilar?"

"Might've. I know she was excited when he asked her out to dinner. And she did say she might not come home that night, so I should watch out for Tonio. Not that I'm complaining. Jules has her needs."

I pictured Sophia: a plain woman in her early forties whose two children and husband were long gone from her life. She clerked at Safeway, played bingo at her church on Wednesday nights, and cared for Tonio. That was it, as far as I knew. But she was still young. Didn't she have needs, too?

"Well," I said, "I guess Tonio's your responsibility until bail can be arranged. Are you supposed to work tonight?"

"Yeah, but there's an old lady upstairs who can take him."

Tonio was a bright, cheerful eight-year-old who did well in school and didn't seem to suffer from being shuffled off to the various caretakers who helped Julia and Sophia juggle their complicated schedules. All of us at the agency were fond of him and encouraged Julia to bring him to the pier when no one else was available to look after him. "If I can help in any way—"

"No, no. I got it under control."

After I replaced the receiver, I looked at my watch. The wheels at the Hall of Justice turned slowly. It might be hours till Glenn returned to tell me what he'd found out. I could read the Aguilar file. I could start plowing through the week's paperwork.

I could visit the mail room.

Because of the size of the pier and the number of tenants, a mail room had been established near the front entrance, to which the post office and parcel service delivery people had keys. Only one person from each firm had access to the room and made pickups. In our case, it was Ted.

I went along the catwalk to his bailiwick and found him seated behind his desk, working on a crossword puzzle. As long as I'd known him—going back to the days when he ruled the front office at All Souls Legal Cooperative—he'd been a crossword enthusiast, and now I wondered how many words he'd fitted into the little squares over the years.

"Why're you still here?" I asked. "It's Friday night."

"I'm waiting for Neal to pick me up for a weekend getaway to Monterey." Neal Osborn was Ted's life partner. "I've also been waiting for you to ask for the key to the mail room."

"Julia's sister said the police seized a lot of merchandise at their building. I have to know if there's more here."

"I understand. I've had a hard time resisting going down there myself." He stabbed his pen—the showoff always did his puzzles in ink—at the newsprint, then dropped it. "Let's see what's what."

The pier was Friday-night quiet. A light glowed in the offices of the architects on the opposite catwalk, but all the others were dark. Ted and I walked silently toward the mail room—actually a chain-link cage to the left of the pier's arching entrance. He worked the lock, opened the door, and flicked on the overhead light.

The room was divided into bins with shelves above them. Most of the bins were empty. Beside ours sat a couple of cases from Viking Office Supply. "Copy paper," Ted said. He leaned over them, reached into our bin, and grunted in surprise as he pulled out a Jiffy bag.

"What?" I asked.

He held out the bag up so I could see. The return address was Coach Leatherworks. The recipent was Ms. Julia Rafael, c/o McCone Investigations.

"What should we do?" Ted whispered, in spite of there being no one to hear us.

"Put it back. That's all we can do. It's evidence. Put it back—and leave it there."

In the three hours before Glenn Solomon arrived at the pier, I read through the Aguilar file and completed my paperwork for the week, but my concentration wasn't all it should have been, and my thoughts kept turning to Julia.

Last year she'd responded to an ad I'd placed in the *Chronicle* for an investigative trainee, no experience necessary—the idea being that I could mold said individual to my own standards while paying a modest starting salary. The application she presented me was the most off-putting I'd ever seen, listing two incarcerations by the California Youth Authority for drug-related offenses and two firings from subsequent jobs, one by a close relative. On the plus side, she'd gotten her GED during her second stint with the Youth Authority and had a solid recommendation from the former director of a federally funded neighborhood outreach program where she'd worked for four years until the government pulled the plug on it.

In California, juvenile records are sealed in order to give the offender a fresh start, and it seemed strange that Julia would choose to reveal hers. When I questioned her about that, she said she feared her history might come out somewhere down the line, and thought it was best to be honest. During the rest of the interview I'd found her honesty to be brutal in the extreme, so brutal that I suspected she was working the angles. But jail time, even in a juvenile facility, teaches you a certainly slyness, and it was an ability that would stand her in good stead as an investigator. In the end, mainly because none of my other applicants had standout qualifications, I hired her; she'd proved a fast learner and was also picking up on the interpersonal skills that would make her an asset to the agency. During the time she'd been a member of our little family—as we often referred to ourselves—she'd opened up, begun to trust in her growing friendships with us, become more confident. Now—

Glenn knocked on the door frame and came in. As he sat on one of the clients' chairs—which creaked under his weight—the set of his mouth was grim.

"It's bad?" I asked.

"It's bad."

Normally Glenn cut an imposing figure: tall and heavyset, with a lion's mane of silver-gray hair, he was always impeccably and expensively tailored, even in his most casual clothes. Although generous and kind to those close to him, he was capable of unleashing scathing sarcasm upon his opponents, and had a cobra's sense of when and how hard to strike. A man you would want as a friend, never as an enemy, and during the years he'd been throwing business my way, I'd learned to walk a fine line with him. Tonight, however, he was tired and looked nothing like the aggressive defense attorney whose thundering voice could quail prosecutors and their witnesses.

He slouched in the chair and ran his hand over his reddened eyes, then over the stubble on his chin. "God, I'd forgotten how much that jail depresses me," he said. "Normally I send one of my associates to handle the preliminaries."

"But you went for Julia."

"As I said on the phone, she interests me. Or maybe she reminds me that I come from humble roots, which is not a bad thing. And, of course, I'm concerned for you, my friend."

His words touched me. "Thank you."

"No need for thanks. Anyway, your Ms. Rafael: They're housing her in Jail Two, on the seventh floor of the Hall.

High security, no bail until arraignment, and no visitors allowed except me, as her attorney."

"Why high security?"

"Because it's a high-profile case—involving a city supe—and because of 'behavioral problems.' Meaning she resisted arrest and is considered a flight risk."

"You speak with her?"

"Briefly. She claims that the arrest came as a total surprise. Says Aguilar took her to dinner at the conclusion of the investigation, and they parted on amicable terms. Denies making any sort of pass at him, or taking his credit card."

"You believe her?"

"I do. I've got a damned good internal shit detector. She strikes me as a very straightforward young woman."

"Maybe not as straightforward as she appears." I told him about the search and seizure at Sophia Cruz's apartment, and the package in our mail room.

He frowned. "Something's not right. I've never known my shit detector to go on the fritz. She claims she and her sister haven't gone into their storage bin at the apartment building in at least three months. I believe her. But by all indications the D.A.'s got a strong case. I'll know a little more tomorrow, after she's processed and I can take a look at the paperwork, but you'd better be prepared: a source close to the investigation, whom I happened to encounter in the men's room, tells me they have plenty of evidence—and that it leads straight back to your firm."

"Jesus. Because the packages they seized at her apartment house were sent here?"

"That's what I'd guess. Who brings them up from the mail room?"

"Ted."

"He still here?"

"No. He and his partner, Neal Osborn—"

"I know Neal. I've bought books from him." Neal was a secondhand bookseller, dealing on the Internet; Glenn was in the process of amassing a collection of out-of-print volumes dealing with criminal law.

"Well, by now they're on their way to Monterey for the weekend. I don't know where they're staying, and neither of them has a cellular. They won't be back till Monday morning."

"Too bad. I wonder if Ted's noticed an unusual number of packages arriving for Julia."

"He said the one we found in our bin tonight was the first he's seen, and I'm sure that's correct. What about Aguilar's credit card? Did it turn up?"

"Not yet."

"So what happens now?"

"I go over the paperwork when it's available tomorrow, and then we wait till she's arraigned."

"When will that be?"

"Tuesday morning."

"Tuesday!"

"It could be worse. Because she was arrested before four o'clock this afternoon, the case has to go to the D.A. by four p.m. on Monday. If he decides to go ahead with it, it's a Tuesday arraignment. If they'd come for her after four, the arraignment wouldn't've been until Wednesday."

"Poor Jules. So I can't visit her over the weekend?"

"No."

"That's outrageous!"

He shrugged. "Sheriff's department runs the jail and makes the rules. Frankly, they're more generous than most; as you may recall, the sheriff used to be a prisoners' rights attorney. But Julia made a bad mistake when she resisted the arresting officer—even though it wasn't much resistance."

This was going to be a very long weekend—for all concerned.

Half an hour later, when I arrived at my house in the Glen Park district, I left my car in the driveway, illegally blocking the sidewalk, as everyone else did on this congested tail-end segment of Church Street. Parking control understood that we residents settled our disputes privately and politely, and seldom ticketed anyone.

As I hurried up the front steps, I heard the patter of paws behind me and then a yowl. Alice, my calico cat. She nosed frantically at the front door while I unlocked it: *Food! I need food!*

"Hold on, will you?" She streaked down the hallway. I dealt with the alarm system, hung my jacket on the wall rack, and dumped my briefcase and purse on the chair in the sitting room. When I went into the kitchen, Allie was pacing impatiently in front of her food bowl.

"Where's your brother?" I asked her.

For the past few months, Ralph, my orange tabby, had done poorly—weight loss coupled with a huge appetite for both food and water, listlessness, back legs so shaky that he had difficulty climbing up onto the couch. He and his robustly healthy littermate were getting on up there in years, and this sudden decline worried me. We had an appointment at the vet's tomorrow morning.

Hearing his name, Ralph crept tentatively from under the table. This was the cat who once could top the back fence in a single leap, who would run to greet me, tail wagging like a little dog's. Now his tail drooped to the floor. My spirits drooped in a similar fashion, but I patted both cats and babbled with false cheer as I filled their bowls.

In the sitting room I checked the answering machine. A

couple of routine calls—I was three weeks overdue picking up my dry cleaning, and even more overdue for my MG's servicing. Nothing from Hy.

My longtime love's silence was another reminder of a troublesome issue, and one I didn't want to dwell on just now. I went back to the kitchen, stuck a frozen lasagna in the microwave, and when it was ready, took it and a glass of Chianti to the table, where I ate as I read my mail. A post-card from my mother and stepfather, mailed at the end of an Alaskan cruise from which they'd now returned. A note and sample menu from my sister Patsy, who, in partnership with her husband, Evans Newhouse, had just opened their third restaurant in the Sonoma Valley. A weird, scribbled card from my half brother, Darcy Blackhawk, in Boise, Idaho. Catalogs and other junk mail that I took to the recycle bin. On the way back, I detoured to my briefcase and extracted the file on the Aguilar case. Went over it again while I finished eating.

As before, I noted nothing unusual. The investigation had proceeded in a straightforward manner. Computers and other equipment had disappeared from the Mission district job-training center Alex Aguilar and a partner had founded. Julia went undercover there, posing as a new client. She studied the dynamics of the other clients for a week, identified a pair of brothers as the probable thieves. Maintained a surveillance at night and photographed them exiting the premises with stolen goods. Followed them and photographed them turning the goods over to a third brother. Called the SFPD Burglary detail, who had arrested the brothers and seized the goods. The trial was scheduled for August, barring a complete breakdown in our overcrowded legal system. End of case.

Until today.